I0747809

AMBER OATH

SARAH URQUHART

AMBER OATH is a work of fiction. Names, characters, and places are products of the author's imagination or used fictitiously. Any resemblance to locales or persons, living or dead, is coincidental.

Cover design by Untold Designs

This book is a steamy, small town, shifter romance and is for mature audiences only. It contains sexually explicit scenes and adult language that may be offensive to some readers.

All rights reserved. This book is intended for the original purchaser. No part may be reproduced, scanned, or distributed in any manner without written permission from the author, except in the case of brief quotations.

Copyright © 2021 Sarah Urquhart
All rights reserved.
ISBN: 978-1-7773011-7-0
eISBN: 978-1-7773011-4-9

This is for our dog, Valkyrie. And for the best veterinarian we could have ever asked for.

ACKNOWLEDGMENTS

I always have such amazing support. I have a husband that supports my career and friends that back me up. There is always more to learn and I have a great tribe of writing colleagues who work together to lift each other up and push each other to do the best we can and more. I can never give a big enough shout out to my beta readers and my cover designer. They really are the best people!

PROLOGUE

Holly dragged her sleeve across her eyes as her mother opened her bedroom door.

"Hey sweetie. How do you like your new room?" Her new room in their new house in a new town. Holly turned away to hide her eye roll.

"It's nice." It was kind of cool, shaped like a triangle and the highest room in the house, but that didn't mean she liked it. Not yet. Not today. She'd turned eight yesterday and had to say goodbye to her best friend. It made for a crappy birthday. Holly fingered the necklace Zachary had given her before she left. She missed him—her big brother.

"Why don't you go check out the yard? We have even more space here than we did in Hull Creek. I know you love to explore."

"Sure." If it would keep her mom from seeing how upset she was, she'd leave her room for a while. Her mom probably wanted her out so she could unpack and organize Holly's room herself.

Her dad was sitting on the floor emptying boxes in the kitchen when Holly ran past him. She skidded on the floor in her socks and turned around. Wrapping her arms around his neck, she kissed his cheek.

"Bye, Dad."

"Where are you off to?" He turned his head over his shoulder.

Holly stopped with the screen door in her hand and slipped on her rubber boots. "To check out the yard."

"Don't wander far."

"I won't." The door swung shut behind her. Her feet itched to run out of habit, but her mood slowed her down.

She looked around. Some trees lined most of the house. Holly wondered how far back they went. The lawn had a small hill—enough for sledding in the winter and rolling down in the summer. The people her parents bought the house from left a playset in the yard. Yellow swings on one side and a green slide that came down from a tiny house on the other. It looked boring. She hoped to find some good climbing trees. The yard itself only had flimsy ones, like her mom had always wanted at their old house.

Holly stuck her hands in her pockets and walked toward the bigger trees. A faint three-toned squeak slowed her steps. Tilting her head, she listened again. This time, a longer and higher fourth one followed the three squeaks. As soon as her foot passed the line of the trees, a swirl of mixed colours rushed across her path like the four-year-old little girl that lived across the street—hair and dress trailed behind her as she'd played tag when Holly and her parents arrived earlier.

The squeak called her forth and a colour swirl appeared again, twirling once before dashing off. She saw it before, yesterday, when she was in the field with Zachary. Up at the top of the hill, the pinkish orange glow rushed around and disappeared before Zachary could see it. Holly had thought it must have been a glare from the sun on something. Not much sunlight was coming through the trees now.

Her ears carried a steady rhythm as they pounded. Still, she kept walking toward the distressed squeaking. She stopped when the sound came from the right. She'd passed it. When she turned, the colourful cloud moved a bush back and forth, just as if it was blowing in the wind. The colours came toward her. Her hair flew back like the little girl's. It was warm on her cheeks and neck.

Holly walked toward the bush. Looking down, she saw something struggling on the ground. Grey feathers poked out between white ones, and darker feathers dotted the wings. It was a baby owl. Holly looked back at the house. She should get her dad to come help her. She knelt down to the ground, sitting on her feet.

The owl's foot was caught between a couple branches on the bush. Holly looked up. She wondered if the baby could fly yet or if she fell. Moving closer, she watched—the owl might get mad at her. It wouldn't take much to free her foot. She only needed to lift it up a little. And the owl wasn't struggling. Holly could do this.

Slowly, she reached one hand forward, then followed with the other when the owl didn't move. Holly tried to remember what she knew about owls. They'd been the last animal her class had learned about before the end of the year. A new baby was called a fledgling and an older one was called an owlet. This one looked nothing like the new babies in pictures their teacher showed them.

Holding her breath, Holly lifted the foot up. As soon as it was free of the branches, the owlet pulled it back.

"There. You're free." Holly pulled her legs out from under her and sat on her bum. With her elbows on her legs and her hands holding onto her ankles, she waited to see what the owlet would do.

The colours came back, winding around first Holly and then the owl. The gentle wind fluffed the owl's feathers, and its colours changed as it moved, creating the look of the rising sun. As it disappeared again, the owlet hopped up onto Holly's knee. Her shoulders tensed with the urge to pull back, but she stopped. She didn't want the sudden motion to scare her. Holly hoped it was a her, but she couldn't be sure.

"You're really pretty."

She tilted her head—her eyes the colour of Holly's mother's favourite jewelry.

"I'm new here. We just moved. I miss my old home."

The owlet tilted her head the other way.

"My mom and dad both got new jobs. And I'm supposed to go to a new school and make new friends. I don't want to do that."

She took a step closer up Holly's leg, her talons tiny sharp points poking through Holly's pants. The owlet's eyes were big and round, reminding Holly of a girl from her class back in Hull Creek. She had really light blonde hair and wore big circle glasses. Perfect circles like the owlet's eyes. Her name was Chloe.

"I guess I'm okay making friends with you. You're a lot better than other kids."

Holly reached out to touch her feathers. As soon as she made contact, the wind of colours came back, weaving around them and in between them. It warmed her skin. Her cheeks felt red, like when Tommy had embarrassed her at school, making fun of her for being the smallest in the class. But Zachary had picked her up from school that day. Tommy said nothing about her again.

The wind squeezed her, pushing at her back to lean her forward toward the owl on her lap. The owlet hopped off her leg and everything inside Holly changed. Tingles, like her entire body was asleep, shot outward from her bones. Holly closed her eyes, trying to shut out the sensations, but then her body ached. The ache grew. She cried out, but the sound changed to mimic the owlet's three-toned squeak.

Holly fell to the ground with something covering her head. She struggled for a moment, but the wind picked up the fabric to drop to the ground beside her. Her shirt piled beside her as the wind disappeared. Holly looked down at herself to see what was wrong with her. Feathers that matched the owlet's covered her. She tried to stretch her arms and spread out wings instead. Her vision sharpened and the scents around her were strange.

She wasn't sure she liked what happened to her. Looking over at the owlet, Holly watched her hop closer. Everything was large around her. The bush now loomed over them, the trees were bigger than giants. She was an owl, an owlet.

The owlet came closer and touched her head to Holly's. She needed the comfort in the chaos. The owlet spoke, but the sound carried through the air and settled inside Holly.

How did you do that?

Holly didn't know how to answer so she made the motion of shrugging her shoulders which lifted her wings up and down.

Can you fly yet?

When Holly still couldn't figure out how to answer, the owlet tilted her head.

I'm just learning. That's how I ended up down here. I can help you learn too. The owlet spread her feet and stretched her wings. *Like this.*

Holly mimicked her movements although neither of

them made it off the ground. Warmth encased the area and rustled the grass and bushes. The colourful wind was back. It charged toward Holly and whooshed under her feathers, fluffing her up. Then it did the same to the owlet.

I get it now. The owlet touched her head to Holly's once again. A connection she hadn't felt with anyone other than Zachary sparked between her and the owlet—between her and Chloe. *Sister.*

1

———

Hell of a day, eh, Tony?"

ANTHONY GLANCED at Morton getting into their vehicle. Nothing out of the ordinary had happened that day, but the calls had been non-stop. He turned the heat down in their too hot truck when the dry heat blasted his face. Morton had started his annual complaints about the approaching winter, and with that came burning extra gas by turning on every type of heater the truck had from the heated seats to the defroster that hit a windshield with no ice. "I'm beat." He looked forward to a cold beer with some TV.

The radio sounded and Hazel's voice from dispatch echoed in the cab. "I've got one more for you boys." Anthony picked up the receiver, inwardly wincing with acceptance that the day wasn't quite done.

"This is Anthony. What have you got, Hazel?" Hazel had been working dispatch for the past forty-five years, ever since her eighteenth birthday. They'd all heard her stories from her younger years.

"An injured owl. Some hikers called it in." She rattled off the location.

"Got it. I'm on my way." He put the receiver back and pulled away from the lake. "I'll drop you off on the way. We don't need two of us for an owl. You might as well go home."

"If you're sure. I don't mind going with you." Morton shrugged, but his shoulders had already slumped against the leather seat.

"I'm sure. It's up near my place, anyway." Morton wasn't lazy, but once he clocked out in his head, he clocked out completely.

Anthony pulled in behind Morton's truck. "See you tomorrow."

"Have a good one."

"You too." As soon as Morton closed the truck door, Anthony left, taking the road toward the edge of town closer to the mountains. He found a couple hikers bouncing to keep warm on the side of the road. The bright colours of their jackets made them look like flags waving in the wind. When they saw his white truck, they hailed him down unnecessarily. Anthony pulled to the side as much as possible without driving into the ditch and parked. "Hi there. You called about an owl?"

"Yes, we did." A slim guy wearing bright blue stepped forward.

"I'm Officer Green with Fish and Wildlife." He extended his hand, and the guy shook it.

"It's up this way." He led Anthony into the trees. "It doesn't look good. We didn't dare touch it."

"You did the right thing."

"I don't think it's been there long. Wonder what an owl is doing out at this time of day."

"Not all owls are nocturnal. Some are active at dawn and

dusk, and even some are active during the day and sleep at night." Most people blanketed all owls into one category, but there were more species of owls than people realized.

"I didn't know that. It's hunkered down next to that bush." He crouched, his eyes squinting and his arm outstretched to point.

Anthony bent down. Stained white feathers poked out from around the bush. The pattern of black speckles over the oddly positioned wing told him it was a snowy owl. Not rare around here, and not nocturnal.

Anthony stood and realized he now had a group of four hikers crowding around him.

"Thanks for the call. I'll take care of this. You enjoy the rest of your hike." He watched them walk away, moving fast to warm up, then he stalked closer to the bush, moving around the side to see what he was dealing with. Blood stained her feathers on her outstretched wing and on the feathers along her side. Only one feather-clad foot touched the ground beneath her. More blood stained the underside around her legs. She was balancing precariously. Eyes that should be yellow glowed a bright orange, and she blinked at him, trying to focus. The poor thing must be in a lot of pain.

"Hey there, beautiful. It's okay," he crooned. With slow movements, he stepped closer, within reaching distance. As quick as the bird of prey she was, her head lurched and she snapped, her beak clacking together. A defensive move, lashing out in fear. She swayed from the movement. "Shh. None of that. I'm only here to help."

Anthony crouched down and tilted his head from side to side to get a good look at her. "You're not in good shape, are you sweet owl?" He'd kept his voice at a calm monotone in hopes to soothe her.

He watched her struggle while trying to figure out the

best way to go about this. He didn't want to cause more harm when he didn't know the full extent of her injuries. An injured wing and he assumed a broken foot, but with the scrape along her side, he couldn't be sure what else.

Her chest puffed in and out and her eyes fluttered. Anthony slowly stretched out his hands, but she didn't snap at him again.

"It's okay. I've got you." He caught her as she fell forward when her eyes closed. She'd lost consciousness.

He gently felt her body for more injuries before lifting her. Standing up, he cradled her uninjured side against his chest and used one hand to support underneath her. His heart ached for the pain she must be in. What she must have gone through.

There was a rehabilitation centre about two hours north and he knew she'd be well taken care of there, but he wasn't so sure she'd make it. The next best place to take her would be to Asher Morestead, Alder Ridge's resident veterinarian. When he'd passed Morestead Clinic in town, it had been closed. Anthony hoped Asher was home.

He hiked back to his truck and positioned himself in the driver's seat, continuing to cradle the owl against him. Frowning, he twisted to reach the opposite side of the steering wheel to switch gears with his left hand. He drove one-handed toward Asher's. She didn't stir until he parked his truck.

JARRING PAIN LANCED THROUGH HER. Holly woke with a gasp and found herself engulfed in large, warm hands. She tensed and looked up. Rich brown eyes filled with comfort looked down at her. The hand beneath her lifted and one finger stroked over her head. His touch, that simple gesture, took some pain away.

A breeze that should have been chilly with encroaching winter rushed around them, creating a pocket of warm air. It was her wind. The unique coloured swirl circled above her and around his head, ruffling his chestnut hair. Seeing the wind meant something. It was always a sign or a warning. But Holly didn't have the strength to decipher its meaning right now.

"I'm going to get you some help." He took a few stairs, then knocked on a door. He was the only thing in her line of sight, and she didn't want to look anywhere else. His scent filled her again as it had back in the woods. The sensations it created mixed with her pain left her floundering, drunk on a potion.

He knocked on the door. Holly recognized the voice of the man that answered.

"Hi, Tony." It was Asher, a friend of Zachary's, who'd helped them escape from the underground fighting ring and had also fought against Tyrone in the woods today.

Guilt crashed on her chest and filled her lungs, clogging the way for her to breathe. She'd fled. She'd fled like a coward. Violence had filled those moments in the woods. Holly did what she needed to do, gouged Tyrone's eye to keep him from shooting her best friends, but as soon as the danger was over she got out of there. Tyrone had broken her leg trying to get her off him. She'd regretted fleeing, trying to find her way back to Zachary, but she'd been too weak.

"Hey, I need your help. Some hikers found an injured owl, and I don't think she'll make it all the way to the rescue centre without being treated first. I hope it's okay I brought her here. I saw your clinic closed when I passed on my way out here."

"Of course it's okay. I'm glad you brought her here." Asher let them in, then started digging in a closet by the door. "In the kitchen. We'll set her down on the table."

The Fish and Wildlife officer, Asher had called him Tony, held her close and waited for Asher's instructions.

"There."

"I'm pretty sure she has a broken foot and an injured wing. And there's a large scrape on her side." Tony explained her injuries while he set her down on the table.

"You'll have to keep holding her for now." Asher said to Tony, but his eyes glanced toward the stairs.

"I can do that."

Asher looked at her wing first. It was tender with his touch, but the pain wasn't unbearable. Tony's hands steadied her on the table. Footsteps on the stairs pulled everyone's attention. She recognized two of the three scents that entered the room. Zachary, Ezaray, and another odd wild scent that held a similar tinge to Ezaray's. She must be Asher's mate.

"Hol..." Zachary started, but Asher cut him off.

"Officer Green brought in an injured owl. These are friends of mine, Zachary and his... Ezaray." Even Asher stumbled over the introduction. Zachary couldn't walk in here and call Holly by name in front of a human, and Asher couldn't call out someone's mate in front of him either.

"Hi there. Anthony." He introduced himself with a nod, but then turned his eyes back down to her. One finger left his hold and stroked over her head. He'd called himself Anthony rather than Tony. It suited him.

"Is she okay?" The fear flowing from Zachary hit her with such force, it filled her. It brought forth panic as she lay on a table surrounded by what felt like giants when in her small state.

"I think she will be." Then Asher reached for her foot. Holly screeched the second his fingers touched her. The pain stretched, covering her leg and more like a spider web.

"Shh. Sweet owl. I've still got you." Anthony crooned as his grip firmed, but his finger still stroked her head. His voice and the heat from his hands helped calm her. But it didn't last as Asher continued to prod at her leg.

Zachary and Ezaray crowded closer the more she squealed and whined.

"What can I do?" Zachary's frantic question barely cut through the nauseous fog swirling through her body.

"Nothing."

"Damn it, Asher." He cursed and ran his hand over his head. Ezaray came into view beside him, her hand on his arm. Zachary was her childhood friend, her hero. He'd rescued her and Ezaray. And while Holly flew off to be alone, he'd mated Ezaray. They were now more connected than she was to either of them. Of course, she was happy for them, but it didn't help the loneliness encasing her heart.

When she'd been fleeing in the woods, she'd tried to get back to Zachary, knowing she'd needed help. But now that she was here, panic overwhelmed her. It hurt too much for Asher to continue to treat her. Zachary's frustration bled into her. He tried to reach for her, shushing and soothing her as he always used to do, but Holly squirmed harder.

"She needs to stay still." Asher's calm command only worked on Anthony.

Anthony readjusted his hold and took a seat in one of the chairs surrounding the table, never losing contact with her.

"We're going to make you all better, sweet owl." Then he

hummed. His warm palms surrounded her and the vibrations coming from his throat sent a calm rhythm through her. The pain was still strong, but it was with Anthony that safety surrounded her.

Why wouldn't she feel safe with Zachary?

His scent, so strong and dizzying, her wind ruffling his hair, and the way his hands warmed her. The pieces hit her all at once. Anthony was her mate.

Fate was a fucking bitch. Holly was in no state to have a mate. She still refused to shift, preferring her freedom as an owl while she healed from her time in captivity. From what she'd learned from Zachary, it was pointless to fight it. And that just made her angrier at Fate and her meddling. She could have sent any other conservation officer to get her, then she'd be in Zachary's hands and perfectly comfortable. But no. Panic at the thought of anyone other than her mate touching her pulsed hard.

"Okay," Asher spoke to her, "I'm going to give you something for the pain so I can reset your leg and bandage you up. It will probably put you to sleep, too."

She pushed herself further into Anthony's hands. There was nothing she could do but accept their help. As long as her mate didn't leave, she knew she'd be okay.

ASHER INSERTED the needle and the owl screeched, her muscles tensing for a moment before she relaxed against Anthony's palms. She'd have a reprieve from her pain. Only moments later her swirling eyes drifted closed, and she fell asleep. Anthony loosened his grip but kept one hand near her head to continue to stroke her feathers. The others that had entered the room were beside themselves, clearly having a strong connection to the animal on the table. He found their behaviour odd, but Anthony let it go. His concern was for his owl.

His owl.

She'd calmed in his arms, in his hands. He felt he had a responsibility toward her. She'd pushed toward him when the others tried to reach for her. Anthony had intended to take her to the rescue once Asher had treated her, knowing that would be the best place for her to recover, but he could no longer do that. Besides, he suspected the other men in the room would argue with his plan.

Was he really going to take her home and care for her himself?

Zachary paced the room while Asher worked, and Ezaray sat at the opposite side of the table. Gwen, Asher's wife, cooked dinner behind them all. The room felt filled with noise, a hum of anxiety, but no one spoke until Asher finished.

"I set her leg. It will heal fine. She has a sprained wing and the scrape in her side isn't deep. It will be sore, though." Asher stretched his back, then started cleaning up.

"Thanks for looking after her, especially in your own home."

"It's not the first time."

"What do I need to take care of her?" All eyes in the kitchen turned on Anthony. He'd figured he'd get some resistance based on the reactions of all the extra people that worried for the owl.

"She can stay here. We'll look after her." Zachary took a few steps toward him, his eyes darkening and ready for a fight. Anthony twisted his lips while mulling over his options. It would be easier to leave her here. She'd be in better care with a veterinarian. He wouldn't get in a fight with an angry guy. But that sense of responsibility for her jumped to the surface. He wanted to take care of her.

"That's a nice offer, thank you. But it's no burden. I found her and am responsible for her." He hadn't meant to admit that.

"I'm responsible for her." The words sounded like they hurt.

"How so?"

Zachary clamped his jaw shut and looked to Asher, who only raised his brow. They knew what each of them wanted to say, but they left Anthony in the dark.

"Have either of you seen this owl before?" Alarm bells installed by his career piqued his curiosity.

"Yes," they answered in unison.

"No rehabilitation centre, please, as we know her home is here. She'll heal well." Asher stepped in front of Zachary. The silence stretched before Anthony answered. Zachary struggled behind Asher who remained calm with steady eyes on Anthony. Gwen and Ezaray both held their breath while looking between Anthony and the other men.

"No centre," Anthony agreed. Asher and Zachary both had strong opinions about this specific owl, but he didn't much care for the idea of parting with her. "What do I need to take care of her?" Anthony pulled out his officer voice to warn them both he was serious about taking her. She'd put her trust in him. He couldn't abandon her.

Zachary tensed, but Asher sighed and gave him instructions. "A large space, no small cage. You can feed her chicken or fish until she's able to hunt on her own. But at that point she'll be on her own, anyway."

"Thank you. I'd appreciate it if you came to check up on her."

"Of course. I'll swing by in the morning."

Anthony cradled the owl as he lifted her.

"I'll come with you and hold her while you drive." Zachary offered, his tone subdued.

"Thank you." Anthony took the peace offering. "I don't live that far. I can drive you back once I have her settled."

"No need."

Anthony said his goodbyes to Asher, Gwen, and Ezaray. Zachary followed him out to his truck. He passed the owl over to him, surprised at his own reluctance to let her go, but pleased she was still unconscious. Her reaction to Zachary inside worried him.

"How long have you known Asher?" Anthony backed out of the driveway and turned the truck around.

"Not long." Zachary looked down at the owl with concern. His eyes never left her.

"You're not from Alder Ridge, are you?" There weren't many people Anthony didn't know, but Alder Ridge wasn't so big you couldn't tell who didn't belong.

"I'm from Hull Creek."

"What brought you down our way?"

"That's a long story." One he didn't want to tell. Anthony let the conversation drop. Zachary didn't want to talk, and Anthony couldn't figure out why he was trying so hard.

Reaching the end of the long lane that led to Asher's, Anthony slowed to look for traffic on the main road before cutting across to the next lane that led to his place. He wasn't so far into the woods as Asher, but he had the same privacy. Something he needed. The time to be alone, away from the town, from prying family and neighbors. Oh, he enjoyed living where he grew up, but he'd been here long enough and chose a profession that kept him under scrutiny. Coming home was his heaven, his peace.

He parked his truck under his tree. When he reached the other side of the truck, Zachary had his door open and was stepping out. "You go unlock. I can carry her in."

Anthony opened his door and allowed Zachary to follow him in. He stopped in his living room and spun around, trying to think of the best setup. Mentally snapping his fingers, he grabbed the spare playpen his sister left during her last visit. He set it up against the wall by his back door that led to the deck and lined the bottom with a couple blankets.

"There. What do you think?" He slapped his fists on his hips and looked at Zachary.

"She'll hate it. She'd be fine with just the blankets on the floor."

"True, but I don't want her doing anything that will cause her more harm."

"I suppose so." His reluctance to agree was evident in the pinch of his lips and the tightening of his jaw.

Anthony took the owl from Zachary and placed her in the centre of the playpen. "I can give you a ride back to Asher's."

"That's okay. It's not that far. I'll walk."

"If you're sure."

"Yeah." He hesitated. "If you need any help with her, you can call me, too." He lifted a pen and paper off the end table and wrote on it before setting it back down. "That's my number."

"I will. Thanks for the help getting her here."

Zachary nodded, and after one last glance at the owl, he left.

"Well, I guess it's just you and me." Anthony stroked her head to see if she would stir, but not a single movement other than her tiny breathing. He eyed his couch, happy he went with comfort rather than aesthetics because that would be his bed for the next few nights.

2

Holly came to, a haze filling her mind and her senses. She tried to stretch her body and winced as fresh pain cut through her. Forcing her eyes open, she tried to make out where she was. Beneath her were soft blankets. The events of the evening flew back into her mind. Being saved by a Fish and Wildlife Officer. Anthony. Her mate.

Her eyes adjusted to the dark. By the scent of the house, this was where Anthony lived, and he'd put her in a pen. It looked a lot like a child's playpen.

She was fully awake now, whatever medicine Asher had given her had worn off. She looked around the room for a clock, knowing not much time had passed. Things like medicine and alcohol didn't have the same effect in small amounts in shifters as it did in humans. It's possible Asher would have given her a higher dose, though.

As she turned her body, she put weight on her injured wing. The painful squeak rushed out of her as she tried to right her body.

Movement on the couch caught her attention.

"You're awake." Anthony turned on a lamp on an end table. Holly winced as it shone in her sensitive eyes. "Oh, sorry." He rushed around the couch and stood between her and the light.

Holly looked up. He wore only his boxers, his muscles on display. She couldn't think. His chest had a thin smattering of hair that didn't hide the lines of his pectorals that sat above a full set of abs. Deeper breaths pulled his scent inside her. Mixed with her pain, dizziness ensued.

"I thought you would have slept all night after the medicine Asher gave you." He ran his hand through his hair, a frown marring his features. For a man who'd been so confident when helping her, he looked so lost now. "He didn't give me anything else to give you. Are you in pain?"

Holly cocked her head.

"I'm sure you are." He leaned against the back of the couch, crossing his feet at the ankles and resting his palms on the furniture. "I wish you could tell me what happened."

Not a chance. He may not be a police officer, but he worked in a law enforcement profession. She hadn't known him long, but any man that would help an owl the way he did and still keep her to look after her would be someone with a specific sense of justice. Besides, she knew nothing of what happened after she'd fled. But she could assume. No way would Zachary have called the RCMP to let them handle the dead bodies of Tyrone and his guard. Not with the circumstances surrounding their deaths. An event that Anthony himself may have been called in on.

Zachary had lured them into the woods after Tyrone had captured Ezaray and Maggie, another girl Holly'd been in captivity with. An easily laid trap with shifters and their pairs around.

Her pair.

Panic tightened her body, every part of her protesting the unrest. Chloe would be searching for her. The magic that changed them matched every shifter with an animal, a twin in animal form that couldn't shift, but their aging changed to match their shifter. Chloe was more than a sister or twin, and after over two years apart, they'd reconnected only for violence to separate them again. Separated by Tyrone and Holly's cowardice.

Holly needed out. She needed to find Chloe. Screeching escaped her lungs and as she spread both wings and put half her weight on her splint-trapped leg. Pain shot through her. She tried to flap, but only had the strength for it in half her body. The other half begged her to stop.

Anthony leapt off the back of the couch. "Hey. Shh. Calm down." He stood over the playpen, blocking her way out, despite the fact she wasn't getting any air.

Please, let me out, she begged him even though he couldn't hear her.

"You're going to hurt yourself, sweet thing." He continued to shush her, but it wasn't enough. Then he hummed, and he bent forward, his hand outstretched. His tentative movements and the calming tune helped her breathe through her worry.

Holly stopped her flailing. Although, she didn't settle. Her wings were still out, and she still had her weight on her broken leg, trying to ignore the pain. The last thing she wanted to do was hurt him.

"There. That's it. You're safe." His fingers reached her head, and he moved them over her in the direction of her feathers. Her breathing turned steadier. The worry for Chloe still throbbed, but she had to trust that Zachary or Ezaray, or somebody would find her and explain where she was, that she was okay.

Anthony was more than kind. Every word from his rich tone settled inside her in ways she didn't understand. But she wanted to curl up in his lap.

"You're scared, but I'm going to take care of you." His sleepy timbre had a low rhythm that turned her insides in a somersault.

He had no idea the vow he'd just made. In his mind, he was nursing an owl back to health to release her back in the wild. Only she knew he was her mate, and that vow could mean so much. It was a vow she didn't need.

She folded her wings in, too quickly judging by the harsh pain, and lifted her foot back off the blankets. She hunched in on herself, huffing at Anthony, her beak snapping in the smallest way.

His brows moved in a quick up and down. Another person would have snatched their hand back, but not him. He gave her one last stroke, then straightened himself.

"And now you're in a mood." He shook his head and walked back around the couch. Holly thought he was going to lie back down, but he started moving his furniture. First the coffee table, then he spun the couch around so it faced her. "You don't need to be alone while you try to get back to sleep."

He laid down and pulled a blanket up to his waist.

Holly closed her eyes so as not to get sucked into the look of the man stretched before her. She craved to know what drove him. Why would he keep her and why would he sleep next to her?

HIS PHONE CHIMED and Anthony groaned as he pulled his arm out from under him to flop to the floor. Turning off his alarm, he opened his eyes, although he only allowed himself to look through tightened up slivers. As they adjusted, he saw the owl. She appeared to be sleeping, but as soon as he swung a leg to the floor, her eyes snapped open and her head lifted.

"Good morning." His groggy tone escaped dry lips. He yawned after scrubbing his face with both hands. A sigh noting he wasn't ready to start the day rushed out of his lungs as he pushed on his knees to stand. He stretched then his eyes landed on the owl who seemed to have perked up with the activity around her.

Anthony braced his hands on the side of the playpen.

"How are you feeling this morning, sweet owl? I hope better, but I imagine it still hurts."

As if to answer him, she stretched out her injured wing with only a wince, then settled it back at her side and stared up at him. He swore a challenge shimmered in her amber eyes that were never fully amber.

"Well, I wasn't expecting that." That was some impressive improvement in one night. She'd allowed him to touch her the night before, so he leaned down to do it again. She tensed until he made contact. Her eyes closed, and she nudged her head against his fingers. "You're beautiful."

The speckled pattern on her feathers was oddly unique. Wisps and swirls connected some of the dots. He'd seen nothing like it. And her eyes. They had a gradient of colours culminating to create the shade of amber that they should be. She was a special creature, and he looked forward to seeing her at her full strength.

"I need to get ready for work. Don't do anything to hurt yourself."

He picked up his phone from the floor and called Asher on his way to his bathroom to shower.

"Hello?"

"Hey, it's Anthony. I was hoping you had time to stop by and check on the owl before either of us leave for work." While she seemed to be doing well, it would be reassuring if Asher looked her over.

"I already planned on it."

"I'm just getting in the shower."

"Okay. I'll be over in half an hour."

Anthony hung up, then made quick work of a shower. He pulled out a clean uniform from his dresser. He loved his career, his town, and had a high respect for nature and wildlife. Choosing this life was an easy decision, despite disappointing his father. But as the years passed, his father stopped arguing with Anthony and left his choices alone once he discovered Anthony would never change his mind, that is. He'd inherited his mother's stubborn streak. He'd had no problem standing up to his father, but that didn't mean the lack of support from him didn't pinch.

Ready for work, he stepped back into the livingroom in time to hear the knock on the door.

When he opened it, both Asher and Zachary stood there.

"Come on in." He shut the door behind them. "She's through there. In a playpen."

"Bet she's not too fond of that." Asher's lips twitched.

"Probably not, but she's safe in there."

"True enough." Asher stood over the playpen and looked down at her. "No snapping," he warned her before reaching in. She tensed, but allowed it.

Asher took her wing and examined it before gently stretching it out. She winced, and Anthony wanted to tell him to stop.

"She's sore, but her wing is already doing well. Still no

flying. And even if she could, she needs her leg to heal before she can land."

"It surprised me how well she was doing this morning."

"She's healthy and strong. There's no reason for her not to heal quickly."

"I saw another snowy owl flying around the woods between Asher's and here." Zachary spoke for the first time since entering his house. But he wasn't looking at Anthony. He watched the owl as Asher adjusted her to look at her leg. The owl's eyes met Zachary's.

"They aren't rare around here. I see them from time to time as well. Part of what I love living on the edge of town. The privacy and the wildlife in my backyard."

"I'm buying a house on this side." Now Zachary met Anthony's gaze. He gave him directions.

"I never thought that run-down place would ever sell."

"I plan to fix it up. A lot."

"Good. We need more of that rather than new houses everywhere."

Asher settled the owl back in place and stood. "She's doing good. Make sure you give her something to eat before you go to work. The better her strength, the quicker she'll heal."

"Thanks, Asher." Anthony let them out, then went to his kitchen to search for something to feed her. He had some fish he'd taken out of the freezer the day before. Pulling that out, he cut off a portion to give her. He found a couple old plastic containers and placed the fish inside one of them and put water in the other.

"Here you go, beautiful." He set the containers down close enough she could reach it without moving, but not so close it was in her way. Anthony watched her for a few minutes to see if she'd eat, but all she did was stare back at him, her eyes wider and more alert than he'd seen yet. "Don't want to eat in front of me, huh? Well, that's all right. I have to go to work, but I'll come check on you soon."

Unable to help himself, he touched her head, then turned to leave, lacing his boots at the door.

If he had another day like yesterday, he may not make it back here. He hoped she would keep herself still until he could get back home.

As soon as the door closed, Holly reached for the fish. Her stomach had been throwing a tantrum all morning, demanding substance. But Anthony had been right, she didn't want to eat in front of him. Not the way she devoured the fish he'd left her. It lacked the punch of freshness, but it was delicious all the same.

It had relieved her to hear that Chloe was okay and nearby. When Zachary mentioned another snowy owl, he hadn't been talking to Anthony. He'd talked to Chloe to tell her where she is and that she's okay. Holly didn't have to worry about her, but she hated being separated.

With the fish gone, fatigue took over Holly's senses. She fought off sleep, but it would be the quickest way to heal. She pulled in Anthony's scent for comfort and allowed herself the healing slumber.

Her skin pricked and tensed only moments before hands wrapped around her, pulling her back from the patio table at the pub. He overpowered her with his size. She bucked against him, trying to loosen his grip or get in a hit to give her an advantage. But his hold was too tight. Her eyes searched around her. More men had the same hold on Ezaray and their other friends. Utterly helpless, despite what she was, they pulled them away from the pub and into the back of a van.

Everything happened in a blur. They'd escorted Holly and Ezaray elsewhere while they had taken their friends to who knows where.

Falling onto the tightly woven red carpeted floor after being thrown into an office, Holly looked up. Up into dark, soulless eyes.

"Welcome to your future."

They stood as the man went on about how they belonged to him now, that their handler would be by to claim them, and they'd be thrown promptly into training.

"Do you understand the consequences?" The consequence for not fighting for him would be death. And he didn't promise a swift one.

Holly spat, wishing she wasn't consumed with fear so she could feel the satisfaction of it hitting his cheek.

He wiped his cheek and spoke to the guard over their shoulder. "She fights first."

The guard pulled them out of the office, his grip bruising on her upper arm. Seeing guards everywhere was like a crushing weight. She had no chance to fight, no chance to rescue Ezaray and herself.

They threw them into a room. Single beds sat on opposite sides of the room like a dormitory. But the room was much smaller.

The four walls inched closer. She packed her panic into a cube as she held Ezaray. If she couldn't rescue them, then she needed to be strong. But the tension of the lid on that box of panic inside her was quickly growing.

The walls. So many walls wherever they took her. She needed out. Holly needed the sky.

Holly's eyes flew open as a screech speared from her lungs. Pain exploded as she spread her wings to fly, but her leg couldn't hold her weight. The sides of the playpen warped in her vision and sunk in above her, closing off the opening. She had to get out before she was trapped again.

Her attempts to fly, climb, hop, they all created massive flailing motions. Her failure only fed her panic. She was as helpless as she'd been for the past two years.

The front door banged against the wall and heavy boots sounded on the floor. Holly screeched and tried harder, clawing into the frail mesh meant to contain a baby.

The scent of musk and pine, the trees she loved, filled her senses. Heavy hands landed on the edge of the playpen, pulling them apart from the warped, nightmarish vision. A large chest covered in a green shirt and vest blocked her path.

"Hush. You're okay. You're safe." The firm voice wasn't from her nightmares. She looked up into Anthony's rich eyes.

No, not him. He could stop her. His scent, his touch. He'd calm her down and she wouldn't escape.

"Shh, sweet owl." There it was. His soothing words, and she hopped a little less. Her wings released a bit of their tension. "I know you want out of there, but you're not ready."

If she were a normal owl, no, she wouldn't be. But she wasn't normal. Holly let herself settle back in the centre, hobbling to get herself back into place. She didn't lay her wings to her side, but kept them out and ready. Staring up at Anthony, she commanded him with a glare to move out of her way. He only stared back with a challenge in his upward brow.

"I'm so sorry I can't let you out." And he sounded it, as if he knew how much it pained her to be kept in a pen. He thought he understood, but he didn't. He didn't know she wasn't just an owl or that she'd been kept in captivity for over two years and forced into an underground fighting ring.

She fluffed her feathers and settled her wings.

"That's better, sweet owl." Anthony leaned forward and stroked over her head.

She soaked in his touch, but as soon as she caught herself closing her eyes and pushing back against him, she shook. Holly pinned him with her eyes and snapped her beak. Damn mate bond. She didn't want to be calm. She wanted to be free.

Anthony only pulled away and chuckled. "Grumpy now, are you? Well, that's just fine. As long as you're resting. But I don't suppose you'll let me look at your leg to make sure you didn't hurt it?" He settled against the playpen to reach for her leg. Holly snapped at him again.

He backed off. "Okay. For now," he warned her and left toward the kitchen, but he kept one eye on her the entire time he made himself lunch.

Anthony put more fish in the dish beside her before he left to go back to work.

"Behave."

She huffed to herself. Holly didn't intend on obeying her mate.

3
—————

"I forgot to ask how it went with the owl last night?" Morton shut the door of the truck and met Anthony around the front. They'd gotten a call to investigate hunting on private property. The farmer stood waiting for them by his tractor.

"She's hurt pretty bad. I'm taking care of her."

"You are? Why didn't you take her to the rehabilitation centre?"

"Not sure. I took her to Asher, then thought it would be best not to put her through the drive." That was a lie. Other than Asher asking him not to take her to the rescue, he had no good reason to keep her as he was. Except that he wanted to.

"She'd be better off up there. I can handle the calls today if you want to drive her up. She might be up for the drive now that she's rested."

Anthony didn't want to tell Morton that he'd caught her trying to escape only an hour ago.

"She's fine. Asher is coming in to check on her too." He

looked around the farm at nothing in particular, as long as he didn't meet Morton's gaze.

Morton shrugged, holding his shoulders up. Anthony knew what his partner looked like when he caved. Morton kept his opinion, but was backing off. "Whatever you say."

"Afternoon, Mr. Wilson," Anthony called to the farmer as they approached.

"Tony. Morton." Jake Wilson had known each of them since they were toddlers. And as they got older, he quickly put them, and any other kid rambling nearby, to work on the farm.

"So, they were around again this morning?" Morton asked.

"I don't think they've left. I think they're camping just outside my property and watching the herds. Listen, I don't mind people hunting on my property, saves me some trouble, but not if I don't know the people doing it and they haven't talked to me first."

"We understand. We'll check the trail cams we set up last time and take a hike around to check for camping and where they are coming in and out of." Anthony shook Jake's hand before he and Morton got back in the truck to circle the property. "How's Janie?" Anthony could see his friend was getting serious.

"She's good." And he also didn't enjoy talking about it too much, so naturally Anthony liked to tease him.

"Good? A weekend trip together next week is more than good."

"How the hell did you hear about that?"

Anthony shot a wide eyed look that said Morton could figure it out himself.

"Hazel," Morton muttered irritably, but his lips kicked up in a smirk. No one could be mad at Hazel.

"So, spill."

"I like her. A lot. Happy?"

"Yeah." Anthony didn't hide his grin.

"There." Morton pointed to the treeline beside the road. Broken branches led into the trees, and on the side of Jake Wilson's property. "Circle back and park the truck. We'll head out on foot."

"Agreed."

It took them two hours, but they'd found the hunters camp sites and all their trails in and out of Wilson's property. They even found the hunters themselves, tracking right behind the herd. It took another hour to deal with the hunters before they got back to town.

"No more reports, fellas." Hazel waved them off when they came through the door. As soon as they finished their paperwork, they were free to go home.

Anthony worried about what he'd find when he walked into his house after work. The screech he'd heard at lunch was full of so much terror, it sent chills down his arms. He'd rushed in and found the owl flailing in an attempt to escape. He didn't blame her, but she'd only hurt herself.

When he'd looked down into her eyes, fear hadn't been the only thing he'd seen. Simple panic shone in her swirling orbs. It worried him.

Being more gentle with the door this time, Anthony was cautious as he walked through his house to check on her before even taking his boots off. She was in the same spot he'd left her, puffed up and angry.

"Still mad, huh?" Her eyes had pinned him as soon as he'd come into view. She wasn't resting, and the fish he'd given her at lunch was still in the dish. "I understand, but being grumpy won't do you any good."

She snapped her beak, even though Anthony hadn't

reached for her. He sighed and walked back to the door to take his boots off. As he toed off the last boot, someone knocked on his door. He opened it right away and found Zachary on the other side.

"Hi. Can I come in? I wanted to see how she's doing?" If Anthony hadn't seen the man's reaction to her when he brought her to Asher, this visit would be odd. But the last thing Anthony wanted was to worry anyone.

"Of course." He stepped back, then closed the door behind him. Zachary walked through his house and stopped near the playpen. "She's mad. She panicked early this afternoon."

"Is she okay?" Zachary didn't take his eyes off the owl.

"I believe so, but she hasn't let me look at her to make sure."

Something like remorse filled Zachary's eyes. "I also wanted to tell you, since I'd offered my help with her, that I need to leave town for a bit. But Asher is available if you need anything."

"Thank you. I'm sure I'll get Asher to look at her again soon. I'm surprised she could move the way she was earlier."

"Fast healer, it seems."

"Where are you going?"

"I have to take Ezaray to see her parents." He glanced at the owl from the corner of his eye.

It didn't sound like a happy occasion, but Anthony didn't want to pry. Zachary continued anyway.

"It's been a long time since she's seen them. She's been trying to wait, but it's time."

"I'm not sure I follow. But family can be important. How long will you be gone?"

"Not sure, but not too long as I have the house to deal

with and I'd like to get some renovations done before winter."

"Smart plan."

He turned back to the owl and met her eyes. "It's good to know she's safe."

The owl snapped the air at Zachary, who chuckled.

"I guess she is grumpy, but I'm sure she knows I'm right."

Anthony would question the man for the way he talked to the owl, but he was guilty of it himself.

Zachary nodded at Anthony without another word and left.

HOLLY SHOULD BE beside Ezaray for all of this. But she'd refused to shift and hid from her reality. Not ready to face the world, her job, her parents, or even Zachary. If anyone knew the shame she carried, they'd shake her. It wasn't shame for what she'd been through. She was ashamed of how close to giving up she'd been. If it weren't for Chloe, her parents, and especially Ezaray who had been right beside her the entire time, she would have given up. She fought her best fight every time for them. Not for herself, not to survive. Only for them.

She may not have been able to hold on much longer if Zachary hadn't shown up when he did. Still, she hadn't believed a rescue would be successful. She'd begged him to leave, then turned silent on him when he wouldn't. Holly couldn't have lived with herself if he'd died while trying to rescue her.

But in coming for her, he'd found his mate. There was no stopping Fate. The same Fate that had Anthony answering the call from the hikers.

She needed to be free, but how could she walk away from her mate? She was aware of the pain they'd both be in if she did. Engineering an introduction when she already knew him felt deceitful. Holly didn't want to start a lifelong relationship that way. She didn't want to start a relationship at all.

Holly stretched her leg within the splint. It hadn't fully healed, but it had already improved. Another few days and she might fly. She had until then to decide what to do.

"I grabbed takeout for supper. I'll leave the rest of the fish for you. I'll get more tomorrow." Anthony set more fish in the plastic dish, and sat down on the couch that still faced the playpen. He opened the brown paper bag and pulled out a burger.

Holly eyed him as she picked at the fish, attempting to eat it in as graceful a manner as she could manage.

"I wish I knew what happened to you," he said after a pause in eating. "That was quite a bit of damage for something as simple as a fall or crash, and there were no signs of an attack from another animal on you or where the hikers found you."

Anthony's brow furrowed as he took another bite.

"I'm glad someone found you when they did. I'm not sure you would have made it."

Holly hadn't been sure about that either. He finished his burger.

"Morton, he's my partner, thinks I should have taken you to the rescue sanctuary. Even told me to take you today."

Holly snapped her beak to show him what she thought of that idea. Anthony chuckled. The motion showing the laugh lines around his eyes. He was a man that smiled a lot.

"That seems to be the opinion of everyone else, doesn't

it? Myself included. I'm unsure what it is, beautiful, but I couldn't take you there and walk away."

Holly knew what it was, but it surprised her he felt that kind of connection already. She had to leave at some point, sooner rather than later, but she didn't want to hurt Anthony. His kind heart was fierce, and the career he chose suited him well. She'd miss the way he treated her when she left. The way he talked to her, his calming commands. The way he touched her, never afraid she'd hurt him, and always soothing.

Deep down, Holly didn't want to leave. She closed her eyes and hunched in on herself. The thought of leaving soured her mood and appetite. But now that she was healing, she would soon be able to shift. Although if her leg hadn't been broken she still would have remained as an owl. Having a mate was forcing her to face reality.

"Tired, huh? You're not the only one."

Holly opened one eye while he continued to talk.

"Tracking down hunters on private property isn't easy when the property is well over a couple hundred acres." He stood and looked down into the playpen, his head cocked to the side. "I'm going to change. How about I get you some fresh blankets after that?"

This time when he reached down to touch her, she straightened and met his hand. He stood with a grin and she realized what she'd done. Holly shook her feathers and hunkered back down while he walked away.

When he came back, he wore a black t-shirt and grey sweatpants, and he carried a clean blanket over his arm. His bare feet padded across his hardwood floor. Hanging the blanket over the side of the playpen, his eyes squinted in hesitation.

"You're going to have to let me pick you up."

Him holding her again, both scared and excited her. She may snap at him, but she'd never hurt him.

He reached down and started by petting her head. She allowed herself to lean against him, giving him assurance she would allow what he was about to do. Gently, his hands ran down her sides and he lifted her.

"There, that's my sweet girl."

Holly wished he knew who she really was when he said that. But she couldn't be his. Not when she hadn't been herself in years. Instead of taking the time to heal alongside Ezaray and with the help of Zachary, she'd remained an animal and refused to face whatever person she'd become since being captured by Tyrone. Holly feared that person. That person wouldn't know how to function to reunite with her family, her friends, her contacts for her job. Flying around the world writing articles for whoever would take them didn't have the same appeal it once did.

"Shh. I won't hurt you." His warm breath from his whisper ran down her back and she realized she trembled. He held her for another moment, shushing her, before turning in a circle. "Now, where am I going to put you while I change the blankets?"

He decided on the floor between the couch and the playpen.

Holly eyed the couch above her. She wanted to test her strength at a time she wasn't panicking. Glancing back at Anthony, she waited until he had a handful of blankets, then braced herself with most of her weight on her good foot and only a fraction on her injured one.

With a deep breath, she leapt, spreading her wings to get some lift.

"What are you doing?"

Holly landed on the couch just as graceful as she'd

hoped. She hopped to the corner with a cushion and turned around to look at Anthony. He stared at her with a slack jaw. Inwardly grinning, she wiggled into the cushion.

"Comfortable?" he asked, lifting one brow and setting a fist on his hip.

She wiggled again.

Anthony shook his head and finished laying out the blankets.

ANTHONY STARED at the pride in her eyes, lost at what to do with her. He shouldn't allow her to stay on the couch, but he didn't see what it could hurt for now.

He threw the blankets in the washer and grabbed a beer from the kitchen. Just as he sat down on the couch beside her, his phone rang. He winced when he saw it was his mother.

"Hey, Mom. How are you?"

"I'm well. And I'd like to know how my son is. It's been too long since you called your mother, Anthony."

Anthony winced, and he always would when his mom scolded for not calling or visiting often enough. He never meant to wait so long between calls. Work kept him busy, but he hated using that excuse on his mother. "I'm sorry. How's dad?"

"He's fine, too. But if you want to know how we really are, you'll have to call us or come visit. Now, what have you been up to lately?" Responsibility, one thing on which his parents had always shown a united front. Anthony looked over to the owl. He'd gone on calls for injured animals hundreds of times, but that sense of responsibility that overcame him when he found her had never reared its head before.

"It's the busy season, with hunting and all."

"Yes, we ran into Jake Wilson late this afternoon. Said you and Morton was up to his place to scare off some hunters."

"We were. Found an injured owl the other night." He hadn't meant to bring up the owl, but as his eyes hadn't left her, it was what was on his mind.

"Oh? Is it okay?"

"Yeah, she's okay. Or she will be."

"The rescue is such a lovely place. I'm sure they'll take good care of her."

"They are, but I didn't take her there. I took her to Asher Morestead. She was in pretty bad shape and needed to be looked at right away. Then I brought her home. I'm taking care of her until she's healed."

"What about when you're at work all day?"

"I come home to check on her when I can and Asher has offered to do the same."

"Well, that's good. He's a good man. And his new wife is sweet. Have you met her?"

"I have." Not only met her, but had to interview her in an investigation earlier this year. Anthony still wondered where those wolves were. He often searched for them anytime work called him to the woods between his and Asher's homes. He ran his fingers over the owl's head. She opened one eye to watch him. Seemed these woods were full of incredible wildlife.

"You'll be at dinner tomorrow, right?"

"Of course." Although he wondered if he'd be comfortable leaving the owl alone for that long. He figured he could call in a favour from Asher.

"Good." She asked more about work, and about Morton, then said her goodbyes.

But her scolding had his lips twitching as he called her back.

"Anthony?" she answered.

"Hi, Mom."

"What is it?"

"I called to ask how you and dad are."

"Oh, you smartass." But she laughed and proceeded to tell him.

When they finished talking for the second time, he realized he was still petting the owl's head.

"You might be getting too comfortable here."

She snapped the empty air in front of her without opening her eyes.

He needed to talk to Asher, maybe even call the rescue to ask some questions. She could have difficulty adjusting if he kept her here much longer. But there was a part of him that didn't want to let her go.

4

—————

The door shut with more force than usual, and Holly sat up straighter. She felt Anthony's irritation before he reached the living room. The words "Hey there, beautiful" didn't come to life as he walked into his kitchen first to retrieve a beer, then sat on his couch. He leaned his head back and stared at a blank space on the wall. He'd just finished dinner with his family. Something she should have already done several times in the past few weeks.

When the silence stretched, she squawked to get his attention. He lowered his eyes. The weight of them hit her. When he still said nothing, she squawked again.

"What is it, beautiful?"

Holly flapped her wings and hopped.

"You want out?"

She repeated her motions. Anthony twisted his lips before setting his beer down and taking the two steps to reach the playpen. Gently cupping either side of her, he lifted her out and set her on the couch before retaking his seat. He picked up his beer and stared back at the wall.

Holly didn't like his sullen mood. And she intended to change it.

Hopping closer to him, she nudged his arm with her head. When he only looked at her, Holly pecked at the sleeve of his shirt.

"What was that for?"

She opened and closed her beak, then nudged his arm again.

"You're one special owl." Awe and sadness settled over his tone. "Your leg hasn't healed enough to go back to the wild, but you're getting too comfortable with me. You won't be able to stay here much longer."

He was right, but not for the reasons he thought. It was becoming more difficult each day not to shift and tell him what she was, what he was. She loved his touch, but craved to touch him herself. To run her hands over his bare chest that she had the pleasure of seeing each night and each morning. While he no longer slept on the couch beside her, he rarely got dressed before getting himself breakfast and often came out for a drink before climbing back into bed. And every time he'd pass the playpen, he'd stop to run a single finger over her head.

"I suppose you have no idea what it's like not to live up to family expectations."

She didn't, at least not until these past two years, but her family had yet to know what she'd been through and where her mind had truly gone. She was an only child and had parents that cherished her, supported every decision she'd made. And as a child, she'd never worried about disappointing Zachary. Maybe if they'd stayed in contact over the years, she may have disappointed him with some of her teenage decisions. She doubted dating would have been easy with him over her shoulder.

"My father never lets the opportunity slip to say how happy he is that at least I didn't join any other law enforcement. Heaven forbid I became an RCMP officer. But at least he doesn't outright state his loathing for my career anymore. You'd think he had a hatred for law enforcement. He doesn't. He doesn't quite have a certain respect, but he doesn't hate them. My father values trade work more. Believes there aren't enough quality trades people. There're lots of trades workers, but not enough quality. He resents the fact that I didn't put my skills and morals into that."

Anthony didn't have support from his father. It may be a minor issue within a loving family, but that could affect a person's self-worth more than they realize. Holly hopped closer to his thigh, not putting any weight on her injured leg. It wouldn't be long and she'd be able to fly. She didn't want to jeopardize that. With another bigger hop, she landed on his jean-clad thigh.

He winced, "sharp."

She balanced, and her talons loosened their grip.

"That's better." His hand lifted and Holly melted with his touch. She wanted to fight it. To fight the growing attraction and connection to him as her mate. But it was useless. At least for now, she gave in.

Holly took the comfort from her mate and hoped she provided comfort for him in return.

For the next three days, Holly had worked on her strength while Anthony was at work. And she had spent the evenings in content listening to him talk. Anthony didn't like silence. He hadn't said as much, but he never allowed the quiet to stretch, except on the night of his family dinner. He'd told her about each day, about the people in his life. She'd heard all about a woman named Hazel that every officer in Alder Ridge adored. She sounded like someone Holly would love, spunky and forceful.

Each day she tested the amount of pressure she could put on her leg and tried to hop and lift herself enough to land on the edge of the playpen. It took the full three days, but she reached the edge just as Anthony walked in the door from work.

"WELL, DAMN. LOOK AT YOU." Anthony dropped his jacket over a chair and stalked into the living room. The owl perched on the edge of the pen, looking healthy and whole. Seems the time had come. With a sigh, he pulled out his phone and dialed Asher.

"Hi, Tony. Everything all right?"

"Hey. Yeah, but you should come check on the owl when you have a chance this evening."

"Is she okay?" Deep concern filled the veterinarian's voice.

"I think she's better than okay. But I can't imagine her leg has healed enough for her to be free."

"I see. I'll be over in about an hour." Asher hung up.

Anthony tucked his phone back in his pocket and closed the distance between himself and the owl. He'd be sad to let her go, but it was no longer safe for her to continue healing with him.

She cocked her head, and the colour in her eyes swirled.

"I'm going to miss you." He reached for her, but his phone rang. Pulling it out, he watched Hazel's office number flash on the screen. "Hello?"

"Hey, handsome. I know you're off, but I just got another

call, and it's right up by you. Are you home? Think you could go take a look?"

"Sure, Hazel. What is it?" He pet the owl, then turned back for his jacket.

"Had a report of a solid black truck with the bed full of cages and other equipment heading past your way, closer to the mountains. The truck wasn't from around here. The caller said it looked way too new, and the plates were from out of province. He said he got a bad feeling and thought we should check it out."

"I'm on it." Anthony looked back at the owl while he listened to Hazel give him directions, then he left. Once in the truck, he called Asher. "Hey, I just got called out. I could be a while. My spare key is stuck under a loose board on my porch. Let yourself in to check on her. I'll call you when I'm done."

"Okay. Talk soon." Asher disconnected.

Anthony saw the fresh impression in the dirt on the road leading north surrounding the back of his property. Large tires with a generic tread. Locals only used this road for hunting. Unfamiliar didn't mean they were doing anything wrong, but Anthony listened to locals often, taking their instincts seriously. If he wanted their trust, he had to trust them in return.

But that didn't always mean they were right.

The hunting road came to a fork, and the tracks showed on both sides, coming in and out. He followed down the right side and came to the end with no sign of the truck. Anthony parked and got out. It was hunting season. Footprints were plenty right here, fading as they entered the trees. It would be dark soon, and he wasn't equipped to hike during dusk. Sighing, he hopped back in his truck and did the same down the left road. Nothing stood out. If the truck had come in this way, then they'd already left.

Scanning the footprints and beginnings of the trails one last time, he turned to go back to his truck when a shine in the grass caught his eye. Frowning, he bent down, pushing the longer grass out of the way.

A chunk of small silver pipe sat in the grass. It wasn't an odd thing to find. But considering the report, Anthony snapped a couple pictures and placed it in a bag and back in his truck. If there was anything suspicious to find up here, he wouldn't find it now. He'd come back with Morton and take a hike in the next day or two.

He arrived home in time to see Asher leaving his house.

"How is she?" Anthony shut the driver's door and met Asher at the bottom of his porch.

"Really well. Her wing and side are all healed. And her leg isn't far behind."

"It was broken. How is it possible that it's healing that fast? It's barely been a week."

Asher pursed his lips, his eyes narrowing with a secret. He gave a small shrug instead of a full answer. "She's strong."

Anthony frowned. This wasn't the first time he suspected Asher of telling him half truths. The incidents with the wolves a few months back sprang to mind. "I wanted to ask if you thought it best that she finish healing at the rehabilitation centre. She seems very comfortable and I worry she'll have a difficult adjustment. Despite healing as well as she is, she can't possibly be ready to fly."

"I think she'll surprise you. Normally, I'd agree with you and would advise taking her to the rescue. But not in this case."

"There's something you're not telling me." He threaded a warning through his voice, drawing on his years of experience in Fish and Wildlife. He'd always considered Asher a friend, going through school together, and having a respectful relationship as adults living in their hometown.

"It's not for me to tell." Asher met his eyes straight on. "Call if you need anything else."

Asher left and Anthony watched him go, mulling over his words. Nothing Asher had said made sense. He personally knew the owl. What information about an animal could the vet possibly have that he refused to say? Anthony stood in his own driveway with his arms crossed until his stomach protested that he'd put dinner off for too long.

Inside, the owl perched on the edge of the playpen again, her leg still in a splint.

"So, the vet says you're doing great. But there's something he's not telling me. I don't like it."

Her eyes widened, as if worried over a spilled secret.

"Yeah, that's what I thought. I bet you know what it is."

Anthony mentally shook it off and went to the kitchen to cook dinner. He set everything out on the counter. His back was to the living room when he heard a faint whoosh. Turning around, he startled at seeing the owl sitting on the kitchen island. She hopped closer to the food he had sitting there waiting to chop.

"Hungry, are you?" And she was strong enough to fly. Anthony ignored that fact. He wasn't ready for her to go, and he couldn't imagine that she had healed enough to be let loose, despite the strength she had right now. He didn't want to let her go until he discovered what Asher wouldn't tell him.

ANTHONY SEEMED pensive the rest of the evening. He treated her the same, but Holly saw his conversation with Asher and her quick healing wouldn't leave his mind. Asher had been right. It was time to go. She'd had no way to tell any of them that Anthony was her mate, but she wondered if Asher had figured it out. He only said what she'd already been thinking.

He'd offered to let her out while Anthony was away, but she refused. She wanted one last evening with him outside of reality. Asher had loosened the knot holding her splint around her leg so she could take it off on her own. The magic of the change would finish any healing.

Holly hadn't shifted since the escape from Tyrone. Except once, days later when she found Zachary. She'd allowed him to hold her, allowed herself the comfort of him after years of missing the only person who felt like a brother. But the longer the air brushed over her skin rather than through her feathers, unease settled. Vulnerability reigned as a human than as an owl. As an owl, she had the sky.

Anthony put the leftovers in a container, but Holly hopped, spreading her wings to close the distance in one movement. She plucked a strip of the chicken he'd cooked and started eating it. He'd offered her both raw and boiled chicken, but she wanted a taste of whatever he'd cooked. And she was so glad she did.

She'd watched him create that cream sauce he'd poured over his chicken and vegetables, and her mouth watered.

"That's probably not good for you. But that's the fastest I've seen you eat."

Creamy with the right dash of pepper filled with the flavour of fresh herbs.

Anthony finished cleaning up, then held out his arm to

her. He hesitated, so Holly did as well. But she wanted to be near him. She leapt and landed gently on his forearm. "You're smarter than the average bird. I have to wonder what kind of life you've had."

She wished she wouldn't have to tell him, but the time would come. Sooner rather than later.

He let her down in the playpen.

"Sleep well, sweet owl." With clouded eyes, he left her there for the night. She listened to him as he readied for bed, hearing every movement he made.

She should leave as soon as he fell asleep. It would be best to make it quick and use the shadows in the night to her advantage if he woke and followed her. But if he woke, he might find a naked woman standing in his living room rather than the owl. He'd taken such good care of her. He had a gentle soul that drew Holly in. It made her wonder what he would do if he found a strange woman in his house.

Holly inwardly smiled. The thought tempted her. Shift now and stay here til morning. Tell all the secrets before she even left.

But she needed to see Chloe.

Asher had offered Holly to stay at his place and also offered the safehouse he'd built where she'd first found Zachary and Ezaray after the escape. Chloe was spending her time up there near Asher's and Zachary's pairs. Holly would stay with Chloe at the safehouse and try to regain her courage to come back to reality as herself. Whatever version of herself was left.

The night hours were long with a sleep that wasn't deep. Knowing that she'd be leaving in the morning gave every sound she heard outside of Anthony's home an ominous impression. She was safe with Anthony, but staying here like this wasn't right.

She sighed as she watched the light from the sunrise show above the trees outside Anthony's glass sliding back door. Anthony's alarm trilled from his room and he groaned.

He was reserved while he got himself ready for work, but he still touched her anytime he passed.

"I'll be home as soon as I can to check on you today. You're too active to leave you alone for so long now."

Holly waited until she could no longer hear his truck, ensuring he was far enough away to give her time.

Lifting her leg and bending down, she pulled at the string over the splint with her beak until it loosened and the pieces fell away. She winced as she stretched it.

She spread her wings and pushed off, landing on the floor. Her heart rate rushed, a sense of urgency to flee before Anthony came back and caught her. She closed her eyes and shifted. But she shook. The more she shook, the more she knew she'd already waited too long. This needed to happen whether or not she felt ready.

Magic and warmth swirled around her and through her, changing her body and shape. The final stages grew painful, especially with her leg, but she'd gotten used to the sensations over the years. Within moments she stood as a woman again. A woman all too aware of her naked state inside her mate's home.

She stretched her leg, no pain or odd movement of the bone from a break. Holly couldn't say she felt as good as new, but she was perfectly fine physically. Asher had said she'd finish healing when she shifted. Taking stock of the rest of her, discovering herself to be healthy and whole, physically.

She turned to the back door and flipped the lock up. With one last look around, she left, sliding the door closed behind her. Holly shifted again on his back deck and took to the sky.

The crisp morning air had a fine layer of frost sitting on the trees and grass. She let out a screech as she approached the safehouse. Chloe emerged from the trees. They circled each other in the air.

They said you were all right. Are you all right? Chloe's eyes widened with worry.

I'm fine. A very kind man found me and has been taking care of me. She needed to tell Chloe who he was. They perched in the tree nearest to the front door. As much as she wanted to stay like this with Chloe, she couldn't allow it. *He's my mate.*

Does he know?

Not yet. Holly leaned her head against Chloe's. *I'm not ready, but I have to be.*

You are ready. And I'll be right here.

Holly pulled away and flew down to the ground. She closed her eyes and shifted, the old feelings becoming more comforting now that she'd done it a few times. With a deep breath, she walked into the house to find the clothes Asher said would be there.

Reality lingered in front of her.

5

———

Asher's secrets hung as a hazy cloud over his mind, occupying Anthony's focus. He'd tried to put the pieces together since he'd seen Asher in his driveway the night before. He couldn't shake the feeling that there was a connection between Asher and the owl. Even between Zachary and the owl. But what any of that meant, he didn't know.

Both Hazel and Morton sent him home for an early lunch and to clear his head. He'd been useless. When normally he was the first of him and Morton to speak up, he'd stayed silent, earning a frown from Morton who took over all conversations.

Anthony let himself in, dropping his jacket, but leaving his boots on. Despite being given the extra time, he wouldn't be here long. Just long enough to grab something to eat and check on the owl. He stalked into the house. The playpen sat empty. A pin prick of panic pinched his lungs, but he hesitated before letting the feeling dig roots. Her splint lay in the centre, the knot undone rather than torn. She was mobile now. She must have moved. He spun in a slow circle around the living room, then went to the kitchen. No sign of her. He searched down the hall and in every room. Nothing. Not a thing out of place, no feathers fallen to the floor.

In denial, he searched the house again. He checked the doors. They'd all been locked. But not anymore. The back door was closed, but unlocked on the inside. Anthony examined it, looking for signs of forced entry. Again, he found nothing.

How the hell had she gotten out? Deciding to take that long lunch after all, he stepped out onto his back deck, determined to search for her. An insane decision. He'd never find her. But the unexpected loss of her didn't sit right with him.

One step off his deck and his phone rang.

"Yeah." He hit his ear with the phone and clipped off his answer with impatience that rivaled his father's.

"You are cranky today." Morton snapped back. "The truck from last night was spotted again. Heading your way."

Anthony sighed as he continued to search the trees. "Okay. I'll meet you there."

Morton hung up.

Anthony clenched his fists, straining the joints in his knuckles. He had to let her go. But he'd figure out her mysterious escape. Despite being an extraordinarily smart animal, she would have needed help getting out. Asher. No one else knew how well she was healing and also knew where he hid his spare key. Those connections he'd been considering were forming stronger lines in his mind. Was there also a connection with the wolves from the summer?

He didn't have time for this now, but he'd be paying Asher a visit later today.

Locking his doors, he hopped in his truck and left to

meet with Morton. At the entrance to the hunting road, Morton got in Anthony's truck.

"There're fresh tracks. The thaw from the frost this morning softened the ground. There's only one set in. Nothing out."

Anthony nodded and drove in, parking at the fork. They got out and looked around. The tracks turned right, but fresh footprints came in and out in both directions. "Let's follow the truck."

At the end of the right road sat the black truck matching the description given the night before. They parked behind it to block him in. It only took a quick look in the truck to see no one was in it. While they couldn't search the truck or the contents in the bed, traps and hunting gear were clearly visible. Trapping wasn't illegal, but there were strict regulations. And it depended on the animal one intended to trap. The traps looked to be homemade. Well done, but Anthony didn't recognize their structure.

"You ever seen traps like those before?"

"Nope." Morton shook his head once, then nodded into the woods. They hiked in silence, watching for any tracks. Or traps.

A rustling under a bush had Anthony turning his head. "Morton," he called, keeping his voice hushed.

The trap was better hidden than Anthony would have imagined. If the mouse in the small cage hadn't been panicking, he may never have seen it. The bush wasn't rooted in the ground. They had built the trap within it as camouflage. It was difficult to examine without getting down on the ground. One pull on the small cage holding the mouse would spring the trap, throwing a net over the animal. Lots of smaller animals would go after the mouse. Many of which were legal to trap with the proper licenses, but the use of net made Anthony believe this trapper was after birds.

Anger rose as he thought of his owl snared in this trap.

Morton pulled out his phone to snap all the necessary pictures. When he nodded, Anthony hooked a stick inside the cage and pulled, springing the trap. While Morton took more pictures and collected the equipment, Anthony continued to hike, keeping a closer eye to the ground and other bushes for more traps.

A twig snapped in the distance, but complete silence followed it. Anthony cocked his head in the direction of the sound. As soon as he started moving in that direction, he heard running.

"Morton!" He yelled for his partner and pointed right, back toward the trucks, hoping Morton could cut him off.

Anthony didn't see the bush behind the tree in front of him. As he rounded it, his foot caught the edge of a cage, springing the same type of trap they'd just found. The bar on the round hoop holding the net hit his ankle. He fumbled, catching himself on another tree. He kept running, but saw Morton skidding to a halt as the black truck maneuvered around Anthony's and sped off, leaving deeper rivets in the dirt road.

"Damn it." Morton cursed, then looked at Anthony and down toward his feet. "You all right? I heard a snap."

"I'm fine. Sprung a trap and tripped, but I'm fine. Guess we have an illegal trapper to track down. Did you get the license plate?"

"I did."

"Good." He turned back into the woods to collect the other trap and search for more. In the end of their search they found, documented, and collected four more traps. Heaving the last trap into the back of the truck, Anthony stretched his back and looked up into the trees. It would be late before he could get out to search.

Bright eyes shone from between branches. It couldn't be her. He started into the trees, keeping his sight on the eyes.

"Tony?" Morton called after him, but Anthony ignored him.

The eyes disappeared and Anthony kept chasing where he thought they were, but all he saw was a flash of white between the trees.

Writhing determination rose to two peaks in Anthony's gut—one pointing toward the owl and the other toward the trappers. No way was anyone trapping birds in his territory, not with his owl out there.

HOLLY FORCED every emotion out of her. She tried to anyway. Pacing the bare safehouse, she'd screamed, cried, talked to herself. She'd dug down deep and searched through the trash pile of emotions from the past two years to pull them up one by one. Some of them came kicking and screaming and others wouldn't budge, shying away from the light.

Anger was the easy one. She'd stomped and screamed with a wild ferociousness that had been bubbling low for a long time. So much anger and at so many people, herself included. Anger at the people in the world that would abduct women, hell abduct anyone, to use for any reason. Anger at herself for her attitude toward Zachary when he'd shown up to rescue her. There was even anger at Ezaray for following along with Zachary's plans when Holly wouldn't. A strain pulled at her heart from losing her two best friends, despite knowing that wasn't true. She should be with them right now, reuniting with her family as well, standing by

Ezaray's side as she reunited with hers. But being a coward, she wouldn't face reality. Fate didn't care of her cowardice and forced reality on her.

Holly shook as she forced herself to think on the things she'd been through, fighting other scared women and having no choice but to win. She forced the thoughts into her head, digging into memories that had buried themselves deep. As more of them flitted across her mind like sped up images of an old black and white independent film, tears jerked from her eyes. And once they began, they wouldn't stop.

Collapsing to the floor, she wept, full sobs of ugly crying. She was grateful no one was there to witness her, because when she tried to reign them in, tried to stop the barrage of images, no barrier formed.

She'd had no idea of the time passed when the sobbing turned to painful hiccups. Hollowness filled her. And she had only herself to blame.

Holly fought the urge to shift, to hide inside her animal. It would be easier, but she feared she'd never find herself. She hadn't faced any of this flying with her pair while Ezaray and Maggie started new lives. The support system had been there for Holly, but she'd refused the help. And now she was alone.

Holly stood and made her way to one of the small bathrooms. She showered and found fresh clothes. Zachary and Ezaray must have stocked this place with clothes that would fit her in the hopes she'd come around. If it hadn't been for finding her mate, she wouldn't be here now.

A sixth sense sent a tingle over her skin. Someone was approaching the safehouse.

Holly closed the cupboard door she'd been searching through silently. She couldn't hear much. They had excellent control. She'd known Zachary to be that quiet, but Zachary wasn't in town. The likelihood of it being someone dangerous was slim, but her body didn't listen. Every muscle tensed.

Footsteps tapped on the wooden stairs and someone knocked lightly. Holly sniffed, realizing too late she could have done so sooner. It was Asher.

He opened the door before she made a move from the kitchen. "You made your escape."

"I did. Thank you for letting me stay here." She hadn't actually met the man before, not as herself.

"How's your leg?"

"Better. Just as you'd predicted. The shift finished the healing." She tried to smile at him, but her lips wouldn't lift.

"Good." He hesitated, but his eyes pierced her. Determination filled the space around him. He wasn't here to just check on her and go on his way, leaving her to suffer alone. "You found everything you need? The cupboards don't have much."

"Yes. Zachary or Ezaray must have left clothes for me. But you're right, the cupboards are pretty bare."

"They did. I talked to him this morning. He says they'll still be a few more days. He wanted me to tell you he's talked to your parents."

Her chest throbbed, an unwelcome burning flared despite knowing it was the right thing to do. It wasn't fair to keep them wondering what happened to her, not when they'd see Ezaray safe. They'd disappeared together. Her family deserved an answer too.

"He only said you were safe and needed more time alone. I believe he promised to bring you back to them himself."

She nodded.

"Holly, Gwen and I aren't far away. We're here for what-ever you need."

"Thank you. I appreciate the help." She tried not to sound so stiff, but when Asher pursed his lips and sighed, she knew she hadn't been successful. "I'm not ready to leave. Baby steps."

"Fair enough. How about I bring you some groceries later? You can have decent food while you're staying here."

"Thank you." She followed him to the door. When he stripped, she averted her eyes into the trees. Chloe flew in from somewhere and perched herself above. A soft thud of paws hitting the ground made Holly look back at Asher. A white wolf with piercing blue eyes stood in his place. He nodded and ran back through the woods toward his home.

Holly looked up at Chloe.

"Where have you been?"

Chloe lifted her wings in a shrug, a gesture Holly had taught her when they were owlets.

Holly sent her a look that said behave, then went back inside. Asher may not have pushed, but her instincts told her they wouldn't leave her alone anymore.

ANTHONY DIDN'T GO HOME after he and Morton finished submitting their reports and all the traps they'd found. He stayed long enough to do his part and left Morton there to run the search on the license plate. Anthony pulled into Asher's driveway and waited. His truck wasn't there, but Anthony wouldn't leave until he talked to him.

It wasn't long and Asher parked beside him. Gwen got out of the passenger side.

"Hello, Officer Green."

"Hi there. You can call me Anthony if you'd like." If he was about to confront her husband, the least he could allow was a first name basis.

"Okay, Anthony."

"What can I do for you, Tony? How's the owl?"

"I believe you already know how she is." Because he only had a working theory, only guessed there was a connection, he tempered his tone. He'd hoped Asher's expression would confirm it, but nothing.

"She was doing really well this morning."

"When you let her out?" Anthony poured the accusation slowly, calmly, but he made sure his meaning was clear.

Asher frowned. "I didn't let her out." He helped Gwen with bags of groceries from the back seat of his truck.

"If you've got some time, I'd like to talk." This would be best not to do in front of Gwen. He grabbed onto control before he continued to accuse her husband in front of her.

"Sure. I'll be right back." He followed Gwen into the house with an armload of groceries, but still carried one when he came back out. "What's up?"

"I was hoping you would tell me. The owl is gone and I can't figure out how. My gut is telling me there's a connection to you." Anthony resisted the urge to step closer to Asher. He wanted honesty from him. He didn't want to intimidate a friend, not that anyone could intimidate Asher.

"So the owl escaped?"

"I'm not sure how. All doors were closed and locked before I left for work. When I went home to check on her, the back door was unlocked, but closed. Someone had to have let her out. The only possibility is you. What's the connection, Asher? Why?"

"I didn't let her out. But she had healed enough to be on her own."

"You're trying to tell me she did it herself?" Anthony gripped the back of him neck and turned away for a moment. "There's more. She's smart. Smarter than the average owl, or any bird of prey. She's smarter than any other animal I've seen, except maybe the wolves we found here on your property earlier this year."

"Is that so?"

"Asher." Anthony's frustration let loose. "Tell me what I'm missing. There's a reason both you and Zachary kept checking on her. And there's a reason you didn't want her to go to the rescue. Why?"

"I have a question for you first. Why were you so determined to take care of her? Why didn't you leave her here with me?"

"I don't know. I felt responsible."

"You've searched for her, haven't you?" Asher's eyes narrowed.

"No time, but I intend to."

"Want to go for a hike?" Asher's tone changed to something resembling jolly. He stood and lifted the last grocery bag, pulling the long straps onto his shoulder.

"What?" What the hell was the man talking about about? His abrupt change in conversation left Anthony reeling.

"Let's go."

Even more confused than when he'd first arrived, Anthony followed Asher across his yard and into the trees.

"Where are we going?"

"You'll see." They hiked side by side in silence, mostly. Anthony recognized the well-beaten trails he and Morton had found when searching for the wolves, although they looked less used now.

"You know something, don't you?"

Asher looked at him from the corner of his eye. "You know how I'm going to answer that."

"You know lots of things. Asshole." Anthony turned away to mutter the insult.

Asher chuckled, but sobered after a moment. "I think I'll be free to tell you everything soon, but right now, it isn't my secret."

His cryptic words only pissed Anthony off. He didn't bother asking any more.

The hike was long, and Anthony's legs had tired when a building came into view over a rise.

"Since when is there a house up here?" With no road to get to it.

"It's new. And it's mine. It's not common knowledge."

He meant it was another secret. "What's it for?"

Asher's lips twisted before he answered. "Safety."

Anthony shook his head.

Asher took the steps and knocked on the door.

"If it's yours, why are you knocking?"

A woman opened the door. A young one with wavy brown hair and stark hazel eyes that widened when she saw him standing beside Asher.

"I brought you some groceries."

"Thank you." Her voice squeaked.

"Officer Green, this is Holly."

"Anthony." He held out his hand and Holly only stared at it.

"That's what I thought." Asher muttered and stepped into the house. "I'll help you put these away." He ushered Holly back inside and left Anthony to close the door behind them. Asher leaned down and said something to Holly that he couldn't hear. She gave him a shaky nod.

Anthony took in Holly's small frame and the way she

held her body. Her muscles tensed and the flesh around her eyes was swollen. She'd been crying at some point. Asher said this place was for safety.

Her eyes cut across the room to hit him in the chest. There was something familiar about her, something that made him take those few steps to be closer to her. She and Asher finished with the groceries.

"Tony came to talk to me about an owl he's been taking care of. She's escaped, and he thought I let her out."

"Oh? Why would you do that?" She raised her brow at Asher. His lips twisted.

"I didn't. But Tony doesn't believe she escaped his house on her own."

"You must have left a window open." She looked at him and her eyes brightened. Her challenge vanished as she looked down.

"It's too cold to leave doors and windows open." Anthony still had questions, but he didn't want to ask them in front of Holly. "Asher said this place was his. How long are you visiting?"

"I don't know."

"I need to get back. Stay if you'd like, Tony. I'm sure Holly would like the company."

Holly glared at the back of Asher's head. "Thank you for bringing the groceries."

"You're welcome."

"It was nice to meet you, but I need to discuss some things with Asher."

Holly followed them out the door and stood on the step.

Asher stopped and turned to him. "You should stay."

"You haven't answered my questions."

"And I still won't. You should stay." Asher left, disappearing over the hill and between trees.

Anthony turned back to Holly, but a flash of white caught his eye. He looked up.

"There you are." His words pitched with relief and excitement. The owl looked down at him, indifference in her eyes. They looked dull compared to the flare and fire he'd seen in her for the past week. "What? Gone only a day and you want nothing to do with me?"

"Do you always talk to animals like that?" Holly had crossed her arms over her chest and had taken one step down away from the door. Despite moving closer and speaking to him, she'd erected strong shields in front of her.

Anthony smiled, more at himself than her. He'd grown attached to the owl. "I've been taking care of that owl for the past week. Hikers found her injured, in pretty awful shape."

She pointed up at the owl. "That owl has been here for weeks. Every day."

"You're sure?" Anthony stepped sideways to see the owl's wings. The same swirled pattern of speckles dotted her feathers.

"Positive."

"That pattern is so unique. There can't be two with the same."

"I've never seen another like her." The first signs of a smile danced on her lips.

"I didn't think so either, but apparently I have." And with discovering the owl he looked at now wasn't his owl, disappointment settled hard. A solid rock that pulled him down.

"I doubt you'll catch up to Asher now. You're welcome to stay and I'll make us something to eat."

She sounded so shy, and it was difficult to judge if she wanted him there. He didn't want the company right now. He'd rather be searching for his owl, but she looked so vulnerable, he couldn't walk away. "That would be nice. Thank you."

With one last look at the owl in the tree, Anthony followed Holly into the house, knowing she was part of what he wasn't seeing, part of Asher's secrets.

6

Why the hell did she invite him in? She'd enjoyed teasing him about Chloe. And seeing him again sparked happiness inside her. But now that she was within close proximity, his body following behind her, it all crashed down. She twisted her fingers in front of her to the edge of pain, keeping herself from turning around and sticking her nose against his chest to inhale his scent. She had no plan of what she was going to do or say. Her emotions were still raw from the jailbreak from wherever her subconscious had locked them away.

Asher had just taken the first steps for her to tell Anthony the truth. Why else would he have brought him up here to his super secret safehouse for shifters? As Asher had guided her inside with the groceries, he'd leaned down and whispered in her ear.

"Is he your mate?"

All she could do was nod. There was no point in lying. The emotions and sensations scattered chaotically through her system. She'd been comfortable as an owl, but the second her human eyes landed on Anthony, it all intensified.

"That's a lot of bedrooms."

She didn't answer him. It wasn't hers to comment on. She was only staying here for the purpose Asher had intended.

"Are you visiting Asher?"

"Not really. I'm a friend of Zachary's." Holly answered everything with as much truth as possible. She'd have to tell him all and it would be easier if she didn't let it drag on.

"Can I help with anything?"

"Sure." Holly had seen the way he cooks and it wouldn't be a hardship to have him help. She passed him ingredients for the pasta sauce while she started chopping for a salad. She watched him put the butter in the pot and slowly melt it while adding garlic and onion. He worked effortlessly to whisk in the flour, then milk. "You're not a bad cook, are you?"

"My mother wouldn't have it any other way."

Holly smiled, remembering the phone call he'd had with his mother just the other night.

Anthony continued to stir the sauce while Holly finished the salad and started the water to boil. "Where are you from?"

"Originally Hull Creek. That's how I know Zachary. But we moved away when I was eight." And because he didn't know how much she knew of him she had to add, "You grew up here in Alder Ridge, right?"

"Is it that obvious?" He scrunched his nose, but the smile said he loved living here.

Holly smiled back, warmth seeping into her with the exchange.

"Asher said he built this place for safety." He paused, and

she didn't answer, not when she predicted what he would ask next. "Why are you staying here?" His stirring slowed and he turned toward her, but Holly kept her eyes away, despite how comforting and rich it was to look at him. He hadn't asked with his tone full of accusation. He'd asked with concern for someone he didn't even know. Mate bond or not, she could fall in love with this man.

"To get back on my feet." She put the noodles into the boiling water.

Anthony didn't pry further, but she felt his eyes on her more while they finished cooking.

"I think there's beer in the fridge that Asher has left here if you want one."

"That would be nice, thank you."

Holly pulled out two beer, realizing this was the first one she'd had since the night they had captured her and her friends. She hadn't had enough then to affect her, but she still blamed herself for her slow reactions to the men closing in on her.

A heavy hand covered hers. She jumped at the pressure and tore her eyes from the glass bottle.

"Are you okay?" His voice dropped an octave, and she was no longer thinking about her past. She was thinking about all the things she'd like to do to Anthony. Attraction grew and zinged between them. It wasn't only her. His eyes widened and his hand squeezed hers.

"Yes." She nodded, the motion shaky. She pulled her hand away.

"Where do you plan to go after you've gotten back on your feet?"

She took a bite of her salad before answering him. To buy her time. "I don't know."

"Where's home?"

"You've got me at an odd time in my life. I think my home is about to change."

"You're full of just as many cryptic secrets as Asher."

"I probably am." She stopped herself from letting out a sigh of regret.

"So, that owl out there. She's been up here this whole week?"

"Yes, she has."

They finished eating. Anthony mulling over the owl and Holly struggling with how to tell him or if she should at all right now. He was a conservation officer, after all. What if he intended to out shifters?

Holly had only gotten a glimpse of his character. Could she be so sure he wouldn't do anything to harm her or the others?

"You've got something on your mind." Holly looked up at Anthony. He leaned back in his seat with his hand around his beer bottle resting on the table. But his focus was solely on her. His hair hung down over his forehead, but not enough to cover his eyes. His skin was tanned from working outside for what she assumed was his entire life. The angular features around his cheeks and jaw gave him the authority he needed to do his job and left Holly melting to the floor when she remembered the calm authority he'd had over her when taking care of her.

Her lip hurt and she realized she'd been chewing on it and she clenched her hands into fists.

"Why did Asher bring me up here to meet you? I had a lot of questions for him, but this was his answer." Anthony leaned forward and even further over the table. His hand lifted and tucked a strand of her hair behind her ear, the gesture more than just kind and gentle. An arousing heat transferred from his skin. The way he clenched his jaw, he felt it too. "I'm sorry."

His apology confused her until he leaned closer, his lips brushing against hers. He waited there with the faintest touch, and Holly couldn't wait any longer. She pressed her lips against his, then he took over the kiss. Anthony's hand firmed around the side of her neck, holding both of them in place. His scent infused her senses, and she had to clench her thighs together to stave off the arousal he wasn't ready for.

With a low growl, he pulled his chair closer and angled his head. Holly allowed the kiss to sweep her away, giving herself a moment of joy when she'd been so deprived of it for so long. The taste on his tongue as he slid it against hers exploded in her mouth. She brought her hand up to anchor herself to his arm. Holly squirmed in her chair and let out a moan. The sound ripped her from the heat pooling inside her. She pulled away.

"I'm sorry."

"You're sorry?" His voice grated over rocks, thick with the same arousal running through her. "I kissed you."

She watched him struggle, his hand never leaving her face. This wasn't fair to him. He should know what she was.

"And I'm going to kiss you again."

It was too easy to melt into him as he took control of her lips. He brought them as close together as possible without either of them getting out of their chairs. The second they did, their hands would get involved.

She needed to tell him. She needed to rip the bandage off.

Tearing herself away a second time, she met his eyes. She panted. "I'm the owl you've been taking care of."

"What did you say?" Anthony didn't let her go, but he pulled his head back to rid himself of the haze of arousal.

"I'm the owl." This time she hadn't rushed her words, but they carried a soft lilt. A whispered confession.

"I don't think I understand what you're saying." A woman, as plain as day in front of him, one he'd kissed and enjoyed, was telling him she was an owl. Not just any owl, but the one he'd had in his home that still has a broken leg.

Holly closed her eyes. "I'm a shifter. I can change between human and animal." She spoke clearly enough, yet Anthony still couldn't understand what she was saying. Something found in fantasy.

"Like a costume?"

"No." She didn't explain further. Wide eyes over soft features stared at him, willing him to understand what his logical mind wouldn't allow. Her breathing lengthened, and she picked at her fingers.

"I'm going to need a bit more." He leaned back and let go of her. At the loss of their contact, he almost pulled her into his arms. Insane attraction to this woman throbbed all the way to his groin, but it was possible that she was the insane one.

"Ever since I was eight and moved away from Hull Creek. Something happened the day we moved. The owl outside is my pair, my twin, but she can't shift. She isn't the owl you've been taking care of, I am. It's how I escaped your house, and why I healed so fast."

Anthony's face scrunched until it hurt. Running his hand over his face didn't help. He pushed his chair back.

"If you've been in my house this past week, prove it."

"What can I do to prove it to you?" She was utterly

adorable as she nibbled on her lip with concern. Anthony mentally shook his head. He should feel violated right now. It was no different than having a spy within his home, his place of peace.

"Well, you could show me or tell me something only the owl would know." He leaned his elbows on his knees and quirked a brow, challenging her. He was curious what she'd come up with to prove her story.

Holly smiled like someone confident in themselves to win a game. "You slept on your couch the first night, and you even turned it around to face me. You fed me fish. You calmed me down when I panicked."

Anthony sat up a little more with each word she spoke.

"Your mother scolded you for not calling and refused to tell you anything about her and your dad until you called her. Then you called her back."

"It explains so much, but it's not possible." Denial hit him hard in the face, harder than Morton punched. That man had a good arm. It didn't matter the truth she laid out for him, he refused to believe it.

"Most of your boxers are green, like your uniform." Her lips pursed and mischief sparkled in her eyes. And her eyes danced with the familiar swirls of the owl. "I find it cute that you match your underwear to your uniform."

He chuckled with his tongue in his cheek and pointed at her. "That's not fair."

"You're the one that brought an owl into your home and walked around almost naked."

"You were an animal." A flush filled his cheeks as he raised his voice to defend himself.

"Do you flash all the animals you find?" Holly pinched her lips between her teeth.

Anthony had to admit, he enjoyed this cheeky side to

the solemn woman who'd invited a stranger in for dinner. But this little piece of information made all of them fit together. "It is true. How? I mean, how do you do it?"

"I'll show you sometime." Now, her skin flushed, and she looked away. Here he craved the chance to kiss her again, get his hands on her, and she turned out to be some paranormal creature that already knew him. Knew a lot about him. "Anthony?"

He didn't answer her, too busy trying to figure out why he even believed her. She left him alone and gathered more beer from the fridge. Absentmindedly, he reached for it and drank.

Asher brought him up here. Asher was supposed to answer his questions, but only gave cryptic answers, like going for a hike to meet Holly.

"Asher knows." Anthony met Holly's eyes. She nodded once. "He knows what you are and knew who you were when I brought you to him. That's why he made me promise not to take you to the rescue. You really healed that fast?"

"Yes. All shifters can."

"All shifters?" He kept his hand down instead of slapping himself in the face. "Of course you're not the only one." He said it more to himself. "How did Asher know what you are? What about your friend, Zachary?"

Holly stared at him with wide, beautiful eyes, but didn't answer. It was all he needed to realize everything in front of him.

"Asher's a wolf." Everything that had happened over the summer had been an unsolved mystery in his mind, but the answer was right here.

"How do you know he's a wolf?" Holly leaned forward. It was nice to see he wasn't the only one getting surprises.

"I'm right, aren't I?"

Holly nodded.

"We had a few incidents with a couple wolves this past summer. It involved both Asher and Gwen." And as the events replayed in his mind, he added the new information that Asher was one of the white wolves. There'd been a report of a grey one, too. Inwardly shaking his head, thinking the grey one must have been Zachary, or his... what had Holly called it... his pair.

"Anthony?" Holly's voice quaked.

He looked at her and saw not only the woman Asher introduced, but as the companion he'd made having her in his home. Petting her as she settled on his lap, feeding her chicken in the kitchen the night before. Remembering the things he'd confessed to her about his family. "There's an unfair advantage. I don't know that much about you, but you know the colour of my underwear."

Her fingers covered her lips, but her smirk still appeared in the tightness of her cheeks. "You know the most important part of who I am. It's the only thing I am right now."

"That can't be true." He ran a knuckle down her cheek, causing a warmth of arousal to hit him.

"I want you to kiss me again, but I understand if you don't want to." Nervous breathlessness quieted her exclamation.

"This is strange, all of it, but I don't think it's enough to keep me from kissing you again." Despite being something paranormal, Holly was a sweet woman and very attractive. Small frame with the curves of well-toned muscles, but all her softness showed in her features, in her eyes. Bright hazel swirls turning to amber before melting into the colours of a sunset.

Because he couldn't stop himself, he took her hand and pulled her up to stand with him. He laid his hands on her waist and bent his head. Her sweet taste poured into him as he took her mouth, claiming her with his tongue. His attraction to her was unlike any he'd ever felt before, and part of him knew it wasn't natural.

Holly's hands splayed over his chest. Anthony pulled her against him and angled his head, supping at her lips before painfully lifting away.

"Since you know where I live, come by for dinner tomorrow." Lifting his hands from her waist, he stepped back.

"Okay."

"I have a... a wolf to go talk to." He left, feeling guilty for not helping her clean up, but darkness had already fallen. The need to confront Asher a second time kept him from spending the night. Who was he kidding? The strength of his attraction to her scared him. He'd just discovered there was a different species living in his own back yard. And he'd wanted to stay there, locking her in his arms. It was best he stepped away. Maybe it would be best if he stepped away entirely, pretend he never found out the owl he couldn't let go of was actually a beautiful woman.

With the long hike back and the time to think, Anthony realized the secrets stretched further back. He could have helped Asher if he'd told him. The crazy man that had been after Gwen had a vendetta against the wolves. Anthony never would have harmed them, but he would have helped them. He considered Asher a friend, although Anthony understood now why he mostly kept to himself growing up.

His thoughts flew to the paranormal creatures he'd discovered existed. He'd asked a shifter on a date, one who'd spent more time with him than he had with her. Anthony knew nothing about her, other than she was getting back on her feet, but from what? He'd wanted to ask, but he wouldn't pry, not yet. He'd ask tomorrow evening. Just as he couldn't turn away from the owl, he couldn't turn away from the woman.

Asher's house came into view through the trees. Only a couple lights remained on inside. At least he wouldn't wake them when he banged on their door.

"Made it back down, okay?" Asher asked after opening the door.

"Yeah, the trail is visible enough." Anthony stood there, trying to find the best way to approach this when what he really wanted to do was punch someone simply out of frustration. "Why didn't you ever tell me? I know we weren't close friends, but with my job, I could have helped."

"Tell you what?" he asked carefully.

"Cat's out of the bag, Asher. No, wait. The owl and wolf are out of the bag."

"She told you." Asher opened the door wider and let him inside.

"Yeah," he snapped.

"And you're mad?" Asher crossed his arms and raised one all knowing brow.

"Yes. No. I'm confused, that's for sure. Why didn't you tell me this past summer?"

"I made the judgment call to not tell anyone. We're safer that way." His logic made sense, and Anthony really couldn't fault him for it. He wasn't lining up to tell the world what he'd discovered. In all honesty, he saw them as part of the nature he vowed to protect.

"Why did Holly tell me, and why did you leave me there for her to tell me?"

"You deserved to know after taking care of her. You were more than upset that she escaped."

"I worried about her." His thoughts returned to the trapper.

"Why?" The single syllable stretched, fishing for an answer. Anthony doubted Holly told him everything. Asher wouldn't supply the information.

"You have more questions than answers." Irritation bled through his tone.

"I've accepted that." Asher shrugged. Anthony sighed and caved with the information.

"We found an illegal trapper coming up into these woods. He's trapping birds." Anthony fought the urge to shuffle his feet in embarrassment.

"Did you tell her? She needs to know."

"My mind has been a little preoccupied." They had bombarded him with a lot of information in one evening. "I'll tell her tomorrow."

"There's a phone at the safehouse. I'll give her a call."

"Thank you." He looked at Asher and saw him in a new light. Picturing the wolves. They'd been amazing. "I want to be mad."

"But you're not. You're curious." Asher grinned and went to the kitchen to pull out a couple beer, ready to talk and give at least some information. And Anthony was eager to listen.

"Yeah." The owl had fascinated him, and now so did the woman. But maybe learning some things about Asher would help him understand Holly.

THE CHILLED wind kept Holly below the trees as she flew toward Anthony's. Chloe followed behind her. Holly carried a bag with her clothes. Well, some clothes that Zachary and Ezaray had left for her. All new, and she had no doubt they intended her to keep them. Ezaray knew what Holly liked, what she used to like. But Holly needed to face her own world soon, to collect her own things. Right now she would start with her mate as Fate wanted her to.

Chloe continued to his house, perching on the railing of his back deck. Holly landed on the ground just inside the trees to shift and dress. Shifting felt intimate to her, and she wasn't ready to show him. She'd never shown Ezaray, and they'd been best friends.

The warmth and magic from the shift subsided and Holly shivered in the air. She pulled out her clothes and dressed in a pair of jeans and a soft sweater. She slipped the flats onto her feet. These wouldn't be enough soon. They were barely enough now. The weather alone would force her to face the world just to get winter boots.

Holly walked across Anthony's lawn and saw him already standing on his deck. He'd pulled his hand back from Chloe and crossed his arms. Chloe's head reared back as if to say, "No way are you touching me, boy." Chloe was solitary.

"She just doesn't trust you yet." Holly climbed the back steps. Chloe trusted Anthony after the way he took care of Holly, but she was stubborn and dug in her heels. If things hadn't happened the way they did, Holly would have had the same initial reaction to her mate.

"And what about you?" The speed with which his eyes landed on her stopped her next step. His gaze, full and rich, begging for an answer, clashed with his tall and rigid frame. He'd already changed out of his uniform and stood in jeans and a t-shirt.

"I trust you. How could I not?"

He put one hand around her waist and pulled her against him. Chloe flew away. "Please wait."

Holly frowned. "Chloe, come back." She looked up at Anthony. "What is it?"

He waited for Chloe to land again. "Has Asher talked to you since last night?"

"Yes. He called."

"Good. So he told you there's an illegal trapper in the area, specifically trapping birds of prey. I'd hate for Chloe to get caught. Or you." His fingers flexed around her waist.

Holly stepped out of his arm to go to Chloe. Wrapping a hand around her back, she leaned her head down. Chloe nuzzled against her in unspoken conversation. Chloe had the same intelligence as Holly, part of the magic that changed the two of them. She wouldn't fall for any traps, but she'd take extra care, anyway. Chloe flew away when Holly let her go.

"She'll be okay?"

"She'll be fine."

Anthony put his hand on the small of her back and led her into the house. The scents coming from the oven assaulted her nose and earned a growl from her stomach. The kitchen looked clean except for two clean plates, a bottle of wine, and two glasses.

"It smells amazing."

"It's pot pie." He winced, worry over what she might like evident on his face.

"Sounds great."

Anthony relaxed and poured the wine, handing her a glass and gesturing to the living room where the furniture sat in its original position. The space by the back door was empty, the playpen put away. "It will still be a bit before it's done."

Holly sat in the corner and Anthony took the other, leaving much more space between them than necessary.

"I feel bad for having put you in a playpen now that I know what you are."

"You don't need to. You did what you thought best. And you took good care of me."

"Still. Asher's and Zachary's comments make sense now. I've been thinking over all the conversations with both of them from the past week. When it seemed as if they were talking to you rather than me, they were."

"Yeah. Their way of telling where they were, where I could find them if I needed them, where Chloe was and that she was all right." She looked away, not wanting to see his expression as she admitted this next part. "When you came home and found me panicking to get out, I was worried about Chloe. I would have hurt myself if you hadn't calmed me down."

"You were scared too." He was too damn observant.

"Yes. I... I don't do well being stuck inside."

"And the playpen acted more like a cage." He moved closer on the couch and reached his hand up to run his fingers over her hair, the same way he'd done over her feathers. "I'm sorry."

"Don't be. I needed that time. And I wouldn't have been able to handle it if anyone but you had put me there." Holly still needed to tell Anthony one more thing, and it hovered on the tip of her tongue. Neither of them were ready for that. He was her mate, and she wouldn't fight it, but Fate asked too much of her to embrace it.

"I've been dying to ask. How did you get hurt?"

Holly had dreaded that question, the one without a simple explanation. Not telling him would only harm their relationship. The secrets from Asher had already upset him.

"There's a long version of that story that I'm not ready to talk about."

"Does it have anything to do with why you're staying in Asher's house in the woods to get back on your feet?"

"Yes. A short version?" she offered.

He nodded.

"There was a fight with a terrible man." She didn't like how she paused between each word, creating a stutter she didn't have. Even a shortened tale was difficult to get out. "He broke my leg and hit my wing. I got the rest of the scrapes from trying to fly away."

Anthony moved closer again, his leg touching hers, without her noticing until she finished speaking. His hand rested against the back of her neck, firm and protective. "Is he still a threat?" She'd heard him use that tone when talking on the phone for work, only this time it drummed deeper, angrier.

"No." She allowed herself to look up at him, and her breath left her lungs. His nostrils flared. Awareness of their proximity and his touch rushed through her. Sensations built as his fingers drew circles on her nape. Their conversation should turn them away from such desires, but the mate bond grew. It had grown while she'd been healing, but now that she spent time with him as a woman, it exploded as if they had held it on a spring and she moved the barrier to release the tension.

Musk and pine filled her as she searched for air. He bent his head, but his lips didn't touch hers, only his breath. His eyes didn't close. They raked over her face and lower to the exposed neckline of her sweater and further, only to do it all again. Her eyes followed his, memorized in the heat they propelled.

Trapped by him, she only felt safe. Desires she'd hoped weren't gone forever rose. Needing to touch him, but not willing to start the kiss, she raised her hand that had been between them. Nervously, she pressed her fingers to his chest. She licked her lips, supplying an invitation for him to do what he wanted.

The oven beeped, shrill across the room. Holly gasped and pulled her hand away. Anthony jumped, his jaw hardening. His hand released her nape and he stood.

Holding out a hand, he helped her stand. "Dinner is ready."

7

———

His phone buzzed in his pocket. Anthony set the pot pie on the stove and shut the oven before pulling off an oven mitt and reaching for his phone. Hazel's name flashed on his screen. Anyone else and he would ignore it, but if Hazel was calling while he was off duty, then it was important.

"Sorry, I have to take this." He answered the phone. "Hi, Hazel." He walked into the living room to keep from talking in front of Holly.

"Hey there, Tony. I'm sorry to call you, but that truck was spotted again, near you. We need someone to go check it out. We think he abandoned it. You're closest and can get there quicker, but I'm sending Morton your way too."

"I'm on it, Hazel."

"Thank you, handsome." She gave him directions and hung up. Anthony went back to the kitchen.

"You have to go." Holly spoke first.

"Yeah, I'm sorry. The trapper I mentioned..."

"They found his truck."

Anthony frowned.

"Shifters have exceptional hearing. Sorry, I didn't mean to eavesdrop."

Anthony smiled. He stepped closer, but hesitated, wondering if his gesture would be well received. Shrugging, he did it anyway. He placed a kiss on her forehead, then turned to get what he needed from his bedroom. He didn't have enough time to change, but he grabbed his vest, belt, and badge. Back in the kitchen, he paused.

"Please stay." His voice hardened more than he intended, demanding her.

Holly nodded.

"Good. Eat if you're hungry. Don't wait for me. But I just want you to still be here when I get back."

"Okay." Her eyes flashed for a moment before she leaned against the counter.

Anthony left, eager to find information on the trapper and eager to get this over with, to return home to Holly.

The location Hazel had given him was still up toward the same hunting trails, but further east. They had driven the truck off the road and it sat with its front end against the tree. He called in what he saw from his own truck, then got out to approach with caution. The cab was empty, as was the bed.

Warmth covered his palm when he laid it over the hood. The truck hadn't been here long. Less than an hour, a lot less.

Garbage lay across the front seat. Twine sprawled in the truck bed with a full roll in the cab. Scraps of steel, wire, and PVC pipe were everywhere. Walking around the back, Anthony bent to see if the license plate matched the truck that drove away from him and Morton. The space was empty.

Inspecting the tracks that led the truck off the road, they

weren't deep. Frowning, he walked back to the front of the truck to check the damage. Some, but nothing that the owner couldn't have fixed. The road wasn't slippery, nothing to make someone lose control. He searched the ground for animal tracks, any reason the driver may have swerved, but found nothing fresh. He'd run his truck off the road on purpose, to abandon it. But why?

Another vehicle pulled up, and Anthony walked toward his truck to meet up with Morton.

"What did you find?"

"More than it looks like. I think he did this on purpose. He didn't hit the tree hard enough to cause major damage. He could have backed up and kept driving. All that's left inside is some garbage and scraps."

"Why would he do that? What about his license plate? At least we can get a good look at the fake."

"The fake?"

"Yeah. There's no match or record of the license plate. We suspect it's a fake."

"He took that too."

"Fuck." Morton cursed and walked toward the black truck to do the same inspection Anthony had just done. They snapped pictures and gathered what they'd need from the truck. By the time they finished, the tow truck had arrived.

They helped him get hooked up and watched him drive away.

"Do you mind dropping all this off at the office on your way home?" Anthony had already put it in Morton's truck.

Morton turned to him. "Sure. You look a bit dressed up. Didn't you come from home?"

"Yes."

"And?"

"I have a date waiting for me."

"You never take dates to your house."

"First time for everything." Anthony slapped Morton's shoulder and left before he continued the interrogation. Holly's secrets were her own. And if he were honest with himself, he didn't want to admit how attracted he was to her. It was a lot too soon.

He waved and drove away as Morton got behind the wheel of his own truck.

Anthony stepped inside to find Holly putting the pie back in the oven.

"Hey. You didn't eat."

"I wanted to wait for you." She leaned back against the counter and shrugged a single shoulder.

"But you were hungry." He toed off his boots.

"I had a few bites." Her rounded cheekbones pinkened as she tried to suppress her grin.

"Oh, I see." He rested his hands on her hips, blocking her against the counter. "You tried it and it was so bad you put it back in the oven to burn it so it became inedible and we'd have to order takeout."

"You caught me."

Anthony looked down her body. "It seems I did."

Her pink tongue ran along her lips. He hadn't been sure how he'd resisted kissing her earlier on the couch, but he couldn't stop himself this time. Capturing her lips, he started slow, licking the seam and nipping at both lips. Heat swamped him and his cock hardened against the fly of his jeans. Desire wasn't a strong enough word to describe how he felt toward Holly.

He'd lost his control with the kiss. His tongue swiped in and stroked over hers as he pulled it back out. Pushing her harder against the counter gave him freedom to move his hands. Up and down her sides. Her breathing shook beneath him the closer he came to her breasts. But he didn't touch them. Not until he slid his hand down far enough to go under her sweater. Though the fabric was soft, it felt abrasive against his hands when he craved to touch her skin.

Her skin seared his fingers—he didn't dare increase the pressure, not until he adjusted. Anthony slowed the kiss while he concentrated on the up and down patterns he traced over her ribs. Her hands landed on his arms and he growled. He wanted her hands everywhere on him. He flattened his hands and ran them up until his thumbs slid against the underside of her breasts. Her bare breasts. She hadn't worn a bra.

A long, low rumble travelled up his chest, and he lifted his head so he could see her face as he cupped her. Their eyes locked, and he watched hers change colour.

She gasped as the oven beeped behind them. He closed his eyes and dragged himself away from her.

"Damn oven. Apparently cooking for you only creates interruptions."

HOLLY STILL COULDN'T TAKE her first full breath since she heard Anthony's truck return. She hadn't expected the intensity of their arousal. It sizzled through her until reaching the surface of her skin, ready to explode. A mating chant started in her head and hummed through her heart.

Anthony stepped away from her and pulled the pot pie back out of the oven, and she clenched her fists to keep from pulling him back. She had no control of herself. The steam that rose around the cracks in the crust filled the kitchen with the aroma once again, giving a moment to ground herself. Holly hoped the mate bond wouldn't control him the same way it controlled her.

"I suppose we should eat." He flashed a smile as he stepped closer to her. Her mind travelled in a different direction than his intentions when he brushed his body against hers to reach behind her for the plates he'd set out earlier. Turning back to the stove, he froze. "You took some right out of the dish."

"Sorry?"

"You're not."

"I'm not. It was good." Holly braced her hands on the counter to keep from reaching for him. Anthony dished up two portions and carried them to the small kitchen table on the other side of the island. Holly poured the wine and followed him. She sat down and waited for Anthony who went back to the kitchen for the bottle.

"How long have you been in Alder Ridge?" Anthony said before taking a bite.

"A few weeks." Although her time hadn't felt real. Wild and free, she'd explored, always returning to the area near the safehouse and checking in with Zachary and Ezaray.

He wanted to ask more, she could see it in his face, but she'd already answered his questions about why she was here. Answered what she was willing, anyway.

"Do you have any siblings?" It was the only familial connection she couldn't determine while staying here before. She wondered how he came in possession of a playpen, but didn't think it was his.

"I have a sister. She's married and has twins. The playpen is hers. With so much to carry around as is with the twins, she leaves a playpen and other things wherever they go."

"Smart woman." Holly saluted her with a slight lift of her wine glass.

"She is." His head tilted, but Holly could still see his fondness for her.

"How old is she?"

"Twenty-four."

"And how old are you?" Holly inwardly rolled her eyes. She hadn't thought about his age before.

"Thirty."

Holly froze, staring at her plate with her fork lifted in the air.

Anthony chuckled. "And how old are, sweet owl?" She had to close her eyes as he called her by the name he'd used for the past week, acknowledging the truth of what she was.

"Not thirty." She took a sip of her wine rather the bite of food waiting on her fork. The sweet alcoholic taste sat on her tongue, giving her a moment to digest.

A finger under her chin lifted her face. "How old?"

"Twenty-two," she squeaked, but shook her head. "No, twenty-three."

"You forgot your birthday?" He teased, his grin playful. He kept his finger under her chin.

"Yeah, I did." Her birthday had been a couple months ago. She hadn't even known it had passed until she came to Alder Ridge. She'd shifted almost immediately after being rescued, and she'd fled. Seemed to be what she was good at.

Anthony's playfulness vanished. "I'm here if you ever want to talk about whatever it is you've been through."

"Thank you." But she couldn't, not yet. She was still taking baby steps. "What made you decide to become a conservation officer?"

"Wildlife, hunting, fishing. It has all fascinated me since I was very little. My dad didn't realize how deep that went until my teen years when I started talking about a serious career."

"What is his opinion now?"

"Still hates it. Just doesn't voice it as much, but he doesn't need to." And Holly knew it hurt him every time. He covered his rich eyes by looking down at his food and scooping a bite.

"How does your mother feel about your career?"

"She's proud of it." Cherishment lifted the corners of his eyes. He adored his family, particularly his mother, and that made him all the more attractive.

Holly lifted her wineglass and realized they'd both finished eating. The air between them sparked to life. Their earlier encounters returning to memory and pushing through their conversation. If she reached out to him, she'd get burned. But there was nothing to stop her.

Anthony pushed his chair back and stood. He took her hand and pulled her up. "We can take our wine into the living room and talk a little longer."

"Or?" She said it when he cut himself off. The word hung in the air.

"Or we can finish it after." A lust-filled roughness coloured his voice.

"Finish it after." Holly didn't know her voice could dip so low. Her husky tone turned her on, adding to the lust pumping through her system.

Anthony bent, his hands sliding to the backs of her thighs, and he lifted her. Her legs wrapped around his waist as he walked across his house and to the hall that led to his bedroom. She rested her hands on his shoulders. His hands splayed under her ass and she felt as light as the bird she was. He didn't put her down on the floor. Instead, he lowered both of them to the bed, settling his weight on top of her, and captured her mouth.

Holly held on and tilted her hips in a wanton invitation. She couldn't hold herself back. Bracing himself on one elbow, he used his free hand to roam her upper body, not wasting time to rid her of her sweater. That wasn't enough for her. She pulled at his shirt until he gripped the back of the collar and pulled it off. While that occupied him, Holly lifted the hem of her sweater. Anthony sat up on his knees. Holly bowed her back, then lifted her head until she got the sweater off.

He undid the button on her jeans before lowering himself back down. Their chests made contact and Holly's nipples hardened. With her jeans loose, Anthony slid his fingers down. He froze as she gasped and stopped breathing. The touch down there foreign, but oh so good. She needed more of him, but didn't know how to tell him, didn't know how to say what she needed when she knew it would be too much.

After a moment, he continued. Her hips bucked at the first circle around her clit.

"Easy, sweet owl."

Nothing about this was easy.

Anthony bent his head and captured a nipple in his mouth. The strong pulls sent waves down her centre to add to the fire he built with his fingers. Her jeans were too tight. She squirmed and whimpered. Her hand reached for the waist, but she didn't have the strength for a decent grip to push them down.

A feminine pitched growl escaped through her teeth, and she huffed loudly through her nose.

"Want some help with that?"

She didn't need to answer him, didn't want to answer

him. Holly moved her hands out of the way, lifting them above her head, while Anthony sat up and peeled her jeans off of her. "Please hurry."

"What's the rush?"

"Don't you feel it?"

"I do. But I don't want this to end." He stood as he pulled them off her feet, then started on his own jeans. Holly knew her eyes didn't look normal as their precision spiked while she took in his body. Every dip and valley between his muscles, the V pointing to his erection jutting toward her. The muscles on his legs were something she'd never seen so defined on a man. Every piece of him was made for her, to hit all her hot spots. She licked her lips, eager to taste his skin. "You can have whatever you want. When I'm finished."

His dark promise shot through her system until every inch of her skin heated.

He put his knee back on the bed and lifted her leg in the air until her heel rested on his shoulder. His eyes trapped hers as he placed a kiss on the inside of her leg. He trailed them upward, adding his tongue and teeth to the sensations. They tickled, but she was too aroused for it to bother her. She only wanted more.

Using his thumb at her centre, he pulled up to expose the sensitive nub that throbbed in anticipation. His mouth drew closer, and she had to fist the pillow above her head to keep from rushing him. When his mouth closed around her clit, she lost control. Her hands gripped his hair, and she lifted her hips against him. Anthony released her leg and used both hands to steady her body.

His strength was enough to control her. Her body had been revved and on edge for a long time. The right pressure and pattern from him had her leaping over the edge of her climax in moments. She cried out, his name a litany in the air.

Swiping his lips with his thumb, he looked up her body to catch her gaze. The sight of his head between her legs sent a new spasm of lust through her core.

He crawled up over her body. Reaching over to his nightstand, he fumbled with opening a small cardboard box and pulled out a condom. After making quick work of putting it on, he kissed her.

When he lifted his head, he angled himself at her entrance. He ran his knuckles down the side of her face. She felt cherished, just as she had when he'd taken care of her as an owl.

But it was his next words that sealed her to him unequivocally. "I've got you, Holly."

HIS COCK WAS ready to burst, but there was more than pure lust running through his veins. The need to care for her ran deep and seated itself in his chest. He could spend all night admiring her body. Such smooth skin over fit muscles, but softness in all the places he'd imagined. Her hips flared just enough for him to grip. Sliding one hand down her body, he angled her to give him better access, ensuring he'd hit the spot that could drive her wild.

He watched her eyes swirl and flutter, and her head rocked from side to side as he pushed in. Tight heat encased him, and he had to push his control to the limits to keep from exploding too soon.

Words, they normally came out of him by now. He was a talker, especially dirty talk. He loved to watch women flush and writhe from his words alone, ramping up the experience for both of them. But he didn't have it in him this time. His focus was on one thing, pushing them both to the peak.

He buried his head in her neck and nipped her as his hips picked up the pace on their own. A strong need to claim her and make her his rode his spine. Lifting his head, he captured her lips to keep from saying or doing anything crazy.

Her walls fluttered around his cock until they squeezed. Holly cried out beneath him and with strength she must have been hiding, pushed against his chest. She squeezed his sides with her thighs and flipped them on the bed until she straddled him. He marveled at the fact his cock never left her heat.

Holly rode him with abandon. Wild ferocity firing in her eyes. Her hands locked on his chest, nails biting into his skin. She leaned down to kiss him and her lips moved along his jaw and toward his neck.

Anthony waited until the first pulse from her cunt ran along his cock. She cried out with her climax, but Anthony didn't let it continue like this. He wanted to make it last. He flipped her back over and gripped her wrists. Holding them above her head, he slammed into her. Frustration leaked from her, but her orgasm skyrocketed, bringing on his own. He held it back until she'd finished.

She was beautiful, panting satiated under him. He adjusted his grip to hold both hands in one and lowered his other to her core. Pinching her clit, he let himself go, thrusting until all he felt was Holly. He roared with his climax, but moaned when she followed him with another one of her own.

Anthony held himself above her until he caught his breath. He held his lips against her forehead when he kissed her, giving himself another moment before leaving to get rid of the condom.

When he returned from the bathroom, Holly was sitting up in bed staring at the door. He crawled across the bed to pull her back down, but as soon as his weight registered, she startled and scrambled from the bed.

"You have to stay away from me."

Her limbs shook, and she tripped over her own feet. Anthony reached out to catch her, but she pulled away.

"No, you can't touch me." A shrillness entered her voice that sounded nothing like her. It resembled the panic he'd caught her in her first day here.

"I'm pretty sure I just did a lot more than touch you." It was a little late to concern themselves with their intimacy.

"No, no, no," she chanted as she scoured the floor for her clothes. She grabbed only her jeans and sweater, pulling them on with jerky motions.

"Holly." Firming his voice to match what he used to calm her before, he stood from the bed to step between her and the door.

Her eyes widened when she saw his attempt. Abandoning her clothes, her jeans left undone and her sweater falling off one arm to the floor, she darted forward to beat him to the door.

"Woah. No." He couldn't let her go like this. His hand clasped her arm as she just made it through his bedroom door. With short pulls, he tried to bring her closer while she gripped his wrist with her other hand. The look in her eyes cut him at the knees. Whatever she was going through, he didn't want to let her go through it alone. "It's okay, Holly. Don't run from me."

"You don't understand. You can't understand." She

continued to pull away from him, but not with the strength she'd used at first.

"I can if you talk to me."

Her head shook with short, quick movements. "No, let me go."

He got an arm around her back, held her against his chest for only a moment before she jerked from his grasp and ran. Anthony chased her through the house. Shutting the back door behind her, she leapt off the deck. The door slowed him down long enough that she had time to shuck her jeans in the cold grass. He reached her jeans as she reached the treeline. Seconds later, a snowy owl soared high. Holly perched at the top of a tree long enough to catch his eye, then took flight further into the woods.

Anthony stood naked in his yard, holding her jeans in his hands. He'd known there was more he didn't understand. And the one person who could give him the answers just flew away from him. She panicked, and whatever she'd been through gave her every right. But it didn't justify leaving him in the dark, not when his gut told him he was more involved than simply having rescued an injured owl.

8

____

Holly refused to shift back when she reached the safehouse. How could she have let that happen? If Anthony hadn't flipped her over and pinned her to the bed, it would have been too late for him. She was thankful for the time she'd spent with Zachary and Ezaray. She never would have known what she had been about to do if it weren't for them.

Mate. Mark. The chant still ran through her head. Her teeth had sharpened. Not in the way Zachary had described. All her teeth had taken on a thin sharp edge whereas the wolf shifters' and the bear shifters' canines lengthened and sharpened when they marked their mates, sealing them together. Hers sharpened to a thin edge similar to her beak.

She'd buried her face in his neck, her mouth open, ready to bite down. Holly would never forgive herself if she took that choice away from him. They'd had a single date. He must be so confused right now, and she wouldn't be able to explain it to him, because she wouldn't shift until she had control of herself.

Settling herself in the tree, she breathed. Her lungs

filling and releasing with measured control. It was the only thing she felt she controlled.

Chloe circled above her before landing in the closest tree. *What happened?*

Too much. I almost marked him. The strained voice in her head sounded foreign. Harsh and beaten down.

But you didn't. Chloe always had a calm cadence. She was who Holly sought when she needed grounding. Like when her boyfriend had cheated on her in high school and Holly had gone on an emotional rage.

Not my doing. He stopped me just in time.

He stopped you? He doesn't want to be your mate? Her head rose and her chest puffed, ready to protect Holly.

He doesn't know about mates. He doesn't know that he stopped me. It's better that way. The next breath Holly pulled in sank deeper.

How is that better?

What do you mean?

What is it you're really concerned about? Thin eyes that matched hers pinned her like an older sister scolding the younger one before taking her to their mother.

I'm not ready for this and it isn't fair to ask him to hand over his life to something he knows nothing about.

Then shouldn't someone tell him about it?

It wouldn't matter. I'm not ready! I'm not even me. I became someone I don't recognize. Holly's heart exploded. It hurt not to understand who she was or who she was meant to be. Even if she tried to return to her life before being captured, it wouldn't be the same. Having gone through what she has has shaped her into a person she's not sure how to handle.

You won't rediscover yourself as an animal. You know this side of yourself. This is who you are at heart and always have been.

Even if I was fine, I'm not ready for a mate. Fate did this. Fate can take it away. She can hold onto her cards and wait with the patience she demands in all of us. She took her sweet ass time engineering a rescue out of that fighting ring. Those pieces could have been put together for Zachary a lot sooner, but no. So Fate can wait. She couldn't cry, yet tears leaked through the cracks in her words.

Chloe flew over to land beside her and rubbed her head against Holly's.

Holly closed her eyes and went back to controlling her breathing.

I'll be ready when you are.

Chloe left. Holly felt as if she'd pushed her away, but she knew Chloe didn't hurt easily. She'd apologize later—when she could move.

HE'D TALKED himself around in circles until he dressed for work in the early hours of the morning and drove to Asher's. Only minutes after he arrived, Anthony saw lights turn on inside and he got out of his truck. He refrained from banging on the door this time.

The door opened, and Asher stood on the other side in only his boxers and ruffled hair.

"I woke you up when I drove up, didn't I?"

"It's okay. Is something wrong?"

"Yes. Holly came over last night, but after we... uh... she panicked and left. I don't understand and she refused to tell me."

"I'm not sure what to tell you. I don't know what's wrong. But she's been through a lot, and I can't imagine she's completely healed from that. And that has nothing to do with her injuries."

"She didn't tell me what happened to her. Only that she's trying to get back on her feet. But Asher, I know there's something else, something more that involves me."

Asher's jaw squared, and the muscles around his mouth tightened.

"You know. What is it?"

Asher remained silent, the placate look on his face only feeding Anthony's frustration.

"Tell me, damn it."

"I can't." Asher sighed. "I'm sorry."

"Fine. I'll just have to find her." Anthony stalked across Asher's yard, barely reaching the trees before his phone vibrated. "Fuck." He pulled it out.

"Time to get up. We have some driving to do." Morton's groggy voice filled his ear, but he didn't wait for a response. He hung up, leaving Anthony staring at his phone.

"Tony." Asher raised his voice to reach Anthony across the yard. "You're upset."

"Upset? Fuck you, Asher." He was on his way to furious. He wouldn't usually be so rude to the veterinarian.

"It will all make sense soon enough. She'll come around."

Anthony shook his head. He waved Asher off and hopped in his truck. One last painful glance at the trees and he backed out of Asher's driveway and drove down the lane.

The entire drive in, Anthony replayed the scene with Holly, certain he had done nothing wrong. She'd pushed him away, but not because she wanted to. Something made her panic. He still felt her cold fingers as she'd tried to loosen his grip. Her body had shook against his. Pure panic complete with clumsy movements and eyes searching for exits. She hadn't even cared that she'd left her clothes behind. He had to find her.

Putting the truck into park jerked him from his thoughts. Lifting his head, he looked around, not remembering the drive. With a huff, he went inside to find out what was going on while he waited for Morton to show up.

"Mornin' there, handsome." Hazel held out a coffee across her desk. "Didn't expect you in before Morton. You get his coffee."

"Thanks, Hazel. I was already up when he called."

"Couldn't sleep?" She tilted her head and her eyebrows rose to look up at his face.

"No." He couldn't tell her about Holly. "What's the call for?"

"More bird traps that match the description and pictures of the ones you and Morton found. About an hour out of town." She took a sip of her coffee from the mug they'd had made for her birthday. *Everyone knows a Hazel....and she's usually fucking awesome.* "Tony, hun, I've got a bad feeling about all this."

"You and me both." Anthony waited for Morton.

Still strapping on his vest and jogging to the front, Morton stopped behind Anthony. "How the hell did you beat me here?"

"I was already up when you called."

Morton huffed. Hazel gave him the same run down she'd given Anthony, including her instincts, then sent them on their way. He considered letting Morton drive today, but Anthony couldn't let go of that control.

Morton talked the entire drive, mostly about nothing. The man wouldn't shut up in the mornings. As soon as the caffeine drop hit him in the afternoon, Anthony wouldn't hear another word out of him unless needed. Anthony tuned him out.

"Yo, Tony." Morton waved his hand up and down.

"Huh?" Anthony mentally shook himself from the images of Holly beneath him in his bed, then her panicked escape.

"You didn't hear me, did you?"

"Sorry, I'm distracted." He took the moment to check out their location and gauge how much longer to get there.

"Was your date that good you didn't get any sleep?" Morton laughed at himself. He let himself smirk at his friend. The joke annoyed Anthony, but he had to just let it slide.

Anthony waited until he finished. "What did you try to tell me?"

"Another kilometer until we turn left."

"Got it." Anthony leaned his head against the headrest while he watched the road. The painted lines from late spring were already fading away on the two-lane highway.

"You sure you're okay?" Morton hadn't looked away.

"I'll be fine." It was a lie. He wouldn't be fine until he found Holly.

The tracks weren't as clear as the last time, let alone multiple sets littered the road. They had no idea what kind of vehicle the trapper used now that he'd ditched the black truck. Parking as far in as possible, they did the same search for footprints, but the ground left nothing to follow. They found five more traps, all constructed the same way with the same materials as the first ones.

All Anthony pictured as he sprung each one to collect them, was Holly and her pair struggling beneath the nets. If nothing else came from this trip out, they at least rid the woods of these traps. But how many more had he set, and where? And what was he after?

ONE THING ABOUT BEING A BIRD, it wasn't natural for her to pace. And as her thoughts continued to race, it's all she wanted to do.

Chloe checked on her often. Even Asher had made his way up as the sun rose. He'd called to her from the ground. His eyes settled on several trees for a few moments to a time, as if looking directly at her. But his guess was never correct.

I just want to know you're okay. Tony came looking for you. He got called away to work, otherwise he'd be here instead of me.

He came for her. Flutters grew in her stomach, trying to burst free. They urged her to shift and go to him, to find him and apologize. But nothing would change this. She didn't have control of herself not to mark him. Those flutters floated down in a pit, like leaves falling from the trees, sad and desperately clinging for life.

Asher had left and Holly remained in the tree, her legs continuing to jitter with the need to do something. She couldn't allow herself to shift until she silenced the call in her mind. The hours of the day passed and she became a shaking mass on a thin branch. Spreading her wings, she took to the air. The quietest place she knew.

Holly caught the updraft and soared, steering herself to stay where she wanted. Inside the trees had grown dark, but up here, light still reigned. It wouldn't for much longer. Her gaze landed on the horizon to watch the sun go down. The colours, her favourites, blended in and out of each other, changing within minutes the more the sun disappeared.

Once she'd returned to Zachary after the escape, she'd

flown away each night to watch the sunset. And with each night, a little bit of peace settled in her heart. Her parents had grounded her so many times as a teenager for disappearing. It never stopped her. She'd fly the coop to glimpse the sunset with Chloe all the time. Over time, the words "You're grounded" were said with eye rolls and a wave of their hand, knowing there was nothing they could do to stop her. They didn't know where she went or what she was, but they let her be. As long as she always returned home safe and sound.

The coolness of the air this high up chilled her insides, giving her something else to focus on. As the last of the sun disappeared, Holly closed her eyes and turned back to perch in the tree once again. To stay hidden and find her control.

But the one person other than Anthony that could entice her down from the tree ran into the clearing below her. A dark grey wolf with deep smoky eyes sniffed the air. It was Zachary. He should still be with Ezaray. Holly flew down to a lower branch. She needed to keep her talons in the bark, to keep the wild feeling running through her, the only thing keeping her from going back to Anthony.

What are you doing here?

Asher called.

Why? You should be with your mate. Zachary wasn't hers anymore. She didn't come first with him. Ezaray did.

He didn't tell me to come back. I made that decision myself. He said you'd panicked over something.

How did you get back here so fast?

He lifted his paws up and looked at the two front ones in turn. *It took all day, but I'm here.*

You shouldn't have left Ezaray. He'd left his mate to come for her when she didn't want help. The support system was there, if she wanted it. All she had to do was tell her sad tale to Anthony and it would solve everything, as if describing the horror, pain, and guilt of being forced into an underground fighting ring for a bunch of sick, disgusting men was an easy thing to do. And that didn't change the fact that Anthony was her mate, and that wasn't fair to either of them.

Calm down, Holly. She needed time alone with her family. She asked for it. I'm going back tomorrow to get her.

I'm fine, Zachary. You can go. Talking about what happened with Anthony with him would be like talking to her big brother about her dates. Even more awkward when that big brother hadn't been part of your life for years.

You know I won't do that. Asher said you'd shifted.

I did.

Will you do it again? For me? I want to talk.

We're talking now.

Holly. Other than a deeper voice, that tone hadn't changed since he was a teenager. All those years ago, it served as a challenge for her child-self. It reminded her how important Zachary was to her. Anthony wasn't here. He was safe from her, for now.

She flew to the ground, landing close to the house. Looking back at Zachary, she saw the smoky wind swirl around him and heard his bones pop in and out of place to create his human form. Holly closed her eyes and pulled on the magic within her. Warmth filled her and the wind ruffled her feathers. Once the process finished, she took the steps into the house to find clothes, Zachary coming in behind her. She went to the bedroom she'd stayed in and dressed, while Zachary reached into the closet near the front. When she came back out, he'd dressed in only jeans and a t-shirt and started a fire.

"It's cold without fur."

"Or feathers." She wrapped her arms around herself. He finished with the fire and stood. It took him a few minutes before he moved or said anything. Zachary closed the distance in two strides and pulled her hard against his chest. Holly hesitated, but she wrapped her arms around his waist.

"I've missed you, Squirt." The sound rumbled through her ear that she'd pressed against him.

"I missed you, too." Her voice cracked, and she cleared her throat.

He walked her to the kitchen table, the only other furniture in this place besides the beds. It still needed a lot of work, but at least now it was ready for winter.

Zachary sat adjacent to her and leaned his elbows on the table.

"Let's start with why you flew away after the fight with Tyrone."

"I panicked. Once I realized how stupid that was, I tried to turn around and find my way back. To you. I obviously didn't make it."

"Did the fish cop take good care of you?"

Holly looked up. Asher hadn't told Zachary everything, like how he knew Anthony was her mate. "Yes, he did."

"Good." He waited, his grey eyes never leaving her face. He didn't need to ask to get her to tell him what had happened.

"How is Ezaray? How is she healing? And Maggie, too?" Maggie was one of the girls rescued from the fighting ring with them, but refused to let them take her home. So, Zachary and Ezaray brought her with them. Guilt bubbled again over Holly's absence. She shouldn't have to ask Zachary how they were doing. She should already know because she should have been beside them through all of this.

"Maggie's still in the hospital, but she'll be fine. She was doing well until Tyrone showed up. I'm not sure how she'll be when she gets out. Ezaray saw her before we left town. And Ezaray is better now that she's seen her family. Something you need to do."

"I know, but I can't even see myself, let alone them."

"It will take time."

"I don't have time."

"What do you mean?"

"Anthony is my mate." Holly closed her eyes. She didn't want to see the look on Zachary's face when discussing her mate. He was the closest thing to a big brother. Big brothers didn't need to hear about the undeniable lust between their sister and her mate.

"The fish cop is your mate. The guy who found you and insisted he take care of you rather than leave you with Asher and I. I should have figured that out."

"Asher did."

"Of course he did. The man doesn't stop thinking."

"Anthony doesn't know. I... I almost marked him and he doesn't know."

"But you stopped yourself. We've all been through that."

"I didn't stop myself. He did. Of course he has no idea what happened. He knows what I am, but not about mates. After..." Holly waved her hand in a circle, not wanting to give Zachary details he wouldn't want to hear, "I panicked, again." She'd never let that panic rise and control her in captivity, but since being free, it's all she seemed to do. "I ran away without explaining."

"You're going to have to talk to him."

"Not until I can control myself."

"That isn't how this works, Squirt."

"I can't have a mate!" Her lips curled.

"Again, that's not how this works."

"I'm not ready. Fate can wait."

Zachary laughed. "I'm sorry, Holly." He reached across the table and pried her hands apart until he held them both. "Did you ever think that having a mate by your side is what you need to feel whole again?"

"That's so unfair to him."

"But that's his decision. Ask Gwen, Ezaray, or better yet, Shaye." Zachary listed off the mates of the shifters he knew. "They've all been through it. What isn't fair is not telling him."

"You've changed." She narrowed her eyes.

Zachary shook his head, disgust twisting his features. "I blame it on Asher."

Holly smiled for the first time since being with Anthony.

Zachary tensed, then Holly sensed it too. Footsteps crunching over forest debris. Feet, not paws, so it wasn't Asher or Nathan, the bear shifter. To come up here, they'd all shift to make it quicker. On foot, it was a long hike.

Holly inhaled as the sound got closer. Musk and pine. Thumps on the wood steps at the front sounded heavy and tired. Zachary was already at the door and opened it after the first knock.

Her heart leapt and her blood heated at the sight of her mate. The need to go to him crushed all her will power. Zachary whirled around, pinning her with a frown, scenting her state.

Anthony looked between the two of them, but said nothing. His irritation was clear.

Holly had to think that maybe Zachary was right. It might be easier with him by her side.

9

———

Anthony stared at the man, looking quite comfortable inside with Holly. T-shirt, jeans, and bare feet sticking out at the bottom. A fire crackled on one side of the room and they had pulled two chairs out at the table.

One date, he reminded himself. They'd only had one date. He had no right to the jealousy that surged through his chest, even though he'd taken care of her for a week before that.

Holly stood frozen near the table. Her mouth open and eyes wide, guilt radiating from her in waves crashing against the walls. Anthony stepped inside without an invitation. He'd hiked all the way up here, he wasn't leaving.

"Zachary." He nodded to the other man, but his voice laced with suspicion and a threat. Anthony closed his eyes and mentally shook himself. The emotions roaring to life weren't fair to Holly and were only fueling a disgusting pit in his stomach. When he looked back up at Holly as Zachary closed the door, she'd recovered from her slack jaw guilt.

She took a white knuckled grip on the chair and her eyes swirled incessantly as they glued themselves to Anthony. Until Zachary spoke.

"Anthony. Holly was just telling me what happened."

"Odd. She hasn't told me what happened, and I was there."

"Don't be an asshole, fish cop." His voice deepened to an eerie threat. Anthony had known that personality slept beneath the surface of the Zachary he'd met.

"Shouldn't you be out of town?" Anthony swung his head back to stare at the other man.

"Someone had to come take care of Holly."

"What the hell do you..."

"That's enough!" She cut him off. Holly took one step forward, but with one look at Anthony, she froze again. But her words didn't. "Zachary, if you so much as hint that I can't take care of myself again, I'll tie your balls in a knot."

"Wow, Squirt. I never taught you that." The threats Zachary'd been slewing at Anthony disappeared in rounded eyes.

"Eight-year-olds pay more attention than you think." There was a history between them. It hardened his chest to think he wasn't as close to Holly as it had felt when she writhed in his arms. But as Zachary stalked toward her and pulled her against his chest, he knew he was in the wrong place.

"Sorry, Squirt," Zachary mumbled before holding her away from him at the shoulders to kiss the top of her head. Their exchange didn't seem romantic, but it was cozy. If Anthony didn't deserve an answer for why she ran, he'd leave, despite the daunting hike.

"Zachary, I'd like to talk to Holly."

"Go ahead." He released Holly, then sat down in his chair at the table.

"Alone." He dropped the word so his meaning would hit hard.

Zachary looked between Holly and Anthony, his eyes narrowing. "No."

Anthony took a moment to glare at Zachary, appreciating the one he returned. He'd called Holly Squirt, and she mentioned something about being eight years old. Zachary had been someone she'd looked up to, taught her things. His relaxed position in the chair wouldn't fool anyone, and he didn't intend it to. He stretched his feet out in front of Holly and crossed at the ankles. Arms crossed over his chest. He'd placed himself in front of Holly as a barrier without standing in front of her. Protection.

Anthony's jealousy dissolved. But Anthony wouldn't be the one to make him leave. Only Holly could do that, and he needed to convince her to make it happen.

"You should leave." Anthony took one step forward and pinned his eyes on Holly, effectively ignoring the protective shield Zachary had turned himself into. "I have things I need to discuss with Holly, intimate things. Questions that involve some specific details of last night." Holly flushed, her skin turning a beautiful blush. The swirling colours in her eyes darkened with desire that matched his own. Even hinting at having her under him in his bed was enough to douse his anger with lust. "I don't want to do that to Holly. To discuss those things in front of someone else, in front of another man that has no business knowing what Holly and I experienced together." Anthony let his gaze turn down to Zachary now that he stood above the other man.

"What you have to say won't bother me."

"I didn't say it would. I don't want to do that to Holly."

And he didn't. Despite whatever past these two had, there was something between him and Holly that he couldn't let go, not until she pushed him away and meant it.

"Zachary, please go." Holly's voice was soft, nothing of the spark from her threat about Zachary's balls lingered.

Zachary took in a deep breath and looked at Holly. "You need me here unless you plan on telling him a lot more than you have." So even Zachary knew what Anthony didn't.

"Go." The quiet word held the force he'd expected from her.

Zachary sighed and stood. He wrapped an arm around her shoulders and kissed her head. Holly winced with the contact. Zachary's friendly slap on Anthony's shoulder surprised him. Moments ago he'd called him an asshole and acted as a shield to protect Holly from him.

The door clicked behind him and Zachary's footsteps faded.

Anthony stood alone with a woman he'd only begun to understand, but craved more of. His fingers itched to touch her skin, to run along her jaw and clasp her neck. To bring his mouth down to hers and steal her breath that already laboured out of her ever-rising chest.

He closed his eyes, reminding himself that she panicked and ran from him, and she'd also refused to tell him why.

"Are you okay?" One thing at a time.

"Yes, I'm okay."

Anthony quelled his frustration and reached for her, but it came soaring back as she pulled a chair between them and took a step back.

"You shouldn't touch me."

"I think you should listen to what Zachary said. You need to tell me a lot more than you have." He burned to touch her and she wouldn't let him. "I did a lot more than touch you last night. I feel damn confident saying I moved inside you last night like no man ever has." She flushed and her hand splayed across her ribs. "Tell me I'm wrong."

"You're not."

"I haven't experienced heat and passion like that in a long time. I wanted to crawl back into that bed and do it all over again."

"I wanted that too."

"Did you? Because you couldn't get out of there fast enough."

"It wasn't you."

"I know. You panicked. But you pushed me away." His own hurt surprised him.

"I'm sorry."

"Then tell me. Before I throw that chair and get my hands on you like we both want. Holly, I can see your skin flush, your nipples are hard, and your thighs won't stop clenching." His eyes landed on each part of her as he spoke. He licked his lips as he remembered how she'd tasted.

"There's something else about shifters I haven't told you."

"I've figured that much out, sweet owl."

"Shifters have mates. Fate chooses them, not us. We know what they are when we meet them."

He crossed his arms over his chest, more to keep from reaching for her to allow for him to concentrate on what she was telling him. "What are you trying to say, Holly?" he asked softly, his irritation gone now that she was talking to him.

"You're..." She stopped.

Anthony understood what she was trying to say, but he didn't understand what it meant. He could guess.

She gripped the chair in front of her tighter when he

took another step toward her. Anthony wouldn't allow the barrier to stand between them anymore.

"I'm your mate." His voice dropped to the husky purr of arousal as he pried the chair from her grasp and moved it out of the way. Holly didn't move.

"Yes," she whispered.

"And what does that mean, sweet owl?" He ran a knuckle down her cheek. "Tell me before I kiss you. You panicked last night. Why?"

"Shifters mark their mates. I almost marked you. You stopped me. But it would have been too late and you wouldn't have had any choice."

"It's permanent?" He tilted his head to capture her eyes that wouldn't stay still.

Holly nodded. "As far as we know. And no one has fought it for long either."

"You left, so I still had a choice." She'd pushed him away for his own good. He couldn't be mad about that.

"Yes."

"But why did you panic?"

"I can't have a mate."

His hands fell away from her and he stepped back. He didn't even have a chance to accept what was.

HOLLY FROZE. She didn't want to move, not when she needed his touch.

He stepped away from her, hurt shining in his eyes as they deepened in colour. She couldn't look away from them. They called to her. *Mate. Mark.*

"I'm sorry. I'm not ready to accept this. Fate thinks this is what I need."

"What do you think you need?"

"I don't know. I don't know who I am anymore. I can't ask you to bind yourself to someone in my state."

"I'll admit, it would be nice to get to know you first before being forced together." His tone didn't resonate with resentment as she'd expected. But curiosity clung to his expression.

"That's the problem. There isn't anyone for you to get to know. She's gone."

He frowned. The moment stretched long enough that Holly turned away from the dominance in his eyes that tried to bore into her soul. She had no warning as his hands clasped her hips.

His head bent until he came into view. "Look at me, Holly."

She did. Denying him wasn't possible.

As soon as her face lifted, he kissed her. All the passion that had been brewing inside both of them bubbled under whatever lid Anthony held over it. His kiss spoke for him. If their desire took over, she wouldn't have been able to hear what he wanted her to hear. *It's all right. I've got you. I'm not going anywhere.* His soothing hum echoed through her heart.

"I think it's time you tell me what you've been through. Why you're here getting back on your feet."

"Okay." Holly leaned her forehead against his chest. She choked on the words as she tried to bring them forth. Pulling in a deep breath, his scent filling her, she tried again. A croaking sound whispered between them.

"Holly?"

She dragged her eyes up, uneasy with how warm his eyes were, how simply looking into them made her world feel level.

"Come back to my place. We can at least be comfortable while we talk."

She was sure he had his own reasons, but she'd grab onto anything that delayed this conversation. "Let me grab a few things."

Anthony let her go and waited in the kitchen. She stopped in the bedroom door and looked back at him. He ran one hand threw his hair and his lips formed an 'o' as he let out a harsh exhale.

Closing her eyes, she turned back to him and abandoned whatever things she'd been about to grab. "No. We can talk here." He deserved the chance to retreat after hearing all she had to say.

"Okay." His lack of argument came with a scowl.

Awkwardly, she pointed to the kitchen chairs. Anthony sat, but only when she'd reached her own.

Holly clasped her hands in front of her and used them as a focal point—plain, even nails and slightly dry knuckles.

"Just over two years ago, some friends and I were kidnapped. Two of them I never saw again. They gave Ezaray and me to a man named Tyrone. He ran an underground fighting ring. All the fighters were women." Holly didn't need to look at Anthony to know rage boiled in his eyes. The heat of it burned her skin. "We didn't have a choice. It was fight or die. Even fighting wasn't a guarantee that we'd survive. If we lost too many times, if we became difficult or lost our value, they'd kill us. I never lost, not accidentally anyway. They hadn't caught on that I forfeited or sometimes pulled punches. Not until the end. Right before Zachary rescued us." Pain registered as her fingers twisted around each other. It wasn't enough. "Women died because of me."

"Because of you?"

"I'm a shifter. Every single fight was an unfair one. They lost. A lot. And so they died." Her tongue curled inward as the taste of disdain filled her mouth.

Rough fingers gripped her chin, pulling her face up. "You. Didn't. Kill. Them."

"I would have let myself lose. Every single fight. To save them, even to have saved them for a little longer."

"And why didn't you do that?"

"Because Ezaray was with me. I had to stay with her. I had to fight for her." Holly knew it wasn't likely that she'd have fought as long as she had if Ezaray hadn't been there too. Holly wouldn't be here with her mate without someone to fight for.

"You survived."

"You got the short end of the stick for a mate. I would have given up. I was close when Zachary showed up. A coward. I fled after the escape. I spent weeks as an owl and refused to shift. I still hadn't when you found me. Don't you see? All I am right now is an owl."

"I don't see what you see. But that isn't what matters. You need to see yourself. You're still in there." The grip on her chin disappeared, but his hand didn't leave her face. He cupped her jaw, then let his hand run down her neck, her arm, until he pulled her hands apart. Lifting the one closest to him, he kissed her palm. It marked her, burned her. The heat from his lips raced back up her arm.

"Anthony, you should go now. I won't be able to stop myself. And I can't ask you to tie yourself to me without knowing who I am." She wished she could have him without marking him. But yet again, she wasn't strong enough.

He kept a hold of her hand and locked his eyes on hers, but he said nothing. For long minutes, the silence became a heavy burden on her back. His thoughts and emotions weren't clear. A bonus to being a shifter was the ability to read others' emotions. Right now, Anthony's couldn't be buried any deeper.

"Anthony?"

"I won't walk away from you." His declaration had force behind every syllable.

Holly shook her head. "You're not thinking clearly. It's the bond between us. It's growing. You need to leave and come back to this with a clear head. I won't take this any further until you do." If she'd been talking to Zachary, the only way to get him to listen would be to thread steel through her tone, just as he'd taught her. Ironic. She assumed Anthony would be the same. He had a protective alpha personality. She doubted he'd respond to meek demands.

"Holly," he started.

"No. I mean it. Nothing more until you take all this in with a clear head."

"And what will you do in the meantime, sweet owl?" She narrowed her eyes at his use of his endearment. When said like that, he wasn't taking her seriously.

"Flying into the sun to find my own clear mind." Holly stood, the chair scraping loudly across the wooden floor. "Leave, Anthony. Please."

"I have one condition." He didn't stand, but he nodded at the empty chair. Sighing, she sat back down. "I get to see you every day."

"That will only influence your decision. No."

"I see you every day or I stay here with you every night."

"You don't realize how serious this is. How screwed up I am and what Fate has stuck you with."

"And you aren't taking me seriously." He leaned his head

forward until the steel in his eyes shone through the rich brown.

"Please, Anthony." She begged. "I'll agree to your condition once you've had at least one day away from me with all the information."

"Fine. I'll accept." He stood, and she followed. He turned to leave, moving slowly. Holly moved around his chair to walk him out. His movements were quicker than she'd expected. He spun around and wrapped an arm around her waist, pulling her hard against his chest. Her hands landed on his chest and she pushed. His heat blanketed her front, robbing her strength she needed to separate them. "You underestimate me, sweet owl."

His lips crashed down on hers, firm and demanding. His other hand buried in her hair and he held her in place for his assault. And an assault was exactly what this was. He'd refused to listen to her warnings and had taken matters into his own hands. And she was helpless. The need to push him away was strong, but so was the need to lean into him, open her body to him.

His taste, a flavour only found outdoors, mixed with something rich, something exclusive to him, her mate. Her blood pulsed and heat pooled in her core. He slid his tongue along hers and he controlled every movement of the kiss with firm lips over hers. With a slow nip to her swollen lips, he lifted his head.

"My place tomorrow for dinner. Don't make me come looking for you." A tremble moved down her body, drumming each muscle on its way. She hadn't underestimated his power and authority, but she'd underestimated the kind of man he'd be with a woman. Tonight had proved that. He released her hair and stepped back. "That hike isn't easy on two feet, and I'm betting everyone else that does it either has four legs or wings."

She held back her giggle and shook her head, remembering Ezaray riding in on a grey wolf.

"Didn't think so. Tomorrow, Holly." He backed up several more steps before turning away from her and leaving. Holly watched her mate leave, wishing she was whole enough to claim what she wanted.

ANTHONY ADJUSTED his ear protection and settled his shotgun against his shoulder.

"Pull!" The first bright orange disc angled high through the air. He shot, and it shattered seconds before it hit a tree. The second disc flew low to the ground, grazing unkempt bushes. Anthony made a quick maneuver and caught it in the middle of its path. And the last disc shot forward, moving away from him. His angle was off, but at the last second he realized his mistake and tried to fix it only to have been too late. The disc shattered against the rock pile in the distance.

"Good shots." Morton grabbed his shotgun from the stand and passed the pulley control to Anthony.

"Yeah. Thanks." At least twice a month, the two of them went to the shooting range together. They'd practice whatever caught their attention that day. Today was skeet shooting, one of Anthony's favourites. Other days they'd practice anything from long range rifles or handguns to archery.

But today, he wasn't on his game, despite Morton's compliments otherwise. He may have pushed to stay with Holly and to see her every day, but his true feelings on the matter wouldn't show their faces. It was like something held them all at bay and each fought for a place in his mind. With the day off, he suggested they come here, hoping to settle himself enough to let loose some thoughts.

Holly'd said mating was permanent, and that there was little choice, but she didn't say what happens if you just don't go through with it.

"Pull!" Morton stood ready, his eyes on the trajectory of the first pigeon. Anthony pressed the button. As soon as his shot rang out, he pressed the next, then repeated with the third. They cleaned up their shells and gathered their guns and ammo to move to the next spot. Moving in silence, he considered calling Asher and asking him what happens if either he or Holly refuse to mate. But what would it matter? He couldn't walk away from her when she was injured. He couldn't walk away from her when she'd invited him in for dinner the night he found out what she was. And last night, he hadn't been able to leave without giving her something to think about. He was an idiot if he thought to refuse her. But where does that leave him?

Without a choice. That should bother him. He'd made all his own choices in life and made it clear to anyone who tried to sway him otherwise that they had no say in what he did. Even his own father.

"...move in with me." Morton's voice broke through his thoughts. He hadn't realized his friend was talking while they moved to the next station.

"Sorry. What was that?"

"I'm asking Janie to move in with me."

"That's pretty soon." Anthony inwardly rolled his eyes at himself. If he was with Holly right now, their relationship would be equivalent to marriage.

"Yeah, but that doesn't matter. It's different with her."

"Then, I'm happy for you, man." Anthony slapped him

on the shoulder. Morton's lips twitched up. He'd needed that acceptance from a friend to ensure he wasn't crazy. But his relationship had Anthony thinking. Holly said Fate decided mates. Why is she only controlling the mates of shifters? Morton never moved that fast with another woman. Maybe Fate meddled in other relationships too.

"Thank you. I admit, I'm worried about what she'll say."

"Only one way to find out." And his own advice worked for himself.

They set up at the next station. Anthony didn't allow his head to wander while they made their way through the rest of the course. Trying to force a decision wouldn't give him the right one. He had to let it go, for now.

On his way home, he stopped in to talk to Hazel, despite it being his day off. But first he sat in his truck in the parking lot and called Asher.

"Hello?"

"Asher, what happens if you don't mate?"

"Are you walking away from her?" Anthony expected the protectiveness from Zachary, but not Asher.

"Please, answer me." He closed his eyes, exasperated from not knowing everything.

"Pain. A lot of pain for both of you. And a chance she'll shift and won't be able to shift back."

"Ever?"

"We don't know. There's only a handful of us we've met. The one time a mate walked away, he couldn't shift back until she came back. Once they were together, they were both fine."

"Okay. Thanks."

"What are going to do?"

"I don't know. I don't."

"You've never let anyone make decisions for you. I understand. I've been through this. But I can tell you one thing. It's worth it."

"Thanks, Asher." Anthony hung up and stared at his phone. He didn't let anyone make his decisions. And he didn't want to start now. But it had been Anthony that took an injured owl home and it had been Anthony that stayed with Holly that first night then invited her to his place for dinner. Fate chose them and put them in each other's path, but She didn't force him to accept her.

His head cleared as he understood himself more. With a firm resolve, he walked inside.

"Any reports related to the trapper?" he asked Hazel sitting at the front desk. She was packing her tote for the end of the day, ready to go home to her husband, who picked her up every day at exactly the same time. He glanced at the clock on the wall. In exactly ten minutes.

"Nothing today, handsome. But I doubt he just disappeared."

"My thoughts, too. He's likely moved deeper into the woods or further from town."

"We've alerted all jurisdictions in the province, and in British Columbia. We aren't the only ones on the lookout for him."

He slapped his hand on the counter. "Have a good night, Hazel."

"I will. You have a good night too. Go make some girl happy." She winked and flashed him her sassy grin she used to tease all the officers, male and female.

Little did she know, that was his plan.

10

Holly talked herself around in circles until she cracked and called Ezaray.

"Holly?"

"Zee. How did you know it was me?"

"Zachary recognized the number as the cell Asher leaves at the safehouse. Are you all right?" Ezaray rushed out her explanation and anxious concern filled her last words.

"No. Maybe. I'm fine. I just... What do I do next?"

"We'll be right there." Zachary's abruptness echoed over the line.

"Don't leave your family. I only need to talk, if you have a few minutes."

"We've already left. We're almost to Alder Ridge. Stay at the safehouse. We'll be there soon." Ezaray hung up. Holly stared at the phone in her hand. She'd put herself in a bare den of a house and had nothing to do but pace. The blank walls keeping her safe from reality and from herself, but the light coming through the opening called to her. Called her name and told her to live.

With nothing to do after an hour of driving herself crazy,

she cooked, but she chose the most unhealthy lunch she could find.

All the women in the fighting ring had cooked for themselves. They'd turned the lounge of that floor into a kitchen and food had always been available, but only healthy options. Bland, monotonous, pre-portioned, vitamin-rich, healthy foods. Tyrone wouldn't risk losing money by having fighters who weren't healthy. One of the easiest ways to ensure that was to control what they ate.

Holly found a bag of nacho chips and groaned. She spread them out on a baking sheet and pulled out everything she could find from the cupboard and fridge. Topping it all with a mountain of cheese, she put them in the oven and poured small bowls of salsa and sour cream. By the time the oven beeped and she had them out and dished onto a plate for herself, she heard the thudding of paws outside.

Ezaray walked through the door, her eyes darting everywhere until they landed on Holly. Zachary sauntered in behind her. Holly stood to meet her friend. This was the first time she'd seen her as a woman and not an animal since they escaped. When she expected Ezaray to hug her, she didn't. She grabbed Holly's face and turned her head from side to side, then lifted each arm, inspecting her body.

"No feathers?"

"Very funny. No feathers, for now."

"Not, for now, Squirt. No more hiding."

"I agree with Zachary, Holly. You can't hide anymore. Your parents need to see you, even to at least talk to you."

"I know." To be honest, she had pushed thoughts of her parents to the side while she maneuvered how to deal with a mate she wasn't ready for. But the reminder of them added more weight over her head. Reality was suffocating her.

There was no way for her to just pick one thing from the pile and start a new journey. It all called to her at once.

"Did you talk to him after I left?" Zachary stood behind Ezaray, looking at Holly over her head.

"Yes, he knows everything now."

"And? What did he say?" Holly felt the threat Zachary launched at Anthony without him even being here.

"Not much, but I also wouldn't let him say much. I want him to decide with a clear head, not with the mate bond pressuring him."

Zachary raised his brows and turned his head away. Holly stomped around Ezaray and shoved a finger in Zachary's chest.

"He's getting someone who's broken. It isn't fair to let Fate push him into this."

Zachary's lips twitched. "You don't look broken to me."

"What's that supposed to mean?"

"Broken wouldn't have been able to leap onto the shoulders of one of her captors to bring him down. Broken wouldn't have attacked the source of her hell to protect her friend. Broken wouldn't have gone back to her mate and slept with him. And broken wouldn't dare shove a finger in my chest. Only you Squirt could ever do that and still have her finger intact."

A throat cleared behind Holly.

"And now Ezaray, of course."

Holly didn't want to admit Zachary was right. Doing all those things meant nothing. Not when she only did what she had to in the moment. "You're wrong."

"And you're stubborn."

"Look who's talking." Holly scoffed and rolled her eyes.

Zachary's features softened. "People always thought I was the one who dragged you into trouble. They had no idea I had to follow you to keep you out of it." The intensity in his eyes dispersed as they reached toward the past.

"How did that work out for you?" Holly was proud of her straight face.

"You know exactly how that worked out. I had to sneak out after being grounded to stop you from your next adventure."

"Bet you wished you never showed me how to have an adventure."

"Never." And in that moment, Holly realized just how special those years were to him, just as they had been for her. "Holly, you aren't gone, or broken. But you don't believe me."

"You're not in my head. So, no. I don't believe you."

"You're forgetting someone who went through the same thing you did." Holly turned toward Ezaray. A bead of grief slipped through her barrier in the form of a tear as she looked at her best friend that she had fought for, to ensure she would never leave Ezaray's side.

"Then you understand."

"I do. But I also understand you need to start some-where. You take that first step. It doesn't matter what that step is. There's no right or wrong order. You just have to do something that's living."

"Accepting your mate would be a start," Zachary chimed in.

"I don't want to talk about it anymore." Only her lips moved as she spoke through a tense jaw.

"Holly, you called me." Ezaray's soft hand encased hers.

"It doesn't matter." Holly looked away.

"One step, Squirt. That's all you need to do."

"Even something as simple as shopping."

"I can't do that. I have nothing of my own, no access to

my accounts, no job. I don't even have my best friends anymore." Holly pushed herself away from them, grabbing her plate from the table, surprised it didn't break as she threw it in the sink.

Zachary's steps thundered on the wood. He gripped her arm and whirled her around. "You always have us," he growled.

"You two have each other. You're mated. Ezaray comes first. As it should be." She kept all bitterness from her voice. She wasn't upset with either of them, and she refused to lay any blame toward them.

"What first step can you take?" Ezaray took her hands and pulled her to the table.

She shrugged. "Anthony told me to come over again tonight. I need to do something before I see him again."

"You don't. He's your first step, Holly." Her voice rang with newly gained wisdom. "Trust me."

ANTHONY PACED BACK and forth across his back door, watching for Holly. When he saw her emerge from the trees, he threw open the door and stood on the deck. She stopped in the middle of his lawn.

"Are you coming in?"

"Nope. I'm staying outside."

"Why?" He couldn't keep the smirk from his face. Her eyes narrowed at him.

"You know why. If I come in, things will get out of control."

"If you don't come in, then we'll both freeze as things get out of control out here." He took the two steps off his deck. She took a step back and Anthony chuckled as he followed her. With the time to think it over, Anthony thought more of her reactions, her reasons for pushing him away, than he had on his own feelings toward a relationship. He knew what decisions had been his. But Holly didn't. Holly didn't believe herself capable of being anything but an animal, not seeing her personality coming back to life. Anthony intended to help her see it. And in doing so, he would understand what the right decision was.

"That's close enough, Anthony."

"It's not. I can't keep both of us warm from over here." He took another step, slow and predatory, stalking her on his own property.

"Staying cold is the point." Her next step back didn't land her feet beside each other, but in a stance ready to run.

"I don't much like freezing, and you're already shivering."

"You're not taking this seriously, Anthony."

"And I've told you, you're underestimating me." Two steps closer. Her muscles tensed, and he wondered if her shivering was from the cold or him. "We can go inside, stay warm and comfortable while we talk, eat, watch a movie, whatever you'd like to do. Or we can stay out here and I'll be forced to kiss you just to keep us warm. Touch you to smooth away the chills. I wonder how hot your skin will be when I bare your breasts to this breeze so I can suck on your nipples."

Her jaw dropped and her eyes widened. Even in the fading light, he saw the bright colours swirling. A flush crept up her neck. "You wouldn't. Isn't sex outside against the law or something?"

"In a public place, yes. But this is very much private." His meaning sunk in with her rapid breaths. They wouldn't freeze out here if they repeated what they did the other night. The heat from that night alone could have set his house on fire. Sex in his back yard wasn't a bluff, and he waited for her to call him on it.

With each slow step toward her, Holly only took half a step back. He towered over her and gave her a chance to see just how serious he was. They stood only an inch apart. There was no way Holly didn't feel his heat, because he sure felt hers.

He lifted his hand to tuck her hair behind her ear, but only the tips of his fingers brushed her skin before she jumped back. "Okay, okay. Inside. I'll go inside."

Anthony smiled and reached for her, anyway. "I made it all the way over to you. I'm still going to kiss you first." This time when he reached for her, he didn't move slowly. One hand cupped her jaw, and the other gripped her hip to pull her against him.

He kissed her as he'd imagined in his dreams the night before. Her taste had invaded his senses then, and the reality was so much more potent now. He pushed his hips against her, his erection nestling at her belly. She gasped, and he invaded with his tongue. Hope flared when Holly's hands moved up his chest and over his shoulders.

She had been right about one thing. This could get out of control. The urge to strip their clothes and lift her up to wrap her around him to sink into her sprang to life. Lust spread from his groin, a song that crooned through his blood, enticing him to follow through with his desire. He held his breath. It was too much. With the image clear in his mind to save for another time, he pulled away.

"Inside, sweet owl." Anthony didn't recognize his own voice. He stepped back and nudged her in front of him. Still breathing harshly, she went. Anthony trailed behind to keep some distance. She didn't want things to get out of control, and it was up to him to make sure they didn't. But he couldn't have stopped himself from stealing a kiss after he'd ruffled her feathers out in the cold.

Holly put herself on the far side of the kitchen.

"I'm sorry I didn't cook for you tonight. I picked up pizza instead."

"Pizza?"

"Is that okay?"

"That's great."

Anthony frowned as her face relaxed from her barriers at the mention of pizza. But he wondered what kind of food they had provided her the past two years. And joy at something as simple as pizza made more sense. "What would you like to do tonight? Since you won't let me taste you again." Satisfaction rushed through him with her flush from the reminder of their kiss.

"You mentioned a movie. Can we do that?" Her arousal had faded, and she looked at him eagerly, cutting into his chest with such a simple pleasure.

"Of course we can. You grab the beer from the fridge and I'll carry the pizza." Her lips lifted with some of her tension gone. A temporary state. It would return as soon as he sat next to her on the couch. He may not kiss her again, yet, but he refused to keep his distance.

They both set the pizza and beer on the coffee table, and Anthony grabbed the remote control. He pulled up his streaming service and started scrolling through.

"What kind of movies do you like?"

"I don't want to watch what I normally do."

"What do you normally watch?"

"Things that hit a little too close to my reality. A comedy?" She didn't sound convinced with her choice.

"Sure." Guessing that she didn't care what comedy, Anthony chose the first one that caught his eye with good reviews and hit play. He opened the pizza box and let her take the first slice while he popped the top on the two beer bottles.

"Oh my God," she mumbled around a mouthful of food. "This is better than the nachos I had earlier. You only bought one pizza?"

Anthony laughed. "Only one, but we can get more. If we eat it all."

"I'll eat it all."

Anthony picked up his own slice and turned toward the movie. After a while, he'd finished his second slice and Holly started in on her third. "Where the hell are you putting all that?"

She shrank back and Anthony smiled to let her know he only teased.

"I'll buy you a pizza every day as long as you look like that."

Holly nibbled her lip, then continued to eat, although more slowly than she had been. Anthony leaned back against the couch and felt like a teenager trying to get laid for the first time as he stretched his arm across the back without Holly noticing.

A low laugh bubbled through Holly at the first joke of the movie, and Anthony's attention focused solely on her. He watched her watch the movie and noted every expression that crossed her face. A not so delicate snort escaped on all the crude jokes and the occasional full belly laugh when a woman tripped going up stairs. Anthony laughed along with her, but it wasn't at the movie. It was joy that matched Holly's.

She glanced over at him and did a double take when she caught him watching her. Her smile spread. He pulled his arm down and around her to bring her closer. She tensed for a moment. Anthony purposely looked back at the T.V. and she relaxed.

He placed a kiss on her blonde hair. He had a beautiful and strong woman in his arms. Fate be damned. Holly was all his, with or without Her interference.

HOLLY HADN'T EXPECTED Anthony's reaction outside when she'd arrived. Throwing down an ultimatum, forcing her to choose. Even as he'd reached for her and she caved, she hadn't expected he truly would have followed through with sex outside. But as soon as he pulled her against him and kissed her, she'd known otherwise. Anthony was a man of his word.

The evening had turned into something so simple, something she'd done hundreds of times with friends. Even as a young child with Zachary, minus the beer. It was Zachary's taste in movies that had fed her own. Action, suspense, and some mystery. He'd introduced her to the child appropriate version of that genre and she took it from there as she got older. But most of those she couldn't stomach the thought of now.

Safety surrounded her with the weight of Anthony's arm. A foreign weight settled in her chest. One that made her smile, not because of the movie, but from the simplicity of the night.

Holly snuggled closer to Anthony's side, resting her head against the curve of his shoulder. His arm tightened, and he leaned further back. Gone was her attention for the movie, as was her worry about things getting out of control. For the first time since the escape, Holly's mind cleared and the breath she took burned like the first after a hard run. It filled not only her lungs, but her body. Anthony's scent added to it calmed her instead of driving her mad with desire.

Before she could stop herself, her eyes drifted closed and peace took over.

She woke in the dark. The T.V. was off and the pizza box sat with the lid flung forward to partially cover the food. She had sprawled across Anthony's chest on the couch. He'd pulled them down together and somehow got a blanket over them, although it only covered her. His feet stuck out over the opposite arm of the couch.

She looked up, her eyes already adjusted to the dark to see clearly. His deep browns peeked through narrowed slits. Holly braced her hands on his chest and stretched her neck. She kissed him with the gentlest touch of her lips.

"Thank you." Maybe he understood what she thanked him for, maybe he didn't. But Holly needed to say it. She didn't want a reply. Settling herself back on his chest, she stretched one arm up over his shoulder and the other around him. Closing her eyes, she let the peace take her again, refusing to consider how close she was to her mate she hadn't yet claimed.

It was still dark the next time she woke. Firm fingers stroking her back brought life into her body.

"Good morning, sweet owl." His sleep clogged voice didn't hide his rich tone. She'd quickly learned that all he needed to make her want was his voice.

"Good morning. What time is it?"

"I don't know. This little person fell asleep on me and growled if I tried to move."

"I did not."

"You did. The second I moved for any reason, you

growled and tightened your arms. At one point you hooked her leg around mine to stop me."

Holly attempted to move her leg and found it wrapped around his and trapped under it. She extricated it and braced her hands on his chest and pushed herself up. His fingers gripped her wrists.

"Kiss me, Holly."

With little thought, she did, but she didn't lower herself completely. Now that sleep had left her body, desire hit her hard and the chant to claim her mate returned. She pushed up after brushing her lips against his.

"More," he demanded. She gave him the same light touch, but his hand came up her back and held her down when she tried to lift off of him. It was a kiss and nothing more. They still had their clothes on from the night before. Nothing was going to happen.

His fingers flexed on her hip and he moved his hand between them. The button on her jeans gave way.

"Give me one. Just one, sweet owl."

"Anthony?"

"Shh. I've got you."

Even being on top of him, she felt encased by him. His hand slid inside her jeans, their bodies giving no room for him to move. Except his fingers. He found her clit and put pressure against it while drawing lazy circles. His other hand moved up into her hair and held her against him. His tongue clashed against hers.

Mate. Mark. The words echoed through her mind, through her blood.

She ripped her mouth from his. "Anthony. I can't." Panting, she tried to stand up, but his strength rivaled her own.

"You can."

"No. I can't control it. Please, we have to stop." She

begged for it to end, but the whine in her voice was anything but denial. Pleasure from his single finger zinged in and out of her and piled into her throbbing core.

"You can control it. And you will." He pulled on her hair and met her eyes. He had such trust in her, she wanted to make him proud. Locking her jaw against her sharpening teeth, she focused on the throbbing in her core. "Come, Holly."

She did. Her core spasmed with surprising strength considering he only used his fingers and nothing else. She locked her eyes with his to keep her focus off of biting him. She'd tried to move closer as her climax continued to pulse, but his grip tightened in her hair, holding her back.

Her body slowly receded from its peak.

"I'm sorry." She pushed against him and this time he let her stand. "You stopped me again."

"No, Holly. You could have overpowered me if you'd wanted to. You didn't."

"You don't realize..." She trailed off. Anthony didn't realize the power he held over her. She couldn't always overpower him. In that moment, it had all been him. "I need to go."

"You don't need to."

"I have to." She looked toward the back door and saw the line across the sky where it was turning from dark to light with the sun below the edge of the horizon. "It's almost sunrise."

Anthony's face wasn't quite a frown, but the hard ridge of his jaw tightened.

"I like to watch the sun from above the trees."

"Come back tonight."

"It's morning. You've already seen me for today. Once a

day. That was the deal." She twisted her lips upward and reminded him of his agreement with a haughty tone.

"Cute. But that's not enough. Tonight."

She nodded, despite knowing better. It had been too close only a moment ago.

"I'll come to you."

"Okay. Now turn around." She spun her finger in the air.

"Why?"

"Because I'm leaving my clothes here. I don't want to carry them while I chase the sun."

"I'm not turning around." His eyes widened and his tone dropped.

Squinting her nose, old mischief rising, she took a step back as she lifted her sweater. Another step and she pulled it off entirely, throwing it through the air to land on his face. She pushed her jeans over her hips with her next step backward. He followed her, matching her step for step. By the time she reached his back door, she kicked her jeans off her ankle and balled them up in her hands. She waited, following his eyes down her body. Her nipples puckered and her body heated, renewing a remnant ache from her orgasm.

Holly threw the jeans at him when his eyes had lowered closer to the floor. She caught him off guard and he threw his head back and lifted his hands. As he pulled them away from his face, she opened the door and stepped onto the deck. She shivered, the morning air colder than it had been the night before.

Anthony threw her clothes behind him, landing them on the couch. He lunged toward the door. Holly shrieked with a giggle and leapt off the deck. Anthony stopped at the top of the three steps. With a final look back at him, she waved. Running for the trees, she pulled on the magic, letting him glimpse it before she shifted out of sight.

Thrusting her wings, she lifted into the air until she broke through the trees. The sun was low in the sky and Holly flew toward it with laughter still in her heart. Squeezing it tight, she realized she had just taken her next step.

11

———

nthony didn't wait to see an owl soar into the sky, but he saw wind the colour of her eyes follow her into the trees. His cock was so damn hard. The minx had teased him. And she'd enjoyed it, feeding off the moment.

He darted back into his house and straight to the shower. Any other time he'd douse himself in cold water to take away his arousal, but not this time. Turning the water hot, he took himself in hand and imagined Holly. Her eyes, when she came, darkening to a deep amber. Her heat tightening around his cock. He squeezed himself a little harder, and he pumped from the base to the tip.

She'd pushed against him as he held her back by the hair on the couch. He wasn't as confident as he'd sounded about her ability to overpower him. Anthony would have accepted whatever happened in the moment, but the last thing Holly needed was another reason to feed her remorse.

He'd demanded that single orgasm, but it hadn't been enough. Then she'd stripped in front of him. If he'd caught up to her, he would have taken her wherever they'd stood.

His hands on her ass. Her ankles locked behind his back and his cock buried in her heat.

Anthony roared as he came, the sound echoing off the tile and the water washing away his seed. He had to brace himself with both hands against the wall and let the water wash over his head until it turned cold. Cranking the heat, he washed. He groaned when he realized his hand hadn't been enough for his cock.

He was early, but he dressed in his uniform anyway, deciding to pick up coffee for everyone on the way. Before leaving the house, he cleaned up the pizza box and beer bottles. But Holly's clothes haphazardly thrown on the couch stopped him in his tracks. It wasn't only memories of her stripping and walking out of his house that stopped him, but the memory of her sound asleep in his arms. Trusting him.

She'd felt right against him. Anthony mulled it over as he drove into town and parked at Wood's Bistro.

Behind the counter, Gwen, Asher's wife—Anthony paused and huffed at himself, Asher's mate—served the customers with a smile that brightened the room.

"Good morning, Officer Green." She tilted her head with her greeting as if acknowledging a shared secret.

Anthony raised a single brow and waited a beat. "I told you, you need to call me Anthony now. Or even Tony, like your husband."

"Which do you prefer?"

"Anthony. I haven't liked the name Tony since I was a teenager, but at that point that's what everyone used."

"Okay, Anthony. What can I get you today?"

"Six coffees, black. Cream and sugar in a bag, please."

Gwen rang it up and gave him his total. She peeked around the coffee machine while she poured. "How's Holly?"

"I think she's better than she believes, but I'm still getting to know her."

"Zachary and Ezaray feel the same. He said he sees her in there."

"That's comforting."

She put the coffee in two cardboard trays and set a brown paper bag on top that held the cream and sugar.

"Thank you."

"Have a good day." Her smile never faltered as she waved at him, then greeted the next customer.

Anthony drove to work with one hand stretched out to hold the tray of coffees steady in the passenger seat. Using his chest to help balance them, he opened the door. Hazel looked up at the sound.

"You're here early. And oh handsome, you come bearing gifts. None of this office crap." She pushed her mug to the back corner of her desk and held out her hands like a child waiting for candy.

"I needed something a little stronger this morning, too. And I wouldn't stop at Wood's without getting some extras."

"You're an angel in green."

He passed her the bag of cream and sugar and another of the coffees. "Pass this one to Morton when he gets in then send him back."

"Will do."

Anthony took the last three coffees to the back offices, leaving one on his superior's desk and passing the others to the two early birds.

"Did Hazel tell you what we found?" Demi, one of the field officers, followed Anthony to his desk.

"I distracted her with coffee. What is it?"

"This trapper isn't new. We found old reports, two from the east coast and one in Ontario. They describe similar type trucks with presumed fake license plates. Pictures of the traps are the same construction, although it seems he's improved his design on the ones he's using here."

"Where are the reports?"

"They left them on your desk." Demi pointed at his desk and took a sip of the coffee, her eyes looking at him over the rim.

Anthony looked down and saw a folder sitting in the centre. He was thumbing through them when Morton walked in. He didn't find any information that could help them. Not a single report had a description or name, but had recorded the same details as Anthony and Morton. Suspected of trapping birds with homemade traps using mice and other small rodents as bait. In a couple cases, he abandoned his truck as he'd done here. Anthony didn't believe he had moved on from Alder Ridge, but was only attempting to throw them off his trail. However, it was interesting that he's been doing this for a while. And now Anthony wanted to know what he was doing with all the birds.

"Thanks for the coffee. What have you got there?"

"Anyone tell you they found more reports of the trapper on the east coast?"

"Hazel said she forgot to tell you and told me at the desk. Anything that will help?" Morton leaned his hip against Anthony's desk.

"I don't think so. They're almost identical to what we already have."

"We haven't seen any sign of him in a while. Maybe he's moved on already?"

"Maybe, but my gut tells me no."

"Agreed. Let's get at it. No calls this morning, but we might as well get out of here."

"Not yet. I want to see if we can track where he's been. He wouldn't just show up in the Maritimes, once in Ontario, then Alberta. We're searching for a trail."

Morton nodded and went to his own desk. "Now I see why you got the good coffee this morning."

This hadn't been Anthony's plan, but after seeing these reports, he had to find this guy.

HOLLY HAD everything ready to make tacos. Asher had brought her more groceries while she'd been at Anthony's the night before. She would start the meat when Anthony arrived.

She'd met up with Chloe when she left Anthony's and they flew into the sun together, swooping around each other. It had been the perfect moment. The peace while watching the sunrise differed from any other day. It was genuine. She'd enjoyed teasing Anthony, and that had stayed with her most of the day.

But now nerves settled on top. She didn't want to mark him, and they would get close again tonight. Anthony already made it clear he wouldn't keep his distance.

Holly paced the kitchen, just as she had most of the day, with nothing to do. She admitted she'd taken the first step with Anthony, and now that she had, whatever the next step, it taunted her.

Footsteps made her heart race, but not from fear. From excitement. From the need to see her mate and feel his touch. She opened the door before he made it to the first step. He looked up in surprise.

"I heard you coming."

The look in his eyes changed. His shoulders straightened only a moment before he took the last two steps in one. Lips lifting to the same sexy challenge he'd had that morning, he grabbed her waist and kissed her. A harsh demand as he licked along her lips until she opened for him. He pushed her back into the safehouse and kicked the door closed behind him. His fingers flexed on her waist, pulling her against him. His erection pulsed hard against her belly, and her body started a rhythm of its own to match. The hem of her shirt rose as he bunched the fabric in his hands.

Holly needed to stop this. She shoved hard against his chest.

"I'm making tacos!" She yelled loud enough for the sound to echo off the bare walls of the safehouse. She winced when she saw Anthony holding back his laugh.

"It's a good thing I like tacos."

Holly kept pushing until his hands released her, his fingers clinging in the last second.

"How was the sunrise?"

She sighed and looked back at him over her shoulder as she walked back to the kitchen. "Gorgeous. It's never anything but."

"What did you do all day?" He followed her.

"A lot of nothing. I think I felt bored."

"Seems lonely up here."

"It's not. Chloe is around and so are Asher's and Zachary's pairs. Sometimes Nathan's pair spends time up here too." They were who she was most comfortable with right now, besides Anthony.

"Nathan?"

"Another shifter. Zachary didn't rescue us alone. Asher, Nathan, and the doctor helped."

"The doctor?" Anthony blinked, his head tilting back.

"Tyrone had a single doctor working for him. He'd black-mailed him. The doctor helped Zachary get inside and helped plan the rescue."

A solemn cloud hovered over Anthony as he stilled. "I'm glad they were there."

"I hadn't admitted it then, but I'm glad too."

"Why wouldn't you have been happy when Zachary showed up?"

"I didn't want him or anyone else to get hurt. And if he'd gotten caught, they would have killed him and anyone who'd plotted with him. They would have killed Ezaray. She told him anything he asked when all I did was try to convince him to leave us there."

"If he'd listened to you, wouldn't it have just been a matter of time before they killed you and Ezaray, anyway?"

She knew that. A familiar anxiety built in her chest, but talking about this was easier than she'd thought it would be. "Our last night there, he made me fight until I passed out. He caught me pulling punches in my previous fight. It was the only time he saw enough to be certain. Cameron died that night. And after that, Tyrone never took his eyes off me." Fear had always been a dull presence, but those last few days the scent of it on herself had been pungent and sickening.

"Then Zachary did the right thing."

"Yeah, he did." Holly turned back to the meat frying on the stove and stirred. Turning it down to simmer, she laid the shells on a baking sheet and put them in the oven to warm.

Anthony's hands landed on her hips and his lips heated her neck as he peppered kisses down to her shoulder.

"You expected me to keep my distance tonight, didn't you?" he murmured.

"Yes. You need to."

"I don't want to."

Holly closed her eyes and moaned, soaking in the last moment of his touch before she forcefully shoved her hips back. He hadn't been expecting the move. He bounced off her. "No." She turned and pointed a finger at his chest.

He chuckled and snatched her finger from the air. He brought her hand to his lips and nipped the tip of her finger before kissing it and releasing her.

"Here." She passed him a couple bowls filled with fixings. "You can put these on the table."

He accepted his job and then grabbed the other bowls and did the same with those. Holly stirred the meat and turned off the heat and the oven. She pulled out the shells and set a couple on a plate to pass to Anthony. As long as he had something in his hands, he couldn't touch her.

"What did you do for work?"

Holly paused, realizing she hadn't thought about her job in a long time. It took her a moment to remember she had a life before. "I was a freelance writer." She sounded surprised at her own job. She'd loved it, but it never crossed her mind since the day they had captured her. Work no longer mattered then.

"What did you write?"

"Anything I could get my hands on. I wrote for the local papers, small news articles mostly. I wrote for both physical and online magazines. I travelled. Easy and cheap for me, so why not?"

"What did you write when you travelled?"

"Some investigative journalism, some inspirational articles. I tried to only take jobs in warm places. Easier to carry small clothing than gear for cold weather. I'd buy whatever I needed once I got there and sold it all before I came home."

As she talked of her work, Holly realized how much she missed it. She'd been good too, but still hadn't found her niche. She enjoyed writing too many things and jumped at any job opportunity that came.

Fear slithered into her heart as she thought of what words would come from her after her experience of the last two years. Tyrone was dead, but the people that worked for him were still out there. Exposing her story would expose them, but it would also invite authorities and an investigation to Alder Ridge and to the shifters that helped them escape.

Pulling in a shaky breath, she looked up and saw focused brown eyes. She hadn't had to say what was on her mind. Anthony looked at her with an understanding that comforted her.

"I..."

A distant shriek rang in her ears. "Stop." Holly threw her hand in the air to cut off what he'd been about to say. She tilted her head and stopped breathing, hoping to hear it again, just so she could be sure. There it was. Chloe. She recognized her sound, and she was in trouble. Holly stood and ran for the door, pulling her shirt over her head on the way.

"What's wrong?"

"It's Chloe." She shucked her leggings, leaving them on the ground, and ran. Anthony tried to follow, but didn't make it into the trees before she shifted and took flight.

Her wind blew like a tornado until she reached the top of the trees and it led the way for her to help her pair.

The wind vanished when another screech from Chloe carried up through the trees. Holly changed direction and swooped downward. She used her senses. Her pair struggled in the net of a trap and one man stalked toward her.

Holly inhaled. Strong scent of a wolf, more than one, came in from behind Holly and Chloe.

She silently perched on a low branch, her talons digging deep into the bark and her wings arched, ready to take flight to attack. A crunch of debris on the ground sounded. Holly cocked her head. The wolves wouldn't make a sound unless they meant for someone to know they were here. But the sound came from the opposite direction of Kai and Smoke.

"Got one?" He spoke low as if more raptors would still fly into a trap with them standing there.

"Yeah, a snowy. They always sell well."

How had Chloe gotten herself caught? She was smart enough to see a trap. Holly searched the ground, pointing out the others they had set nearby. They'd camouflaged them well, but to a shifter or a pair, they stood out like a warning beacon.

The first guy crouched to the ground, reaching for Chloe. An eerie growl curled around the area.

"What was that?" He looked back up at the guy behind him.

The wolves growled again. The stench of their adrenaline set an inward grin on Holly. *Be afraid, you assholes.*

"Oh, fuck." The one still standing started to back up. Kai and Smoke were close, close enough their eyes glowed through the bushes. Holly watched their approach and cheered at the men's retreat.

Her joy and relief was short lived as a familiar scent turned her stomach. Gun metal. A third man walked into the area, not masking his approach. He lifted a rifle and leaned his head to look through the scope. Holly acted with no thought put into a plan. She launched herself off the branch. The air moved around her, but she didn't make a sound. She gripped the barrel of the gun only a second before it fired. The heat seared her feet as she lifted it away, tearing it from his hands. Tossing it into a tree, it balanced across a couple branches.

"What the fuck is going on here?" Gun guy kept a low tone. If he'd roared as his blistering red face suggested he wanted to, the wolves would attack instantly, if they had been normal wolves, that is.

Holly winced as her feet touched the bark to land again. The burns would heal, but they stung at the moment.

Kai and Smoke advanced, forcing the three men to back up. Gun guy gripped the shirts of the two in front of him, pulling them closer as shields. Disgusting coward.

To speed this little dance up, the wolves turned more aggressive, snapping and snarling in a way that would have their shifters fearful of the outcome. The first two kept wary eyes, their bodies shaking and their steps barely landing flat. Gun guy, apparently needing something in his hands to feel superior, picked up a stick from the ground. It wouldn't matter what the size of that weapon, it would do nothing against the wolves. But the guy was after Holly's kind. She wouldn't just stay perched while the wolves backed them into their truck. The old blue farm truck sat behind them, blocked in by trees. She was surprised they'd gotten it this far into the woods.

Holly launched off the branch again and swooped for the stick. But gun guy was paying more attention now.

"Not this time." He lowered the stick from her reach and pulled it back. He moved quick enough to land a blow to her side. Pain erupted with the impact and she crashed to the ground. The wolves went berserk, lunging and snapping at their legs.

"We need to get the fuck out of here."

"We need those birds." Gun guy pushed the other two toward the wolves.

"We can get them somewhere else. This is clearly too close to their territory."

"We already have them sold. We don't have time to move our setup."

"Get in the truck, man." The other two turned on gun guy, overpowering him into the truck. Holly sighed as they backed out and disappeared. No one moved until the sound of their engine completely faded.

Smoke turned to her. *Are you okay?*

I'll be fine. But I left Anthony back there.

I'll get him. Kai took off in the direction of the safehouse.

Chloe! Holly called back toward the traps, hoping her pair could hear her.

I'm sorry. I was trying to help free them. Chloe called back, tears in the sound of her echo. Holly would have done the same, just as she was here now trying to save Chloe.

It was over, for now. But Holly heard enough from them that she knew in her heart she had to stop them. And she would.

ANTHONY RAN. He didn't know which way to go, but he ran anyway. As the silence descended on him, he stopped. He couldn't chase her. Helplessness engulfed him. His... whatever she was... his mate flew into who knows what, and he couldn't follow.

He turned back to the house, but froze as a gun shot pierced through the trees. Dread hit his knees, trying to force him to the ground, but his feet had another plan. He continued to run. He chose the direction from which the gun shot most likely came. In the back of his mind he knew he should stalk instead of run, mask his footsteps and his heaving breath. But his only instinct was to find Holly.

A white wolf with familiar blue eyes appeared over a rise, charging toward him. Anthony stumbled to a stop, his arms windmilling to catch his balance. The wolf stopped in front of him.

"I know you, don't I?"

The wolf nodded.

"Where's Holly?"

He swung his head in the motion to follow. He matched Anthony's pace and stayed directly in front of him. Lead filled his stomach with each step they took. And when they broke through to find Holly, the weight intensified, trying to pull him down. A snowy owl soared low toward another in a trap. Her landing faltered and she teetered while using her wings to balance.

Anthony bolted toward them, falling to one knee. He looked between the two owls, wondering which was Holly and which was Chloe. But it didn't matter. They both needed help. He first gripped the one struggling beside him to help her balance. Dried blood clotted in her feathers on one side. Clenching his teeth against his anger, he focused on the one caught in the trap. He pulled out his utility knife.

"Hush now. Try not to move." She calmed beneath the net and Anthony sawed the rope above the knots that attached it to the semi-circle bar. Once loose, he lifted the net off the owl, untangling talons, feet, and wings as he went. She jumped free and huddled next to her twin. Two sets of amber eyes looked up at him. But only one had the colours of the sunset swirling dimly in them. The one with the injured side and dried blood. Chloe had been caught in the trap and Holly flew off to save her, but she came across more than just her pair in a trap.

"Are you shot?" He eyed the blood.

She shook her head.

"Is anyone shot?" Anthony took note of the grey wolf that had been hovering over the owls when they'd arrived. No one else was bleeding and they stood strong. "Good. Let's get out of here. Then you, sweet owl, are going to tell me what happened." He pinned Holly with a heated gaze, ensuring she knew exactly how upset he was. Angry, afraid, shaken. Anthony wasn't sure if he'd ever felt that kind of panic before, where his body wanted to drag him to the ground in utter despair but the rest of him filled with adrenaline.

He lifted Holly and cradled her in his arm. He offered his other arm to Chloe, but instead of accepting the offer to carry her, she hopped up to his shoulder. Anthony stood and hiked back to the house. The wolves followed behind.

As they approached the house, Chloe pushed off him and settled on a nearby branch. Anthony pulled out his phone and dialed Asher. Even without knowing what happened, he was out of his element with the shifter pairs involved.

"Asher. Something has happened. I don't know what yet, but Holly's hurt and there're a couple wolves hovering."

"We'll be right there." Asher hung up before Anthony could ask who else was coming with him.

The wolves laid down, but they didn't look relaxed. Firm muscles tightened under their fur and they pulled in full breaths through their noses. Holly had closed her eyes and leaned her head against him. Anthony was loath to disturb her, but he wanted answers. With no fresh blood oozing at her side, he sat on the front steps and allowed her to rest in his arms for a little while longer. But soon, a small squeak escaped her beak. Holly tensed in an attempt to adjust herself. Her closed eyes tightened.

"You're hurting."

She nodded and squirmed to get out of his hold. He set her down on the ground in front of him. Her gaze lingered on him, giving him the impression she was saying she's fine. Then her wings spread and she took flight, but only far enough into the trees he could no longer see her, but he heard twigs and leaves crunching when she landed. Anthony waited. Holly returned, but as herself, in naked glory. Anthony didn't pay attention to anything but the dark purple bruise on her hip with the healing red line from a cut.

He looked at the woman meant to be his equal. The woman who'd flown into danger leaving him helplessly behind.

12

———

Holly was sore, but the magic of shifting helped soothe the pain. She had a slight limp walking back from the trees. She didn't want Anthony to see her shift, not when it would be painful with her hip. As soon as he saw her, he ran. His hand and eyes instantly sought the darkening bruise.

"Are you sure, you're okay?"

"I'll be fine. The bruise will heal in a few hours."

His hands moved to her shoulders, and he looked down at her with so much in his eyes. It was the first moment she'd ever gotten a clear read on his emotions. Fear, anger, and love? Love for her, or simple love because he was that kind of man? The kind that helped both her and Chloe without knowing who was who.

He moved his hands up and down her arms, and Holly became aware that she stood naked in front of him. And by the change in his eyes and the bulge behind his jeans, he was aware of it too. But he shut it down by looking away.

"What happened?"

"Trappers. There isn't just one. There were three of

them. They'd caught Chloe. Kai and Smoke helped scare them away."

"How did you get hurt?"

"Just the wrong end of a stick. No big deal." She didn't want to admit her foolishness for going after a weapon that hadn't even been a threat, but was more likely a lure to bring her out again. When she'd thought back on it, gun guy had been quick to pull it back.

"And the gun shot I heard?"

"He had bad aim." He hadn't. It had been likely he could have hit one of the wolves, although they'd argue otherwise.

Anthony's hands tightened above her elbows. Holly stepped around him, forcing him to let her go. She limped toward the safehouse to find her clothes. Dressed, she sat on the front steps to wait for whatever happened next. Every fibre of her being screamed at her to follow the trappers. But now wasn't the time.

"Holly?" Anthony sat down beside her. "Can you describe them?"

She nodded. "All three had really short hair. The one with black hair was the tallest, about your height. And the other two had brown hair and were about five foot ten. The tallest had a mustache and the others had no facial hair."

"Any other distinguishing features? A crooked nose, any scars, visible tattoos?

Holly closed her eyes. Her focus hadn't been identifying them so other than a cursory description, she didn't look too hard. She brought their image into view. "Yes. The tall one had a neck tattoo on his right side. I don't know what it was, but it was long and skinny."

"That's good. Did they have a vehicle with them?"

"An old blue Ford with silver lines down each side."

"A dent near the back?"

"Yeah."

Anthony pulled out his phone. "I know that truck. I need to call this in."

"What are you going to tell them?"

Anthony frowned, waiting for her to explain.

"You can't tell them I saw them."

"I won't." He softened, running a knuckle down her cheek before walking away. His low tones filtered back to her, but she tuned him out.

Paws thundered over the ground as Anthony wandered back to her side. Asher and Zachary slowed to a stop so Gwen and Ezaray could climb off their backs. Kai and Smoke stood. The wolves looked between each other for several minutes, conversing as shifters and pairs did.

Zachary's eyes pinned Holly. She looked at Kai and Smoke.

"Tattle tales."

Then the heat of Anthony's gaze burned her cheek. She looked away. She'd lied to him. But he hadn't needed to know what she'd done, didn't need to know how she'd fallen for his bait to grab the stick. Didn't need to know that she'd lain on the ground, defeated, and unable save Chloe herself. She'd let the wolves finish the job of running them off.

Asher and Zachary shifted. Asher retrieved pants for each of them while Zachary glared at her.

"Are you trying to get yourself killed?"

"Fuck off, Zachary. You would have done the same thing." She stood, fists clenched at her sides. She'd cowered on the ground at the first beat-down, but she wouldn't have allowed any of them to get shot if she could have helped it. She'd do it again and didn't have to answer to Zachary.

"And why the hell weren't you there?" He turned on Anthony.

"Two feet doesn't get me very far or very fast. Kai showed me where they were when it was all over." Anthony's eyes left Zachary and turned on her. "What did she do?"

"Tore the rifle from the guy's hands at the same time he shot it. She threw it up in a tree. Then she went for the stick he'd picked up, but he saw her coming."

Heat infused her cheeks, but she didn't look away from Zachary. She couldn't look at Anthony.

Anthony stepped in front of her and pushed her back. She caught herself as she fell back to sit on the stairs again. Down on one knee, he lifted first one foot then the other, brushing a finger over each sole.

"Mild burns." He glanced up. "From the barrel of the gun?"

Holly nodded.

"Why didn't you tell me all of that?"

Holly pulled her ankle back from his warm grasp and stood. "It doesn't matter." She threw the words over her shoulder before stalking into the house.

ANTHONY WATCHED HOLLY STORM INSIDE. The pain from being lied to struck deep. In his profession, people lied to him all the time. He grew to look past that. It didn't bother him. But from Holly, it did. She'd yet to lie to him about anything. Telling him as soon as they met that she wasn't human. When he confronted her about more information, she came forth and told him about mates. But she flew into danger and didn't tell him. She brushed him off as she would a stranger off the street who asked how she got hurt.

He'd deal with her later. For now, he turned back to the shifters behind him.

"I'll start a full investigation. I'll use Holly's description as my own and say I was the one who spotted them up here."

"Why would you do that?" Zachary narrowed his eyes.

"Because I'm not including Holly, you, or any wildlife in this investigation if I can help it."

"We appreciate that. I'd rather no one find out about us or our pairs." Asher stepped forward.

"They'll be back." As Anthony's voice dropped with his warning, he took in his words for himself. He'd already been helpless once. How much of this could he control?

"Kai and Smoke will keep close watch."

"But next time they'll be more prepared." Anthony would if he were in their shoes, although his preparations wouldn't be lethal.

"We can all handle ourselves." Asher didn't speak with boasting, but with genuine confidence.

"That how a psycho stalker got the drop on you with a tranquilizer?" Anthony referred to the incident from the summer. Asher's scowl said he wasn't pleased with Anthony's assessment. Realizing he was pissing off a pack of wolves, he lifted his hands in surrender.

"I'm going to go check on Holly." Ezaray broke the tension and moved around Anthony to go inside.

"We'll be careful." Asher nodded once.

"I assume the answer to this will be the same as last time, but what about trail cams? You decide where they should go to best catch them and you all know where they are and how to avoid them."

Zachary shook his head, the slow motion a menacing denial, but Asher only frowned.

"The other option is stake outs." Something he was willing to do if that's what it took.

"We'll think about it." Zachary cut a shocked look toward Asher's response.

Anthony wanted to argue, but Asher's glare shut him down. That was the best Anthony would get for now. "I doubt they'll come back tonight, at least. I've called in what I know now and I'll get on top of it all first thing in the morning."

"Call us with whatever you find out in the morning." Asher started stripping off his jeans.

"Ezaray and I will stay the night, just in case."

"You don't need to." Anthony lifted his head.

"Don't argue with me, fish cop." Zachary stalked past him. Anthony sighed, accepting he wouldn't have privacy with Holly tonight. He lifted a hand to say goodbye to Asher, but dropped it when Asher's shape began to change. Bones popped, the sickening sound echoing. Then a visible wind encased him. Next Anthony saw was a white wolf in his place. His eyes flashed back at Anthony before surging through the woods with his mate on his back.

Shaking himself from the awe of the moment, Anthony followed Zachary inside. Inside where he had to face Holly and what she'd done. He knew where he stood, but now he wasn't so sure about her. Instead of asking for his help, she flew off on her own. And even after discovering the situation to be dangerous, she flew directly at it. Anthony reminded himself she was saving her pair. He couldn't feel angry at that. Only pride.

But that didn't replace the hurt that pierced his gut when he'd discovered she'd tried to hide what she'd done. He was ready to face his mate.

HOLLY NIBBLED on a cold taco while she cleaned up, listening to the low voices of everyone outside. Closing her eyes, she let defeat sweep through her like a slow wind, just for a moment. But she wouldn't have changed her actions had she the chance. She still would have flown off to rescue Chloe and she still would have torn the gun from his hands to save them.

Shaking her head, her hair fell over her face, she locked her jaw and pushed it away. It was over.

The safehouse cell phone sitting on the counter caught her attention. There was something she needed to do, but had been putting off. Maybe now wasn't the best time, but after throwing herself into danger yet again, she needed to take another step.

Picking it up, she dialed a number she'd never forgotten.

Her mother's voice softly echoed through the speaker.

"Hello?" she said a second time when Holly didn't answer.

"Hi, Mom."

Dead air greeted her back

"Mom?"

"Holly? Simon, get in here." The next she spoke, her mom sounded distant. "Holly, we're here." She'd put her on speaker phone.

"Holly, are you okay? Where are you? I'll come get you right away." Her dad's deep vow warmed her soul.

Tears filled her eyes. "I'm okay. I... I can't come home yet." She felt their pain through the phone.

"Please, come home." Her mother cried too.

"I will. I promise. I just can't yet." Holly considered using what was happening as an excuse. Her developing relationship with her mate could keep her behind. But the truth of it was, it was a step she wasn't ready for. Calling was hard enough. Her heart hurt hearing her parents and not seeing them. But remembering her shameful cowardice and allowing them to see it would be worse. She didn't want to see whatever look would be in their eyes, whether it be sympathy or disappointment.

"Where are you? Zachary came to see us. We saw Ezaray, but neither would tell us where you are. They know, don't they?" Her dad's inflections moved up and down as frustration and sadness warred with one another.

"I needed to call you. To talk to you, hear you. You deserve to know I'm okay. I'm sorry I can't come home yet. But I will as soon as I can." As soon as she got out of her own way. There was no reason she and Chloe couldn't fly back now and leave all of this to Anthony, Asher, and Zachary. They could handle it while she and her pair stayed safe.

But she wouldn't abandon another of her kind.

"I love you." A sob hushed her.

"We love you, too. Keep calling, Holly," her mom begged.

"I will." Holly didn't wait for a reply. She hung up and let full sob crush her to the floor.

"Holly!" Ezaray rushed over, sliding on her knees. She wrapped her arms around Holly and crushed her against her chest. "What is it? What's wrong?"

For several minutes, Holly couldn't answer her. She sobbed with large hiccups of air. Ezaray clung to her, rocking her back and forth until she calmed enough to answer.

"My parents. I just talked to my parents."

"Oh, Holly."

The sobs didn't want to stop, but with so many people here, Holly regained control, holding her breath to push them down.

Ezaray let her go. She breathed in as if to start speaking,

but the front door opened. Holly jumped to her feet, wiping at the last remnants of tears on her cheeks. Zachary and Anthony walked in. Holly started cleaning the kitchen and reheating the meat and shells, not looking at Anthony.

"Maggie came home from the hospital today." Ezaray changed her tone quickly, averting worry from the others. "She's still staying at Shaye's." Ezaray set out clean plates on the table.

"She's okay?"

"She's fine. But scared again. She didn't say much. I'm worried she'll retreat to how she was when we first escaped."

Holly hadn't been around for that. She'd been in the sky and refused to touch the ground for a couple weeks.

"You should go see her. She was asking about you before Tyrone showed up."

"I will." It was another step Holly needed to take. Now that she'd started, it seemed she was taking steps one right after the other. Needing grounding, she caved and looked across the room. Anthony was talking to Zachary, but he must have felt the weight of her gaze. He turned, his eyes meeting hers with undeniable heat.

Holly knew she was doing all the right things, but she felt like an impostor as her heart screamed, saying those small steps felt like leaps.

13

———

Zachary's threat to Anthony's limbs if he ever hurt Holly cast the words big brother in bright letters over the other man's head. Anthony still recognized the darkness in the man, but with the way Ezaray looked at her mate, there was more beyond the surface. And Holly never cowered around him.

They sat on the floor by the fire, his arms wrapped around Holly sitting stiffly in front of him. But as their conversation died, and the chirps and creaks of the night echoed outside, Anthony pulled Holly up. "Time for bed."

"He's right." Zachary stood and lifted his sleepy mate—Anthony was getting accustomed to the term. With a nod, Zachary carried her off, disappearing into a bedroom. Anthony placed his hand at the small of Holly's back and nudged. Her feet dragged as if he'd tied rocks to them. Each step a slow trudge long after Zachary had closed their bedroom door.

"We can't go into the bedroom, Anthony."

"We can and we are. We need to talk." His voice dropped

unintentionally, raw emotion integrated through the sound. She bit her lip and walked into her bedroom.

"What is it we need to talk about?" She crossed her arms and stood as far from the bed as possible, the only piece of furniture in the room.

Anthony shut the door, the click snapping in the silence. "You took years off my life tonight. And you lied to me."

"I'm sorry." Despite her sincerity, a void flattened her apology.

"Are you? Or would you do the exact same thing again?" Reliving it in his mind made his heart race and his head swarm.

"I'd say a little more to you before flying off. But yes, I'd do it again. My pair was in trouble." She lifted her chin. Pride in her for protecting the ones she loves dug roots into his heart. But he'd been helpless to do anything.

Anthony ran one hand through his hair and when that wasn't enough, he ran the other through the same path. He let the need to touch her rise. To show her what it meant for him to react this way. To show her what she meant to him. He accepted where he stood with this fated relationship when he saw the bruise on her hip, and every part of him turned to ice at the thought of her hurt. Closing the distance, he reached for her.

"You lied to me."

"You didn't need to know." She turned a fierce frown up at him, her head tapping the wall and she tilted it back.

"That you literally flew into danger without waiting for help?"

"Kai and Smoke were there. I wasn't alone." Defensiveness crept through her tone.

"*I* wasn't there." The hoarse sound that escaped him was painful.

Her frown dispersed and her face softened, under-standing lightening her eyes. "And what would have done?"

"I don't know. But at least I wouldn't have been wondering if you were hurt, or worse." Needing to feel her, he ran his hands up her arms, stoking the flames of desire in both of them. Showing her he was willing to accept this gift from Fate was the only way for her to understand she needed to come to him for help, to never be afraid to tell him the truth.

"What are you doing?" Wide, panicking eyes shot out at him and she pushed herself back against the wall.

"What do you think I'm doing?"

"You can't do that. You know what will happen if you do."

He twisted his face into fake thoughtfulness. "Then I must not mind."

"Anthony, no. It's too soon for that. You're still upset about tonight. I can feel it. I refuse to let you make that final decision with anything but a clear head." She threw her hand out, flat palm facing him, but he didn't budge when it landed against his chest. "Stop touching me."

"I won't. I'm going to do a lot of things to you. Because that's exactly what I want to do, and not only because I have the need to feel you're okay."

"You can't."

"You keep saying that, but I'm going to do it, anyway. So, if you're not ready to mark me, then you'll have to stop your-self." Her skin trembled as he towered over her. "Do you want to stop yourself?"

"I'm not sure. Please, Anthony." She begged him. For what, he wasn't sure.

He tilted his head and let the silence stretch. He didn't move his touch from her arms, the lack of movement driving both of them mad. Controlling his breathing, he kept himself from panting, but Holly struggled. Her eyes swirling, her chest heaving, and her hands shaking. Knowing he would do anything to earn and keep her trust, he imagined how he could take her and keep her from marking him as she so desperately didn't want.

As the images of how he would do it ran through his mind, his control shattered. He cupped the back of her neck, delving his fingers into her hair to tilt her head back.

"If you can't trust yourself, you can trust me."

He kissed her, forcing his control when her lips firmed to keep the kiss only surface deep. She tried to hold back, but Anthony wouldn't let her. He wouldn't get all of her tonight, not without her giving in and marking him, but he would take everything he could.

Stepping back, he released her. "Take your clothes off, sweet owl."

She shook her head.

"Holly, even I can feel how much you want this. Tell me it's a lie."

"It's not."

"Then one way or another, I'm going to take you tonight. Clothes. Now." Their hushed voices carried a spark through the air, one that if they reached for it, they'd burn.

Holly caved and pulled her shirt over her head. The jeans followed next, but slower.

"I won't let you mark me if it isn't what you want. Do you trust me to do that?"

"I trust you to try."

He chuckled. "Good enough."

"It's not. There's no going back after I mark you."

"Holly, if I was so concerned about that, I wouldn't be here. I wouldn't kiss you or want to feel your skin under my hands. What do you think I'll do next, sweet owl?"

She didn't answer him, but that was fine. He only wanted her to imagine.

"You don't want to guess?" He placed his hands on her hips and pinned her against the wall. His thumbs reached inward to expose her clit. "I'm going to lick what's mine."

"Yours?"

He dropped to his knees. "Yes, mine." His growl of possession roared to life, and he latched onto her sensitive bud, running his tongue up with harsh strokes as he sucked.

She slapped her hand over her mouth as she cried out. Anthony reached up and pulled her hands away.

"I want to hear it."

"But we're not alone here."

"I bet the wolf with almighty shifter hearing already knows what we're doing."

She tried to pull her hands back up, but he pinned them against the wall while he continued between her legs. Now free to move, her hips bucked against him, reaching for what he offered. He followed her movements as best he could and didn't let up until the muscles of her core and legs tightened. She cried out when he tore himself away from her.

"You will not come until I let you." He stood, lifting her on his way up. Dropping her to the bed, he stripped. "Roll over."

She hesitated.

"Now."

As soon as she did, he knelt on the bed and pulled her hips up, then reached around to flatten his hand between her breasts. Pulling her up, he settled her against his chest.

"Touch yourself, Holly. I want to watch." He looked over her shoulder and down her body. Holly moved her hand over her belly and down, splaying her fingers to reach through her folds and back up. She moved too damn slow, but he had her in his arms and under his command, he wouldn't complain just yet. Her strained gasp fluttered as she drew in. Anthony saw her finger begin slow circles around her clit.

"Anthony?" Lost and needy, he gave her more. His hands firmed to keep from taking over.

"Put your other hand on your breast. Do what I would do."

"I don't know what you would do."

"I bet you can imagine. Otherwise do what you'd want me to do."

Her hesitation only lasted a second before she kneaded her breast, bringing her fingers to the tip. He watched her nipple peak with her touch, light twists and pulls.

"Are you really imagining I'm that gentle?"

"You can be."

"That's the truth, but tonight I'm not feeling gentle."

Holly gasped as she pinched harder. Her head slammed back against his shoulder. He held her, one hand on her hip, the other over her ribs, while she pleasured herself for him. With a full view of her face all the way down her front, he saw it all. His cock became unbearable, but he had a plan for this. Listening to her breathing, he'd learned when her climax was close. Her belly quivered, thighs tightened and moved apart. The delicious moans he loved to hear grew quieter. As she reached for her peak, Anthony reached for her wrists.

Tearing away all contact, he pulled her hands away and held them out to the side. Her final moan turned into a frustrated screech.

"You sadistic asshole."

"Not even close."

She struggled against him, trying to pull her hands back.

"Not until I let you." He waited until enough time had passed that she couldn't get there quickly, then he pulled her hands behind her back and pushed her forward. Only when she hit the bed did he release her wrists.

He gripped her hips and held her against him, his cock nestled against her heat.

"Do you want this, Holly? Because I'm dying a little every minute I'm not buried in your tight heat."

"Yes, Anthony. I want this." The sincerity that rang through both of them evaporated the tension from withholding her orgasm.

"I want this too. You need to see that now."

He angled himself and entered her in one smooth thrust. His moan turned into a growl as Holly squeezed him. Anthony didn't need to think about this anymore. Holly was it for him. Fate or no Fate, he was exactly where he was supposed to be.

FLAMES ENGULFED HER. His words penetrated, but as soon as he filled her, all sensibility fled. She fisted the sheets as he moved one hand to her back, holding her down. Relentlessly, he took her, claimed her in a base way they both understood without words. With every thrust, waves of pleasure rippling through her body.

A torrent of longing filled her soul when he'd vowed to not let her mark him, when he said he wanted this. His voice so calm, not taken over by the moment, but his true feelings shone through. Anthony was ready for this, so why wasn't she?

The orgasm she'd been chasing climbed back to life, but

heavier, fuller with the promise of its intensity. She whimpered, scared of the rush when the dam broke.

Anthony paused. Relief warred with frustration. He bent forward and brought his hands back to her front, pulling her up against him again. Once she was secure, he moved, slowly. Much too slowly. He added his fingers to her clit.

"I've got you." His breath tickled the shell of her ear. "I won't let you go."

His promise sunk deep, but it sent a new sensation through her, knowing that it was him that held her, controlled her body.

"Every time you try to fly away from me, I'll be here waiting for you." He spoke in a rhythm with his slow thrusts. The drag of him across her sensitive flesh stretched each sensation. "Every wish and dream you make, I'll be here to push you forward. When you were healing, I said I couldn't wait to see you at your full strength. And I still can't. But now I get to see more."

The promise of a future with him pulled a single tear from her, stroking her cheek with her desire for more. She leaned her head back, grounding herself against him before his words shattered her. His thumb wiped the drop away, but another followed. Then something in him changed. His hand encircled her neck, his fingers under her jaw. His rhythm stayed slow, but he punctuated the rest of his speech with more force.

"Fate created our situation, but She doesn't make our decisions for us. You're with me because you want to be. I'm here because I want you. I want your touch. I want your mark. I want every single climax you give me. This is my oath to you. Every breath, moan, whisper, cry, laugh, I am here to drink them in."

The truth trembled to her core. She wanted him just as

much as he wanted her. But she wasn't worthy of him yet. She would be.

"Come, sweet owl. Give me all of you."

She shattered, bucking against him as he held her tight. Her climax overruled her, and the mating chant sang a chorus in her head. His hand around her neck and jaw tightened when she tried to move forward and turn around.

"I promised you I wouldn't let you." He nipped her ear. Shock waves reignited her orgasm. "You feel so fucking good, Holly. It's my turn." Carefully, he released her and pushed her forward. "Hold on."

He hammered into her, pulling her back to meet him. Holly lost all sense of reality, feeling freer than when soaring high.

Anthony roared before his cock swelled against her walls and the heat of him filled her. The action so primal, she clamped down on him as another, calmer orgasm tore through her.

He collapsed on top of her to catch his breath, then rolled to the side, pulling her with him.

"Don't fly into danger. Not without telling me first." He kissed her neck, inhaling as he lingered.

"I'll try." She reached around to the back of his neck to hold him against her. Anthony pulled at the blanket enough to cover them. Holly fell asleep and dreamed of a future without fear.

Instincts woke her before sunrise. She stretched against a hard male body and sighed. Anthony stirred and rolled her beneath him. Holly lifted her hand to stop him from kissing her.

"No time. I want to show you something. Get dressed. It's cold outside." She watched him from the bed. He stopped halfway through pulling his shirt over his head.

"You're not getting dressed?"

She shook her head. Holly stood, moving slow to give him time to look. His eyes on her boosted her in a way nothing else could. She walked from the bedroom, peeking down the hall to make sure Zachary or Ezaray weren't up. They crept to the front door.

Holding back the chills from the cold proved impossible. When she stopped, Anthony wrapped his arms around her.

"What is it, Holly?"

She pushed away from him and took several steps back. "This." She closed her eyes and pulled on the magic to shift. Warmth engulfed her, and she sighed as the chill of the oncoming winter no longer penetrated her skin. The magic worked hard to change her shape to the point her body could do the rest. Mild pain hummed in her muscles and joints. As the warmth lifted away, she sat on the ground and shook out her feathers.

Holly took flight and flew toward him. He instinctively lifted an arm to shield himself, but Holly took advantage of the offered perch.

"Beautiful."

She pointed into the trees with her beak, hoping he'd walk with her. He started the hike and Holly readjusted herself closer to his shoulder, careful not to pierce him with her talons.

He promised to be by her side. Holly made a promise to herself not to push him away.

ANTHONY HAD WAITED for Holly to chase the sun, then he hiked back to the house with Holly perched on his shoulder again, her feathers warm and soft against his face and neck.

Reluctantly, he'd said goodbye rather than walking her inside. Holding her naked even outside was too much temptation.

Dressed and ready, he drove to work, eager to pursue the investigation.

Papers and maps littered the tables they were working on. X's marked all the confirmed and suspected places across the country they'd been spotted in. And they drew various routes out between them to search for a pattern. No pattern, except they hit towns and parks with high wildlife sightings. Alder Ridge wasn't large, and was close to the mountains. The prime spot for abundant wildlife. And unique wildlife. It was Anthony's job to protect them. To protect Holly.

Last night had been a turning point. Without a doubt, he wanted Holly in his life. What Fate wanted didn't bother him.

"Where does all this leave us?" Morton leaned forward against the table.

"Better descriptions, a likely location, vehicle description, as long as they don't switch again. And we know there's more than one."

"A likely location? They could go anywhere around here to trap."

"Maybe." Morton wasn't wrong. "There's no reason for them not to trap in the same area. They don't know they were spotted and that we're searching for them now."

"I suppose."

"You asked your girl yet?" Anthony changed the subject, needing the momentary break.

"Yeah. She said she had to think about it." With his eyes cast downward, Morton's lips tightened with doubt.

"If you're serious about her, don't back away, but give her time."

"Since when are you a relationship guru?" Morton threw a wadded up piece of paper, hitting Anthony in the head. He caught it before it rolled off him to the floor and threw it back.

"Just my advice. Take it or leave it." Anthony hadn't had a solid relationship in his life, nothing that made him feel the way he does with Holly. No one should listen to his advice. He wouldn't.

"It's good advice. I just want to know where you learned it."

"I've met someone." Anthony mumbled through tight lips.

"This the date that you had at your house? I thought that was odd."

Anthony never took dates to his place, not for the date itself or for overnight.

"Is it anybody I know?"

Anthony shook his head. "And you aren't meeting her yet, either. It's new." He couldn't predict when he'd introduce Holly to others, but that would be up to her. She had to be ready to face the world, and to face their relationship.

Morton lifted a finger, and his mouth opened, but Anthony cut him off.

"Back to work. You can wait."

14

Still shaken from Anthony's commitment, she needed to act and push herself toward the next step. After a short, and awkward, phone call to her parents, she shifted and flew into town. She found a quiet place by the lake to shift and dress.

Ezaray had given her directions to where Maggie was staying. More times than she could count, Holly took a wrong turn or walked straight when she should have turned. Not that the town streets were complicated or that Ezaray's directions weren't clear. Every time she passed someone, she flushed and her skin prickled as if it talked, telling complete strangers what she'd been through, the things she'd done, the people she'd been responsible for. Time slowed with each person passing. Holly shrank in on herself as she imagined hateful and disgusted eyes looking their fill before moving on to their destination. When in reality, no one spared her a glance. No one could see her past written on her skin.

Several times, she closed her eyes to focus, freeing herself from her self-conscious trap for a few moments to find her way again. She found Shaye's house. Nathan's mate was letting Maggie stay there until she was ready to either move on or could pay rent. Holly knocked three times.

"Maggie? It's Holly." Ezaray told her to announce herself when she knocked as Maggie was still nervous of someone finding her, even though Tyrone was dead. Ezaray didn't give Holly details, but Maggie's past was more complicated than just being kidnapped and used in a fighting ring.

Soft steps approached the door. Maggie opened it a crack. When she saw Holly, she opened it wider.

"Hi, Maggie. Can I come in?"

Maggie hesitated, but let her in and closed the door behind her.

"I wanted to see how you were doing."

Maggie nodded. Ezaray warned Holly that she reverted to not talking much, explaining it was her way of self-preservation.

"You look well, considering." Tyrone had shot Maggie in the fight. A half smile lifted her lips.

"I'm sorry I ran off after the escape. I should have been here with you and Ezaray."

Maggie tilted her head, thoughts flitting across her eyes as she examined Holly. "It's okay," she whispered.

"Are you okay staying here alone?" Holly couldn't stomach staying here herself, but she'd visit as much as possible.

She nodded and moved to sit on the couch. Holly followed.

"I'm not staying in town, but I plan to get my own phone today, maybe a few of my own things rather than still borrowing from others. You can call me if you need anything."

"What about you?" Maggie asked with her head still

tilted.

"What about me?"

"Who do you call if you need something? Ezaray said you only just came back. You're just getting started on recovery."

"You're right." Silent Maggie seemed to be the wise one. "I have Zachary and Ezaray, Zachary's friends. And I've met a conservation officer who's been helping me." Holly reached up to brush an imaginary hair from her face, hoping to take her blush with it.

"Ezaray jumped into a relationship fast too." Disappointment echoed in her tone rather than judgment.

"I didn't say it was a relationship."

"Your face did." Maggie smiled.

"I have people, but you're right. I'm just getting started. I'm taking baby steps," Holly blew out a breath, "but I'm taking them awfully fast."

"Is Tyrone really dead?"

"Yes." Maggie had seen nothing from the moment they had shot her. She didn't know an owl had shown up and attacked or how Tyrone had died. Ezaray had explained the shifters away as wild animals, and they'd stepped into their territory.

"I'm surprised you're here. I figured you hated me." Maggie winced as she pulled her feet up on the couch and settled against thick cushions.

"Why would I hate you? You gave us the information we needed to escape. We got out of there because of you."

"Ezaray didn't tell you?"

"Tell me what?"

Maggie's sad eyes widened, and her bottom lip quivered.

"What is it, Maggie?" Holly asked, calm and slow.

Maggie closed her eyes, her cheeks rising as she

squeezed them tighter. "Tyrone was my step-brother."

"But, you were a fighter. I don't understand." They had treated Maggie no differently than any other girl there. She was one of the best fighters and had been there for years. Had been there from the beginning. She must have been Tyrone's first fighter.

Maggie didn't offer an explanation. She fisted her hands in her lap.

"Maggie, you aren't to blame for anything Tyrone did. That's all on him. I don't know your story and you don't need to tell me, but I bet you've been more brutalized than the rest of us."

"I'm still alive. Others aren't." Sorrow filled the room and invaded Holly.

"I can carry the blame for some of them." Holly's admission was low, but no less audible.

Maggie reared back. "If you had thrown fights to save anyone, then you would have died alongside them. They still would have died, and even more once you were gone. Don't you think I've felt the same for years, tortured myself with how many women I saw come and go from there? How many I fought against for their last fight. I may feel guilty that I've survived, but I didn't kill anyone."

Holly reached across the couch and took Maggie's hands. Her grip was tight, but she didn't have enough words. "Thank you," Holly croaked.

Maggie surprised her by leaning forward and pulling her hands free to wrap Holly in a gentle hug, keeping her wounded side away from any contact.

Small silent tears escaped from both of them. They let each other go and swiped at their cheeks.

"Here." Maggie wrote something down on a small piece of paper and passed it over. "That's my phone number.

Zachary and Ezaray got it for me when I was searching for work. Call me, or text me when you get yours. Don't run again. I know it's tempting. I didn't want to come back here after Tyrone showed up, but it's worth it. It will be anyway."

"I'm not running again."

ANTHONY SLAMMED his head back onto his chair. He faced the ceiling, closing his eyes. He and Morton had just gotten back from a couple calls. They had the map done and plans to place trail cams on the back roads into the north woods. And Anthony offered to put some up around his property. When someone suggested the other landowners up that way, Morton shut it down, remembering Asher's response in the case regarding the wolves. Anthony agreed with him. But now he understood why Asher didn't want cameras up there.

There was nothing more to do than wait.

"You have a phone call, handsome." Anthony threw his head up at the sound of Hazel's voice so close to his desk.

"A phone call?"

"A young woman. She's cute."

"How do you know she's cute from the way she sounds?" asked Morton.

"Live long enough, dear, and you'll understand." Hazel patted Morton's arm. "She's on hold." She pointed to the phone on Anthony's desk and went back to hers. He picked up the receiver and pressed the blinking button.

"Officer Green."

"Hi." Soft hesitancy filled his ear.

"Holly?"

"Holly? This the new girl?" Morton leaned across Anthony's desk with an eager grin. Anthony's face hardened and pointed away from his desk. Morton threw up his hands and left.

"Yes. Expecting another young woman to call you at the office?" Although she teased, she didn't sound confident over the line.

"No one calls me at the office."

"That wasn't exactly a good answer."

He laughed. "My mother and my sister are the only women that call me."

She paused. "Lie."

"The only women that call and that I answer." He clarified. Must be a woman thing to sense when there's a lie, even by omission. Or maybe it was a shifter thing.

"Better."

"What phone are you using?"

"Mine. Just got it. And I've been to visit Maggie. And I've called my parents twice today." Her voice cracked the more she listed. She'd faced the real world. No wonder she didn't sound right.

"Where are you?" He stood and grabbed his keys. The metal scraping across his desk turned heads toward him.

"In town. I'm..."

"Are you lost?" She knew the woods. She didn't know the town.

"Yes, but not in the way you mean."

"I'll come get you." A surge of urgency shot through him. He needed to get to her.

"I'm on a park bench."

"Which park? We have a couple." Anthony pulled his jacket off the back of his chair and put it on while holding the phone between his cheek and shoulder.

"The one surrounded by coffee shops?"

"I'll be there in less than five minutes." He hung up and rushed out the door, stopping to talk to Hazel on the way. "Call me if I'm needed, but I need to take the rest of the day off."

"Everything okay?" Hazel's concern was always something to cherish.

"Yes." He gave her a reassuring smile and left.

He found Holly sitting in the centre of a bench, her eyes searching anyone that passed.

"Hey, sweet owl." Anthony sat beside her, unable to keep his hands off her. He laid an arm across the back of the bench and set his other hand over hers clasped in her lap. "Are you okay?"

"Sure." Scared eyes met his.

"The truth, Holly."

"I'm not *not* okay. This was a lot today. People can see me. I used to love people."

Anthony pulled her close, setting his lips to her hair. She didn't need or want words from him. She was facing this on her own. He understood that.

"I talked to Maggie. Then I went to get this." She pulled out a cell phone she had wedged between her legs. "Then I sat here."

"Let's go get a coffee and go home."

Her eyes swirled when she looked up at him, as if he'd handed her a present. He pulled her up with him and held her hand for the walk to Wood's Bistro. If Gwen was working, it would help her to see a familiar face while out in public.

A blast of heat hit them at the entrance. Only one customer stood waiting at the counter, and a handful seated at the tables. They'd just missed the noon rush. Gwen gave her farewell smile to the customer, then turned it on them.

"Hey." Her enthusiasm stretched, but thankfully she didn't bring light to Holly being away from the safehouse.

"Hi, Gwen. Been busy today?" Anthony kept his hand on Holly's back.

"Oh yes. Everyone is coming in for anything hot now that it's colder. We've even had to turn up the heat in here."

"We noticed. I'll have a regular coffee, please."

"Sure." She pressed some buttons on the screen in front of her. "What would you like, Holly?"

"Caramel macchiato, please." She sounded steadier, a hush of relief compared to her uncertainty when he'd found her outside. But her eyes held a dreamy look toward the menu.

"You've got it."

Anthony paid, and they moved to the side to wait for Gwen to make their drinks. "See you both soon, I'm sure."

"Thanks, Gwen." Holly waved and Anthony nodded. He walked them back to his truck. But Holly's pace slowed as she sipped her drink on the way.

"Feeling better?"

"Yes, thank you. You didn't have to leave work."

"I did."

She looped her arm around his and rested her head against his arm while they walked to his truck. He opened the passenger door for her, stealing a kiss before shutting her in. Her eyes didn't leave her cup unless she looked up at him. Once he parked his truck in his driveway, he turned to her.

"I want to return to work. I'm a freelancer. I don't have to take jobs I don't want or I'm not comfortable with. Most of what I do, I can do alone, but it doesn't keep me out of contact with other people." She pulled in a breath. "I'll be able to control my interactions with others. It's a safe way to keep moving forward."

"That's a smart decision" Anthony was in awe with the change in Holly in such a short time. And to take a tough day like today and learn what she needed to do, required resolve. "Is there anything I can do to help you with that?"

"I need to get my things, which means seeing my parents. In the meantime, do you have a computer I can use?"

"Of course." He got out of the truck and ushered Holly inside. With her in his home, the last piece snapped into place. She belonged here, with him. If she wouldn't claim him, then he would claim her.

HOLLY SAT on Anthony's couch, watching the fire through the glass door of the wood stove. The flick, whips, and falls of the flames quieted her mind. Her time in town had been rough, but she'd needed to do it and she felt better for it now that it was over. Her decision to return to work hadn't been difficult to make. It was already calling her, but she worried what path she'd follow. She'd enjoyed investigative journalism, but the stories she looked to expose now carried a risk. But the trappers, they were something she could sink her teeth into and ruin.

Baby steps. Just as she'd done with everything else, her work would come in baby steps.

Leaning her head back, she listened to Anthony in the kitchen. He'd dropped everything to come to her, and the only thing he did was lend a supporting hand. His emotions were getting easier for her to read, so when his fear spiked at the mention of Tyrone's organization, Holly held her breath, not knowing what he would say. Others in her life would forbid her from doing it, not that they could stop her, but they'd try. Not Anthony. Not her mate.

He brought her home. Not only his home, but hers too. The safehouse was just that, safe. Temporary camping. She was comfortable here, like she belonged. Her parents would want her to move home. She'd visit, but she would never live in an urban area again in her life. Grudgingly, Holly admitted to herself that Fate knew what She was doing. But She could be nicer about it.

Anthony brought in a plate and a glass of wine.

"You made homemade pizza?"

"It's easy when I made it ages ago and put it in the freezer." He left and returned with his own plate and a bottle of beer.

Holly lifted a slice and blew on it before taking her first bite. The greasiness found in the restaurant pizza was missing, but the abundant flavours filled her mouth. "That's fantastic," she said around a mouthful.

"Thank you."

"You must keep this cooking talent a secret, don't you?"

"No." He frowned. "Why?"

"Don't women want a man who can cook?"

"You're the first woman I've cooked for."

Holly paused with her pizza in the air between her plate and mouth.

"I don't bring dates home."

"There's no way you haven't dated." An adorable flush filled his cheeks.

"Of course, I have. I just never bring them to my home. It felt like an invasion. Until you." Melted chocolate eyes pinned her to the couch.

"Fate at work." She no longer held as much resentment

toward the all powerful being, but Holly still bit at Her with her tone.

"Maybe, but I think it's that way with a lot of couples, whether or not they're shifters." He'd already made it clear he accepted this, in more ways than one. Holly was the one holding back.

She'd tried to tease him about his cooking and instead got hit with a truth she hadn't seen before. One that made accepting Fate's plans for her as a shifter easier. Fate stuck her claws into all relationships. Maybe shifters weren't so special after all.

Holly was done putting off the inevitable.

They finished eating and Holly grabbed their plates. Taking them to the kitchen, she washed them and set them to dry. The mundane task centred her mind. When she turned around, Anthony was leaning against the counter.

He emptied his beer and set the bottle down.

"You've been doing an awful lot of thinking today." He pulled her against him.

"I have. I needed the quiet tonight to clear my head."

"I have other ways to clear your head." His voice dropped to a delicious purr. One filled with deep promise rather than fun play. Holly was incapable of resisting. She pressed herself against him while his hands cupped her ass. His erection swelled against her, starting a throbbing in her core. Her heart beat hard, and her pulse pounded through her veins. A haze filled her mind, like a shield to block out her past and her troubles of today. She only focused on Anthony.

"I won't try to fight it tonight."

Anthony's fingers flexed, pushing into her. His jaw hardened and his eyes narrowed. The weight of what she'd said hit them both.

With a growl, he lifted her and stalked to his room. Her hands landed on his shoulders. His strength matched hers, and after today, she knew he would always be there to protect her, big or small.

"You're mine, sweet owl. And I'm yours." He kicked his bedroom door shut before letting her slide down his body. He claimed her mouth while his hands pulled at her clothes, reaching for her bare skin beneath them. Heat seared everywhere he touched. Her clit throbbed. Her breasts turned heavy, and her nipples tightened. Now that she'd accepted Fate's desires, every sensation multiplied. Her body electrified. Zings and zaps emanating from his touches.

"Hurry, Anthony," she pleaded. Emptiness consumed her and only he could help her.

"No. I move at my own pace." His breath hit her chin as he moved from her lips to line her jaw and neck with kisses.

Holly whimpered. He added his teeth and tongue to each placement. A single shiver of pleasure ran from her neck down her back. Tired of waiting, she gripped the hem of her shirt and started pulling it up.

"What did I say?" His authority made her pause. But it also made her core clench. With a challenge in her eyes, she kept pulling and threw her shirt to the floor. "Careful what you play with."

With a quick snap at her back, he removed her bra. Now, he moved at a pace she could handle. He pulled it down her arms while his mouth once again claimed hers. She leaned against him, his shirt abrasive against her sensitive peaks. His hands ran down her arms and clasped her wrists. She craved to touch him, to rid him of his clothes too, but his touch was so gentle, she disbarred to disturb the moment.

But the moment changed. He pulled her wrists to the

small of her back and wrapped them in fabric. Pulling back, she tested the bonds. He'd used her bra to secure her.

"I told you I move at my own pace. You will not rush me."

Holly growled, plotting her own revenge.

Anthony laughed. "I'll take whatever you give me. As soon as I'm done." Then he set his mouth to her breasts and his hands at her waist while he took his time to feast. Each pull of his mouth sent a pull to her clit. She struggled, trying to pull free from the restraints. She wanted to touch him, to drive him wild enough to lose control, to give her what she wanted. But he'd tangled the fabric around her too well. "Stop moving."

"I can't."

"You can."

She sighed when his hands moved. The button on her jeans fell open, but nothing else. "Payback is a bitch, Anthony."

"So I've heard." He smiled against her neck and dragged down the zipper. By the time she stood naked in front of him, every inch of her trembled with anticipation. "Exquisite and all mine."

He stepped back and removed his clothes, but didn't take his time. His cock protruded, reaching for her, surrounded by thick muscles. She raked her eyes over him. When he didn't move, she searched for his eyes, warm slivers in his angular face.

"Finished?" She wrinkled her nose at his cocky grin. He pushed her back to the bed, her arms pinned beneath her. With a hand under her thigh, he lifted one leg to wrap around his waist. Holly followed with the other. He angled her hips and pushed in. "Wet and ready. Fuck, Holly." His eyes closed. "You undo me."

She undid him, but he put her back together.

15

Anthony's body tightened, but he held himself back. He wasn't ready for this to be over so soon. Holly's declaration in the kitchen was what he'd been waiting for. Now, he held his rhythm steady and revelled in every stroke, touch, squeeze. With her hands trapped, she writhed beneath him. Angling his hips, he ground against her mound with each thrust, building the tension inside her and adding to his own.

Watching her eyes change colours, all shades of the sunset, his need to bind them together grew. He worked his hips harder, faster.

"Are you with me, Holly?" He didn't recognize his own voice.

"Oh, I am so far ahead of you."

Anthony bent his head and took a nipple into his mouth. He wrapped his arm around her back to hold her against him while he rolled. Helping her sit up on top of him, his cock still buried deep, he pulled at the bra around her wrists. It took some time as he had twisted that in every way imaginable to ensure she couldn't free herself. As soon as her hands were free, she slapped them on his chest and lifted herself up, riding him with a ferocity worthy of the predator inside her.

But she slowed, and tension filled the space around her eyes. He felt the edge of her climax as her heat pulsed around him and her muscles quivered. Anthony sat up and used one hand on her hip to keep her moving. He wouldn't let her control this any more.

He gripped her chin with a bite of pain and turned her face so their noses touched.

"Mark me, Holly. Do it. Claim me like I intend to claim you by slipping a ring on your finger when I marry you."

She gasped and stopped fighting his control with his hold on her hip. Her eyes changed the moment her orgasm took over. She cried out and buried her face in his neck. Sharp teeth pierced his skin while she rode out a harsh climax. Anthony groaned and slammed her down on him. When he couldn't hold back his own orgasm any longer, he lifted them up and rolled her beneath him.

Holly continued to nip and lick at his neck while he buried his face in her hair, inhaling her sweet scent. He pounded into her, riding the river of her receding climax to reach his own.

Anthony roared as he spilled in her heat, pleasure extending throughout his entire being.

When he lifted, her eyes fluttered shut. He pulled out, eliciting a moan from each of them. Collapsing to the bed, he pulled her against him. They dozed in peace until the sun was long gone.

Holly's hand and mouth roused him. Opening his eyes, he saw she already straddled him, but not over his hips. Her mouth moved down his abdomen, and she paused. Sultry sparks looked at him before she engulfed his head in her mouth.

He fisted her hair, following her movements. He threw his head back when she took him to the back of her throat.

"Holly." He tried to warn her. Of his control. Of his climax. She sucked and licked her way up and down. He tightened his hold and moved her head in time with her, but each time pushed her down a little further.

She moaned around him, sending vibrations to his spine.

"Holly."

She shook her head, moving him side to side. He lost himself in the wetness of her mouth. With a growl, he came, and she swallowed in time with his jutting thrusts to hit her throat.

He released her hair as the sensations receded, but Holly didn't stop. She softened her mouth and moved gently over him, over his painfully sensitive head.

"You're trying to kill me. You've had what you wanted and now you want to kill me."

She smiled, but didn't release him. Not until his arousal returned, and he hardened in her mouth again. Then she let him go and moved up his body. "Take me, Anthony. Please."

"Anything for you, sweet owl." He rolled them over and thrust in. Pinning her to the bed, he gave her what she wanted. She cried out and bucked as her orgasm claimed her. But he didn't release her or let her come down from the high. He kept going until he felt another, smaller climax of his own.

Hers built, and she wrapped her arms around his neck, pulling him closer. He only had a moment's warning before she lifted her head to sink her teeth into the opposite side of his neck. She came, her body milking another from him. What started out calm turned ravenous as she bit harder.

Hers. He was hers. He'd be damned if he let anything take her from him.

Grasping for breath, Anthony rolled off Holly and pulled her against his chest. A light sheen of sweat coated each of them, but the only heat he felt was the warmth of having his woman secured to him. Not just in his arms, but with her acceptance. She'd finally stopped fighting what they couldn't control and she'd stopped doubting him. Trust and responsibility were important to him. He didn't know how a relationship with someone chosen by Fate would work if she'd never learned to trust him. Without her trust, he wouldn't be able to protect her and her species. But now he had it, settling his heart into place.

Anthony curled his arm, bringing Holly to face him. He touched his forehead against hers, brushing her hair back that had stuck to her face.

"It's about time you caved. I've fallen hard and fast for you, Holly."

"Me too," she whispered as her lashes settled on her flushed cheeks. She moved down and tucked her head under his chin, nuzzling into his neck.

Anthony stroked her body, up and down over her hip and up to her neck. It only took a minute for her breathing to lengthen. Kissing her hair, inhaling her sweet scent, he followed his mate into a euphoric-induced sleep.

A sleep so sound that it took both of their phones ringing consistently to wake them, but they stopped before either could reach for them. The sun shone brighter than usual through his bedroom window, like a sign that everything was as it should be.

"Good morning, sweet owl."

His only response was a groggy moan.

Anthony stirred her by kissing her forehead, cheeks, nose, to finally land on her lips until she kissed him back. His phone started its loud shrill and shook on the nightstand as it vibrated. He pulled away from the kiss with a groan and reached for his phone. Holly followed him and settled on his shoulder while he answered.

"Yeah." Anthony looked down at Holly who had closed her eyes to fall back asleep.

"It's already a busy morning and we could use you in early." Morton's voice sounded like an echo as if he spoke over speaker phone and Anthony could hear the hum of a truck. He considered saying no, wanting to stay in bed with his mate—he liked the sound of calling her his mate. But Anthony knew if Morton was calling then they really did need the help.

"Okay. Give me a few minutes to shower and I'll be on my way."

"See you soon." Morton hung up.

"Holly, I have to go to work." He tried to wake her by squeezing her shoulder.

"No." Her answer was muffled against his chest as she squeezed herself against him and threw one leg over his.

He chuckled and started to roll her over, intending to push her into the mattress, but her phone rang again. Anthony reached over and passed it to her. He sealed their lips while she answered with a muffled moan.

Holly shoved at his chest until he left her. Smiling, he went to have shower, already thinking about spending his next day off in bed with his mate.

HOLLY WORKED with the other shifters and pairs to keep watch for the trappers. And the entire time, she couldn't get it out of her head that this was the wrong way to do this. Anthony believed this was the best course, and she trusted him. But something called to her. She was meant to do something.

Asher, Zachary and Nathan had discussed in length about the possibility of using trail cams and in the end, it was just too much of a risk to allow them this far up. So the pairs kept watch and the shifters and Anthony would join whenever they could. And Anthony had set up trail cams along the hunting roads.

They'd found several places that gave the shifters the advantage of an ambush. But it would only be luck if the trappers set up in one of those where the shifters and pairs could rid them of their weapons and pin them down until Anthony and his backup arrived. Holly and Chloe would lead Anthony to them just in time for the shifters to disappear and Fish and Wildlife to take over. That would be too easy.

Holly and Anthony had both been relaxed, content with the events of the night before, until reality crashed in with phone calls to both of them. Zachary wanted her up in the woods, and Anthony was needed at work early.

Anthony was no longer calm when he left Holly as she'd hiked into the woods to shift and fly toward the safehouse. But up until that point, nothing could have been more perfect. Holly still had a long way to go, but with him filling her and the mating complete, she was whole. She had everything she needed to continue to survive. More than survive. She could live. She couldn't live as she had before, and she didn't want to. Here, near the mountains with her mate and other shifters, this was where she belonged.

They'd been scouting for hours when the shifters all called it quits. Asher had an emergency at the clinic, Zachary left to work on his house, and Nathan left to get Shaye. The pairs continued to scout a little longer before trudging back to their territories to rest. Holly flew to the safehouse to pack the few things of hers that were there. She hadn't told Anthony yet, but she planned on staying with him from now on. He'd mumbled in his sleep about moving in together. Holly had smiled and shushed him with a soft kiss before going back to sleep. But now she needed to face her parents, not just short phone calls, she needed to see them. And she needed her own things.

As time had passed with her missing, her parents had been unsure what to do. Zachary had packed up her apartment and put it all in storage to spare her parents from having to deal with it. And since he'd promised to find her, in his mind there was no need to deal with her things. The result was, she now had some work to do to go through it all.

Setting the small bag by the front door, Holly heard a screech. She threw open the door and saw Chloe flapping frantically to stay in one spot in the air. Holly stripped, leaving her clothes on the steps. She shifted.

What is it?

I've scented the trappers. They're close.

Tell the others, then go find Anthony.

Chloe flew away and Holly headed north to find the trappers. Their foul scents reached her in the air. She perched in a tree to listen and spy on them.

"This trip has been a waste. We're so far behind on quota." The shortest of the three complained.

"We wouldn't be if someone had latched the cages properly last time. We wouldn't have lost a quarter of our birds. At least we got some today."

"This is it, Paul. We have to ship out what we've got tomorrow. We have buyers waiting. Keep an eye out for wildlife. And people. We can't screw this up today." Their attention was focused around them. Holly silently followed them, watching their every move.

After setting up half a dozen traps, they retreated into the trees, presumably back to their truck to wait.

She followed. They hiked for fifteen minutes to check another round of traps. Her help wouldn't be far behind. But Holly's gut screamed that something wasn't right, that this was a big mistake. She willed for the instinct to go away, to prove her wrong. But the scents that whirled in between the trees confirmed it all. This wouldn't happen the way they thought it would.

Her stomach sank as she watched a hawk stoop toward one of their traps they'd just walked away from. Her heart hurt for the animal thrashing in fear when the net snapped shut over top of him. The trappers came running back.

Holly tilted her head, catching an odd scent in the air. But who she saw next stopped her flight, forcing her to land.

A woman they've all seen at least once. A ghost, with a long dress and hair swept over her shoulder.

"They need your help, Holly. There are two pairs in their storage unit. You need to get to them before they're separated from their shifters for too long."

Anthony and the others are on their way.

"One is hurt and getting weaker. She may not make it until their investigation leads to them. That's why you need to rescue them."

The woman came to her. Why her? In what way could she go against the trappers to rescue the pairs? Help was on the way. But that was the problem. Holly knew what she needed to do. She needed to let herself get captured. If help arrived first, it would take too long to find them. And if the trappers got away, they wouldn't go back and lead Fish and Wildlife to the birds, not so soon when they could be followed. Holly looked at the woman, pleading for there to be another way. But it had to be her. She needed to get to the pairs and trust that Anthony would find her soon.

Her heart raced and her wings shook creating an unsteady flight. She flew toward the trappers. She couldn't bring herself to fly into the trap.

"That owl is back. Get her." The tall one they'd called Paul snapped as he pointed at her. She swooped toward his head, not getting close enough to scratch him, but the man ducked, the scent of panic escaping his pores. One of the others produced a net. Holly flew out of reach and perched, drawing them away from their traps. She glared at them and they took the bait. Swooping in again, she allowed her wing to brush near their hand-net, then turned her direction further still from their traps and toward their truck. They followed, an odd determination in their eyes to catch specifically her. She had their attention. Taking flight again, she closed her eyes and let them catch her.

As soon as the net wrapped around her, she felt the weight of captivity fill her. The dread, helplessness, and cowardice roared to the surface. They slammed her down to the ground and pulled the net tight around her.

"Don't worry. Your mate will find you. I promise." The woman smiled before she faded into the air. Snow floated down in place of her presence. Tiny flakes turning the air white.

"Let's get these ones out of here. Seth, you stay here and watch the traps. We'll leave some cages. Danny and I will take these ones and come back to get you. I'm not chancing losing them as we get them. Not when we're this short on product."

Holly closed her eyes as one of them threw her over his shoulder. She landed with a thump against his back. Holly hadn't thought of doing this on her own before the woman appeared. But thoughts of her days under Tyrone terrified her. Hearing there were shifter pairs in trouble sealed the deal. She'd been separated from Chloe for two years. If these guys shipped off pairs when she could have stopped them, if they'd died because they took too long to rescue them, she'd never forgive herself. They'd never be reunited with their shifters.

Breathing through her panic, she knew she made the right choice.

IT HAD BEEN SNOWING for the past hour, and Anthony wrote his fifth ticket for hunting violations that day. Blatant transparent lies. Sometimes the boldness of some people, even when caught in the act, stunned him. Morton handled the rounding up of licenses. The calls had started early that morning, forcing him to leave the warmth of Holly curled up against him.

Just the thought of her made his neck throb where she'd marked him, sending shocks straight to his groin. The night hadn't been long enough. But now that they'd mated, Anthony intended to move her in with him. He'd made a promise last night to claim her with marriage. And he would, but not until she was ready. She still had things to do to finish getting back on her feet. He'd already requested time off to take her to her parents.

He only hoped they caught the trappers before then.

The investigation was under way. They'd talked to Ryan Morison, the previous owner of the truck, that morning. He'd claimed he sold it to a non-resident of Alder Ridge who'd had his own vehicle stolen. His description matched Holly's of the tall trapper with the mustache and tattoo. There was a search out for that truck. In the meantime, Anthony and Morton had been dealing with hunters.

Waiting at the truck for Morton to finish and send the hunters on their way, a flash of white caught his attention. A snowy owl flew close, swooping in a circle above him. Chloe. Her eyes didn't glow when she looked straight at him.

"Wow." Morton sidled up beside him.

"We have to go." Anthony said we, not thinking that he should go alone.

"What?"

Anthony didn't answer. He got in his truck, and started pulling out before Morton barely had his feet off the ground.

"What the hell, Tony?"

Anthony leaned forward to keep Chloe in sight as she raced over the trees, staying close enough to the road to guide him. She took them past his place and up the old back roads. When she stopped and perched in a tree, Anthony jumped out. Fresh snow even covered the canopied forest ground.

"Wait here."

"No." Morton squared off with Anthony. "You've been keeping something from me. I'm going with you."

Chloe screeched above them, her wings ready to take flight. They didn't have time to argue. Anthony ignored Morton and ran, following Chloe who swerved low in the trees.

"Anthony. What the hell is going on?" Morton chased

after him. "Oh, fuck." His curse had Anthony spinning his head. Asher, Zachary, and Nathan ran ahead of them. But where Anthony saw who they were, Morton saw two wolves and a bear.

Asher looked at Anthony and raised his brow. Anthony shrugged.

"He wouldn't stay."

"Who wouldn't stay. Tony, we need to back up."

"You wouldn't stay. And no. We follow them."

Zachary growled low, looking directly at Morton. Anthony nodded and turned to his friend.

"Morton, there are things you don't know. And if you insist on following, you can't reveal anything you see. If you can't promise that, then you need to turn around now and wait at the truck."

"What is it?"

"Promise me. I don't have time to explain, except we're chasing the trappers."

Morton frowned at him then looked at each of the large predatory animals standing patiently ahead of them. "Why can't I say anything?"

"It will put people, and wildlife, in danger." Morton was as dedicated to his job as Anthony. He needed his friend to understand.

"Okay. Because it's you. You have my word. I won't repeat anything I see or hear."

The shifters started forward. They followed until the shifters spread out. Asher nodded to the right. Anthony took Morton with him in that direction.

"We're catching the trappers." Anthony couldn't keep his excitement from his voice, but in the back of his mind he wondered where Holly was.

"We? I don't think I'm part of the *we* you keep talking

about."

"Hey." Asher appeared behind Morton, surprising him, although Anthony had seen him coming. Morton turned around.

"Woah. Where did you come from? And why are you naked."

"Never mind." He took his attention off Morton and looked over his head to Anthony. "They aren't all here anymore. According to Kai, they were here, scouted around and set up a few areas with traps."

"They aren't *all* here?"

"They left one behind, but the snow is so heavy we don't know how long ago they left or which way they went."

"Any weapons?"

"The one left has a shotgun."

"Any dart guns?" At least those wouldn't harm.

"Not that we've seen, but even if he does, it won't work on us in time." Asher shrugged.

"Again with the *we* and *us*. Someone want to fill me in? The vet here works for Fish and Wildlife now does he?" Morton's head continued to swivel back and forth.

Anthony ignored Morton. "Where's Holly?"

Asher hesitated, his lips pursing in a thin line. "She isn't here. Chloe said she left to find them after sending her off to get all of us."

Two scenarios filled his head, and both of them pissed Anthony off. Either she followed them without leaving a sign for anyone, or she'd been caught.

"Holly? That's who called you yesterday at the office. That your new girl?" asked Morton.

"Yes." Anthony didn't intend to snap at his partner.

Morton reared back at his gruff response.

"Follow m.." Asher paused. "Just follow. He'll lead you

two to the one that's still here." He left, not waiting for a response, but a minute later returned as a large wolf. His blue eyes beckoned them forward. They stalked further into the trees, the still soft snow dampening their footsteps.

A man dressed in black pulled his collar up around his neck. Anthony tagged Morton's shoulder and pointed right.

He nodded and left.

Anthony straightened, his hand over his gun holstered in his belt. He entered the situation as he would any other, start approach and start a conversation, but this wasn't like any other situation.

"Hello, there."

The guy's head whipped up and his body tensed, indecision in his features. Fight or flight. He chose flight, but he didn't get as far as Anthony was sure he'd imagined. Morton's arm swung out from behind a tree, knocking the guy in the nose. He stumbled back, catching on something beneath the snow and falling to the ground. Anthony was on him before he could move.

"That wasn't a very polite response to someone saying hello. But I'm in a bit of a hurry, so we'll worry about that later. We know you're illegally trapping raptors to sell. We also know you aren't alone. You're under arrest and considering we've tracked you across the country, it would be wise to come clean. And you're going to start with telling us where your buddies are."

The guy's jaw locked under a mutinous glare. Idiot.

Anthony flipped him around, not concerning himself with the face full of snow he tried to turn away from. He pulled the cuffs off the back of his belt and snapped them around his wrists. His phone vibrated against his leg. He stood to answer it, leaving Morton to pull the guy up off the ground.

"Officer Green."

"Tony." Hazel's voice filled with urgency. "I have Herb Batemen here, renewing his license. He just said he saw Ryan's old truck heading out of town. Not the first time either. Going toward the old Wentworth highway. Not much on that road, Tony."

"Tell Herb I owe him a bottle of whiskey."

"Will do, handsome."

"I'm on my way out there." Anthony tucked his phone back in his pocket. They had a location.

"What did Herb have to say?" Morton had a hold of the guy's arm.

"What this guy wouldn't. They're on the Wentworth highway."

"Let's take this guy back then we'll head out there." Morton started to pull him away.

"No." His tone was flat, but it stopped Morton.

"No?"

"You take him back then follow me out. There's no time." Anthony didn't know that for sure, but the blood ran through his veins with an energy he didn't understand. But time was running out.

Morton's face hardened, a permanent glare tightening his face while they hiked back to their truck. The snow wasn't letting up, in fact, it fell thicker. The weather report had been so far off the mark this morning. This wasn't light snow. They were getting a blizzard.

The hairs on the back of Anthony's neck stood. He looked behind them and saw several sets of eyes flash through the white blur. They secured the guy in the truck and Anthony kept walking, not surprised Morton followed.

"What the hell?" Morton raised an arm over his eyes as

Asher, Zachary, and Nathan stepped out, all naked after shifting.

"Chloe panicked and flew off, we assume to search for Holly." Zachary's eyes narrowed as the snow flew down around his face.

"We know where they went." Anthony itched to turn back to his truck.

"Hopefully she'll find them too." Asher seemed to always have the reassuring words.

"Why the hell are you three naked and why have wolves and bears been stalking us?" Morton's voice pitched to an octave Anthony had never heard from his partner.

"You knew they were there?"

"Yeah."

Anthony didn't have time to analyze Morton's observational skills. "We need to go. Asher, you know the old Wentworth highway?"

"Of course."

"They're on that road."

"We'll meet you out there." Asher turned back to the trees and Nathan followed him.

"I'm coming with you." Zachary stepped forward.

"Okay. Morton, drop us off at my house and we'll take my truck. Follow us with RCMP after you drop that one off." Anthony hiked a thumb over his shoulder.

"Anyone but you, and I wouldn't go along with any of this. You owe me an explanation." Morton jabbed a finger in the air.

Anthony nodded. Morton would get his explanation, but Anthony would let Asher do the talking.

16

Holly took long breaths, shoving her panic down with air that only added more weight to her chest. But it wouldn't go away. Captured again. Flashes of the early days in the fighting ring played behind her closed eyes. Pulling in more air, she tried to push those visions away. She crashed against the side of the square cage more than once, losing what little grip she could muster on the steel bottom. And she'd thought Anthony's playpen had been bad. She'd rather be in that and with a broken leg than in this cage driving away from her mate. Hopefully Chloe was following and could lead Anthony to her.

She fell back as the truck lurched to a stop.

"Get them out of there quickly. I want to get back to the rest of the traps. Quota is due and we need to ship whatever we have." Paul was always the one giving the orders.

Danny ripped the tarp away and Holly winced at the bright white of the snow, as did the other birds. They released the straps around the cages then they jerked them forward, knocking Holly and the others over. She'd bruise, but she wouldn't take long to heal.

Holly looked around, knowing she needed to take in any information she could. Nausea clogged her throat at the bars in her line of sight. Focusing, she tried to look past them. A large, old barn stood alone at the end of a field. A storage container sat along the side of it between the building and some trees, off the ground on a truck bed.

They opened the storage unit, the large metal doors groaning. Squawks and screeches echoed from within, some protesting the sudden light, others angry at their situation. The sides were lined with cages, only a quarter of them empty.

All beautiful birds of prey, raptors, magnificent beings, held captive. No one deserved this. The cages were stacked on top of each other. They carried Holly and the other two they'd caught inside and hefted them onto the pile on the left.

"Grab food from the barn. We're going back right away. This storm is getting bad." The leader called from outside.

"Can't wait until we ship this off tomorrow," Danny muttered under his breath for only the birds to hear.

The door creaked and groaned again as they closed it. More screeches and squawks complained. Darkness encased them, creating a darkness inside Holly. The same darkness that almost consumed her before Zachary had shown up to rescue them. The darkness that whispered permission for her to give up.

"Holly." A soft voice echoed in the air, not really present. She opened her eyes, blinking to help her sight adjust faster. The woman, the ghost, stood in front of her cage. The sight reminded her again why she allowed herself to be captured. There were pairs to save.

Where are they?

"They're in here. They can see me and they can hear you."

Holly pulled in air, but each breath turned shakier as the walls of the container consumed her and the bars of her cage grew thicker.

"Holly, the winds created all of you to do extraordinary things. Don't let panic beat you."

The winds created us? Created shifters?

"Yes."

What are the winds? Where did they come from?

"I created the winds, in a way. Lost souls filled with magic that needed a purpose. They've had their purpose for a long time, but they were waiting for the right people. And when those shifters find each other, the winds can be reunited again."

The answers that herself, and she was sure others, always wondered about gave her something to focus on.

"You are strong. You can do this." The woman backed away, fading slowly as she watched Holly straighten herself up in her cage. She wouldn't let panic beat her, not when she'd finally found her freedom again.

Examining the latch on the cage, she tried to reach it with her beak, but it was too far out from the bars. Using her beak and feet to climb, she held onto the side of the cage, her head pushing against the top. Holding her weight with one foot, she used the other to push the sliding bar on the latch to the left. Her muscles protested at her position. She reached to the other side and pushed the latch up. It slipped and slid back into place. With a huff, she tried again, but this time when she felt it slipping from her lack of reach, she pushed at the door with her wing. As the latch fell off her talon, it didn't land back in place.

She hopped down and breathed. Pushing the door open

with her head, she lunged out of the cage and spread her wings to lower herself gently to the floor. She'd hoped her panic would disappear after she escaped the cage, but looking around at the metal walls, she realized she had only been in a cage inside a cage.

Shaking her head, she looked at all the birds. Hawks, falcons, owls, a couple eagles.

Hello? She hoped the pairs weren't too afraid to answer. *I'm here to help. To make sure you get back to your shifters.*

Are you one of us? The call came from further in the container.

I'm a shifter. Where are you?

In the back. She heard tapping sounds. With a short hop, she flew to the back. An owl and a hawk sat toward the front of their cages, except the owl leaned her weight fully against the bars.

I'm going to let you guys out. How badly are you hurt? She looked at the owl. Her eyes struggled to stay open and one side of her face seemed to droop.

Hit on the head. But I can move.

Holly wasn't so sure about that. *I need you to move away from your door.*

But how are we going to get free of the container? The hawk asked while the owl inched back to lean herself against another part of the cage.

I have people coming. She hoped she did. She trusted Anthony would find her.

Holly closed her eyes and shifted, feeling her own strength fill her as the warmth of the change moved through her body. She quickly unlatched both of their cages. The hawk flew out on his own and Holly reached in for the owl to pull her out. She shouldn't move until she absolutely had to.

"Are there any more pairs in here?"

The hawk shook his head. Holly settled the owl near the front by the door and shifted back. The last thing she wanted was to be found as a naked woman if they came back.

Now what?

We wait and you two can tell me where you're from.

Learning about them and their shifters kept Holly from focusing on the metal walls surrounding her.

ANTHONY'S HEART RACED, but his focus remained strong. While he grew up driving in these conditions, it didn't mean he didn't need to concentrate to get through them, especially at the speed he'd set.

"There." Zachary pointed from the passenger seat at the truck coming at them. "That's them."

Anthony kept driving.

"You're not going to stop them?"

Anthony lifted the radio. "Passed the truck. They're heading back, Morton."

"Got it."

Anthony glanced at Zachary. "The bed is empty. If they caught Holly, then we need to get to her first." He had a single focus. If he allowed another thought, he'd lose control, allowing fear and rage to rule. He stepped on the gas, pushing through the snow.

Between the blurring white, flat ground between sections of trees with mountains standing strong in the distance stared at them. After three turns in the road, an old barn would come into view, the place Anthony suspected the trappers were using. Abandoned for a couple decades, it would make the perfect storage building, and it was a long drive to the next usable building.

His truck lurched forward. Anthony's arms tightened, keeping him from hitting the steering wheel. Zachary threw his arms out on the dash. Looking in the rearview mirror, Anthony saw Ryan Morison's old truck picking up speed to hit him again. He prepared to maneuver through the snow with the impact. They jolted forward, harder than the first time, sending the tail end of his truck into a fishtail. Anthony took his foot off the gas to give the tires a moment to catch traction. The trappers behind them continued to swerve, the snow pulling them to the side. But they righted themselves and eased onto the gas to pick up their speed. Anthony couldn't avoid the next hit in time.

They hit on the side of his tail end, pushing him into the deeper snow in the ditch. The blue truck swerved back and forth out of control for a moment, while the snow pulled Anthony's truck off the road.

The truck came to a stop and the passenger door opened. He lifted a gun and aimed it at the front driver's side tire. Anthony reached for his own gun, but before he had it out the window, Zachary yanked on the guy's shirt, sending his shot into the snow.

"Destroy the barn and move the unit!" he yelled back into the truck. Anthony jumped from his truck to stop the driver, but didn't make it in time. He drove off with the passenger side door swinging.

"Damn it!" Anthony turned around and saw Zachary had the guy pinned in the snow. He ran to his truck and pulled out another set of cuffs, tossing them to Zachary. He lifted the radio. "Need an ETA. One caught and one got away. We're in the ditch, but will follow as soon as we're free."

"At least twenty minutes out. This is turning into a mighty blizzard."

"Understood." He ended the call. "Throw him in the back seat."

Zachary heaved the guy over his shoulder and tossed him in. "Get behind the wheel and I'll push."

The snow continued to thicken outside, but within five minutes they were out of the ditch. Zachary jumped back in the truck and Anthony drove as fast as he dared. Three turns in the road and he saw the old abandoned barn through the hazy snow. An eighteen-wheeler with a sea-can storage unit on the flatbed sat in front of the barn. The barn that was engulfed in flames. Bright red and orange covered the brown wood and dark clouds billowed thickly above the building.

Zachary grabbed the radio before Anthony could and called for the fire truck.

"Where the hell does he think he's going to go with that truck?"

"He's not going to get as far as he thinks." Anthony's voice cracked, his eyes glued to the fire. Where was Holly? In the barn, or in the storage unit?

He slid to a stop as the truck started to move forward onto the highway.

"I've got the back, you get him." Anthony ignored the surprise on Zachary's face and ran to grab onto the back of the truck. Zachary had the guy out from behind the wheel and the truck stopped in seconds. Anthony lifted the bar across the doors and threw them open. A hawk perked up immediately, ready to take flight, but two owls sat huddled together. One leaned heavily on Holly, severely injured. The drooping face indicated head trauma. She needed help.

Anthony closed his eyes and ran a finger over Holly's

head. She was safe. The heat at his back from the burning barn finally registered. He turned as the walls began to collapse. There wasn't anything to do with it. He'd bet his savings that these guys were illegally selling more than just raptors, and all of it had been in that barn.

Looking at Holly, it was her he wanted to pick up and cradle in his arms, but the other owl needed help.

Help was arriving just time for the guy sitting in the back of Anthony's truck to jump from the back seat. His hands were still cuffed, but were held out in front of him as he attempted to make a run for it. Zachary outright laughed as Asher leapt out of his truck to chase after him.

Anthony watched on, cradling the injured grey owl. Asher knocked the guy to the ground in seconds with Nathan following. The shifters made a pretty good team.

"Asher, one of them is hurt."

Asher passed the guy to Nathan and ran toward him. He took the owl from Anthony. "Head trauma."

"That's what I thought."

"She smells different."

"A pair." Zachary appeared beside them.

Holly came to rescue shifter pairs. Anthony hung his head. Deep down, he knew what had happened. Holly hadn't been captured by accident.

"How many pairs are there?" Nathan took a step toward the storage unit.

Holly pointed with her beak at the owl now held by Asher and up at the roof of the unit where the hawk had perched.

"Just the two?"

She nodded.

Anthony wanted to grab Holly and shake her, hold her, make her shift and touch her, but even through all that he couldn't grasp the hurt he felt at being left behind for her to fly into danger again on her own. There was no time to step away with her. Morton and another conservation officer pulled up with RCMP and the fire truck coming behind them.

But at least Holly never left his shoulder.

TENSION, anger, relief, it rolled off Anthony in waves that had gradually gotten bigger since he opened the door of the storage unit. It didn't matter how upset with her he was, she wouldn't have changed what she'd done, not when it meant saving someone's pair.

He closed the door to his house behind him. Before he started shucking his jacket and boots, Holly flew off his shoulder and landed in the open space by the back door.

The trappers were in custody and the birds on their way to the rehabilitation centre for checkups and release. Except for the pairs. Asher had the owl in his home and the hawk was staying with Chloe near the safehouse. They came from the same area further north and agreed to return home to their shifters together. They promised to bring them back here to introduce them. Holly would love the chance to meet other raptor shifters.

Anthony stood at the side of his coach, his fists clenched and parts of his uniform wet from the blizzard. His hair fell forward in damp curls. Holly looked up at him. She felt the magic shine in her eyes as they locked with his. Pulling it in, she shifted, the process taking longer due to her exhaustion. All adrenaline from her panic had fled and she didn't have any strength left. She shivered as the process completed and the effects of the blizzard sunk into her skin.

Pulling a blanket from the back of the couch, Anthony wrapped it around her shoulders, holding it tight in front of her. He fisted the ends. Holly looked up.

"Antho..."

"Don't talk." He swallowed and pulled her against him. His mouth crashed down on hers. Holly's knees weakened as he fed her everything he'd gone through today. His emotional upheaval was a torrent through to her heart. His fingers bit into her arms, but she didn't protest. "Damn it, Holly," he growled and pushed away from her, leaving her reeling to catch her balance.

Slapping his palms to his forehead, he turned away from her, displaying his broad back.

"You flew into danger. Again. You didn't wait for me. You didn't trust me to do my job. I may not be a shifter or someone's pair, but I'm not useless. This is what I do." His shoulders tightened, lifting higher as he spoke.

"It wasn't like that." He was mad enough for the both of them. She lowered her voice to a cautious tone.

He turned his head over his shoulder. The slim corner of his eyes looking to a blank space beside her, defiantly avoiding her gaze. "Really? You should have waited."

"There wasn't time. I had to get to that pair. I had to get captured and lure them away so you could find them quicker. If you'd only caught them in the woods, it would be too late by the time we found where they kept the birds."

"You don't know that."

"Neither do you." She threw it back. Holly couldn't have taken the chance that they'd have found them in time. All she had to do was picture Chloe in there and never seeing her again because someone wasn't quick enough to save her. "I know this is your job. And I do trust you. That's why I knew it would be okay. That's why I listened to the ghost when she told me I needed to save them. I knew you'd find me."

"Ghost?"

"There's a ghost, a woman from the past that shows up from time to time. I've seen a glimpse of her before, but this was the first she's ever spoken to me. She told Zachary where to find Ezaray and I."

"So many things could have gone wrong. So many things could have kept me from finding you in time. Don't you understand that?" He turned to fully face her. His face rigid in a pain she felt to her soul. She felt everything coming from her mate.

"What is it you're really upset about? Upset I let them catch me? Upset I did it to save that owl? Or upset I didn't talk to you first?"

"You did it alone!"

"I had to." Why didn't he understand that? She'd thought it was only to save the pairs, but part of her knew she'd had to face that on her own for another reason. To prove to herself that she was whole, that she was ready to live again. And not a different life from what she'd had. She wanted to live her life. The only change was with Anthony by her side. But if he couldn't stand her flying off on her own, then Fate made a mistake. "If I could have come to you first, I would have."

"I'm starting to wonder if that's true."

"What are you saying, Anthony?"

"I can't help protect you, and other shifters, if you don't trust me to do my job. I can't be here for you if you don't trust me."

"And I'm not going to stop doing what I do. I've wallowed long enough. I want to return to my job, my writing. And that means that sometimes I'm going to fly off on my own. Not all the stories I write are safe and happy tales."

"You want to do it alone." Bitter acceptance flattened his normally rich voice.

Her heart beat faster as their mating seemed to crack. An ache in her core flared. She looked at him, begging him to understand, to see that she really did trust him. But his eyes dimmed and he looked away. For once, Fate had been wrong.

Holly dropped the blanket to the floor and stepped back toward the door. Sliding it open behind her, she shifted while her bare feet still touched the hardwood floor. Closing her eyes against her mate, the one person she didn't want to tear herself away from, she turned and flew into the snow. She heard his door close only seconds behind her.

As much as it hurt, and as much as the sky and trees called to her again, Holly wouldn't let herself get pulled back. But neither could she stay here waiting for Anthony to understand. She flew to Zachary and Ezaray's house. Landing in front of the door she pecked as hard as she could, hoping they would hear the fainter knock.

Zachary opened and she swooped inside.

"Holly?" He shut the door.

She shook snow from her feathers and then shifted. Ezaray came down a ladder that was currently acting as their stairs.

"I'm ready to go home."

Ezaray brought her a blanket to cover her.

Zachary frowned. "Whatever you need, Squirt. We can leave tomorrow."

Leave the place that has felt the most like home since her childhood in Hull Creek with Zachary. Leave her mate.

17

H ours later, Anthony still hadn't moved from his couch. Empty beer bottles replaced the full ones he took from the box he'd set beside him. He'd turned his couch around the way he had when he first brought home an injured owl. His eyes stung from staring out the back door. There was a physical pain in his chest that he'd hoped the beer would ease. No such luck.

The blizzard raged on through most of the night, but by the early hours of the morning, the air was clear of white and only grey clouds sat in the sky. The ground was a pristine white. Winter was beautiful and it brought out a whole other side to the nature he protected. But the sight didn't hold the same pull today.

Waiting as long as he could, daylight behind the clouds, he pushed himself up. Reaching for his keys, he stopped. He'd had too much to drink to drive anywhere. That left him with two choices. Wait longer or call Morton. If he called Morton, he'd have to explain about the shifters and he could barely form a coherent thought of his own at the moment. His feet dragged across the floor as he scuffled his way to his shower. Under the water was the first time he closed his eyes, reminding him why he hadn't. His tortured mind forced him to watch Holly shift and fly away from him again.

He was an idiot. He still didn't agree with what she did, but why the hell did he have to push her away for it.

Alternating the water from hot to cold and back, jolted his system, but the lack of sleep only aided the alcohol. He stepped from the bathroom and heard his phone ringing.

"Yeah." He blinked several times.

"You're late. Are you okay?" It was Morton.

"I'm late?" He hadn't looked at the clock and he'd assumed morning had barely arrived.

"Yeah. Especially when there's more to deal with from yesterday." Yesterday. The clusterfuck that made him push his mate away.

"I can't drive. I'm still drunk." Anthony winced. He hadn't meant to say that, which told him just how much alcohol he had in his system.

"You're drunk?" Morton directed a hushed mumble into the phone.

"Yeah."

"Sober up quick. I'm coming to get you."

Anthony would have told him not to bother, but Morton had already hung up. He made coffee and left to get dressed while it percolated, the hum and gurgle of the machine throwing the rich caffeine scent into his kitchen. The pot still worked on the brew when he came back in jeans, t-shirt, and bare feet. Morton could show up, but Anthony didn't plan on going in to work.

He leaned against his counter to wait, watching the last of the drops into the carafe. Pulling down a mug, he poured his first cup, knowing he'd need a lot more to get himself out of the house. His front door opened, letting in a whoosh of cold air. Morton thumped heavily on the mat before closing the door.

"Anthony," he called, then poked his head into the kitchen. Anthony didn't bother answering or turning his gaze from the black bitterness in his mug. He cringed at his own thoughts. He loved coffee, but this morning it tasted horrible.

Groaning, he took another sip.

"You really are drunk."

Anthony spun his head around. It wobbled until the room straightened in sight. A pounding started in his temples, the first sign of a hangover.

"What the hell is going on? Look, yesterday was strange and I let it go as we all had shit to deal with. But now this?" His hand moved up and down in the air, gesturing to Anthony's uncharacteristic state.

"Holly."

"You're girlfriend?"

"She's not a girlfriend." Girlfriend hadn't even been a stage in their relationship. One thing Anthony knew was that mates were so much more.

"We never found her yesterday. Do you know where she is?" They hadn't explained to Morton that Holly had been there inside the storage unit.

"She was there yesterday. She left last night."

"Left? Left you?"

"I don't know."

"Okay, start connecting the dots." Morton crossed his arms over his chest and blocked the way from Anthony's kitchen.

Anthony pulled out his phone and called Asher.

"Are you busy? You have questions to answer." He tried to keep his lazy tongue from slurring.

"What do you mean?"

"Morton is at my house and wants to play connect the dots, but I don't know the rules." While Anthony could tell Morton all he needed to know and felt confident he would keep the secret, it still wasn't his secret to tell and would feel better with Asher's stamp of approval.

"I'll be right there." He hung up.

"There. Asher will be here soon." Anthony set his phone down and took another sip. His nose curled.

"Chug that coffee and pour yourself another one. When did you stop drinking and go to sleep?"

"Didn't sleep. Stopped drinking an hour ago."

"Fuck, man." Morton sighed and leaned against the counter. Anthony poured another cup and passed it to him. He took one sip and spit it back into the mug. "What is wrong with you? That's awful." He dumped it down the sink and took Anthony's from him to do the same. Then he made another pot. He'd just hit the button to start it when Asher walked in without knocking.

"Morton, Tony." He stopped and his nostrils flared. "You're drunk."

"Yup." He hit his consonants hard, and tapped his fingers on the counter waiting for the fresh coffee. "Morton wants an explanation from yesterday."

"He deserves one. I have to reiterate how much we appreciate your discretion." He pinned Morton with a glare that didn't match the politeness of his request.

"I'm not telling anyone's secrets."

"Good. The animals you saw yesterday weren't just animals. I was one of them."

"Huh?"

"I'm what's called shifter. I can change into a wolf. A white one."

Morton's mouth worked up and down, his eyes sizing up both Asher and Anthony with a calculating you-two-should-be-in-the-loony-bin look. But when Asher didn't back down, understanding lit Morton's face. "Blue eyes—charged out of a cage last summer?"

"Yes. You met two others shifters yesterday too. A grey wolf and a grizzly bear."

"But there were two of each."

"Every shifter is matched with an identical animal. I call them pairs. The animal can't change, but their aging slows to match their shifter."

"This is... it's insane. You know that right?"

"But it's true." Anthony's words mumbled over a thick tongue.

Morton ignored him. "What does this have to do with him being drunk?" He tilted his head to point at Anthony, who turned away.

Asher didn't answer him this time. Anthony felt two sets of eyes boring into the back of his neck while he stared at the coffee.

"You said Holly was there yesterday. She was the owl perched on your shoulder the whole time, wasn't she? She'd been caught by the trappers."

"She purposely got herself caught to save two pairs that were in the storage unit. The owl Asher took home was one of them."

"At least it all makes sense now, even if it is hard to believe."

"Asher?" Anthony pulled the carafe from the machine and poured. "Would the pair have survived if Holly had found us first and we waited to follow the trappers instead of her luring them away and getting caught?"

"It's hard to say. I can't really answer that. It was cutting it too close as it was."

Anthony's hand tightened around the mug, the hot ceramic burning his palm.

"Tony, Holly left this morning. Zachary took her back to her parents."

"Is she coming back?"

"I don't know. Zachary didn't know."

Anthony let the coffee burn his tongue. A punishment for being selfish. It wasn't her that hadn't trusted him. He hadn't trusted her.

ZACHARY WASN'T PRESSURING HOLLY, but she felt the weight of it from his gaze. She looked out the passenger window of Zachary's truck, staring at her parents house. It had only felt like a home to her for a short time. It had taken years for her to let go of Hull Creek after they'd moved. But that wasn't what stopped her now. She didn't want to face her parents. A few phone calls hadn't prepared her the way she'd thought they would. The thought of explaining to them all she'd been through churned bile in her stomach. Her chest clenched with the weight of her shame. She'd come a long way and knew she wasn't to blame, but her shame was making a reappearance for this reunion.

"It's time to go in, Squirt." Zachary's voice was a low hum meant to soothe, but it only grated through her ears, adding to the nausea.

"Not yet."

Holly had stayed away too long. She should have shifted

and come home as soon as she'd arrived in Alder Ridge. There was nothing to do about that now, but it made facing her parents even harder. She wished she was shackled to the truck so she'd have a good reason for not going inside.

The curtains in the front window moved again, as they had every two minutes since they'd arrived. At least her parents didn't come out to get her.

Closing her eyes, she pulled in a breath. She let it out slowly through the shape of a flat 'o' of her lips.

"Will you walk me in?" Holly turned her head toward Zachary, but looked at the centre console rather than him.

"Of course." Zachary got out of the truck and Holly set her hand on the door handle. He waited outside her door for a moment, but then opened her door for her when she couldn't.

Imaginary shackles attached to her ankles dragged her back to the truck as she moved closer to the front door.

Zachary opened the door and ushered Holly inside quickly, ripping off the bandage of stepping over the threshold. Her parents stood waiting for her several feet away, and as soon as Zachary closed the door behind him, they lunged at her. She was encased in her mother's small arms and then both women were surrounded by her father. No one spoke a word, but their tears created a chorus that echoed off the walls. It wasn't just her parents' tears, but Holly's too. They'd pooled behind her eyes and flooded outward. Zachary stood solid by the door. She'd made him promise not to leave until she said she was okay. Holly wasn't anything close to okay, but the sobs she shared with her parents were a start, like a cleansing of her slate.

But as she slowly let go of the things that had held her back from coming home, the pain of walking away from Anthony grew larger as the space in her soul freed.

All their tears faded away and Holly opened her eyes to look directly at her mother who held Holly's face in her hands.

"You have no idea how it feels to hold you again." Her mother's voice came out a staggered whisper, unable to gain any volume.

"We're so happy to have you home," said her father, gruff with pain. His hand squeezed her shoulder, then he looked behind her. "Thank you, Zachary. I'll admit, I didn't believe you would succeed in bringing her home when you'd promised us you would two years ago. I'm sorry I doubted you."

"It took too long to find her. And I'm sorry for that." Holly heard the anger Zachary kept at bay. She doubted her parents recognized it.

"That's nonsense. You brought our baby home." Her mother pulled Holly against her and spoke to Zachary over Holly's shoulder.

Holly pulled away. "I'm sorry I stayed in Alder Ridge for so long."

"It's okay. We might not understand, but it was what you needed." Her father kissed her temple.

"Well," her mother stood a little straighter, "let's get out of the entryway and get you settled. I have dinner cooking in the oven." She pulled Holly into the living room. Her father and Zachary followed. Not a thing had changed and yet everything looked different. Her parents had painted. Two years ago, the walls had been bright and freeing, and now they were dark and warm.

When her mother saw Zachary hadn't left, she added, "There's lots if you'd like to stay for dinner, Zachary."

Holly set wide eyes on him, hoping he saw her pleading not to leave her. She knew she'd have to tell her parents everything she'd been through and she didn't want to do it alone.

"I'd like that, thank you."

Holly sat on the couch with her parents flanking her. Zachary sat in the armchair, but didn't stay motionless for long. He popped up from the chair. "Can I get everyone something to drink?"

"That would be lovely, Zachary. There's wine and beer in the fridge. Holly, what would you like? We have juice?"

"Anything is fine, Zachary." Holly gave a pinched smile up at Zachary before he disappeared into her parents' kitchen. Her parents began to speak several times while they listened to Zachary search the cupboards and clink glasses. But the silence continued to stretch, growing thick with everything that Holly needed to say.

Zachary returned with a tray holding opened beer bottles and a couple glasses of wine as well as a bottle of water. He set it down on the coffee table and picked up a beer for himself before retaking his seat. His simple nod toward her spurred the words from her.

"You heard about the underground fighting ring in the news and I'm sure you've heard some of what we went through from Ezaray's parents." Holly picked up a wine glass and took a sip to wet her throat.

"Ezaray's parents wouldn't tell us anything." Her mother looked between Holly and Zachary. "We saw the news and knew you'd been found at the same time. We made the connection ourselves. Zachary confirmed that much for us when he brought Ezaray home."

"We'd been taken from the patio of the pub we were at." Holly started telling the tale of her special kind of hell, leaving out any details she felt were too much for her parents to know. She kept everything as short as possible, but she still needed to search for comfort while reliving the rest of it in her mind. It was Zachary, her figurative big brother, that held her gaze when he knew it was too difficult.

Holly wished the eyes looking back at her were Anthony's warm, chocolate ones rather than Zachary's smoky greys. She needed her mate for this, not her big brother. But Holly had been the one to walk away, causing the pain that was twisting her heart.

ASHER AND MORTON stood in Anthony's way. They blocked both doors out of his house. He held a single duffle bag in one hand, packed for a night or two out of town. Anthony was going to bring his mate home.

His drunken state had turned into unrelenting drummers in his head, beating not only on their skins but his skull.

"This isn't a good idea." Asher stared him down, repeating his opinion.

"I don't really care. I want to go get her."

"I know you do. Believe me, I understand what you're feeling." Being a shifter with a mate of his own, he would. "But Holly needs this time with her family. She can't deal with whatever fight you two had and deal with that at the same time." Asher's logic tried to penetrate, but the throbbing muscle between his ears wouldn't let it pass. He had an ache that wouldn't settle. He knew the only way to make it go away was to make things right with Holly.

"I don't know the whole story, but Asher's right." Morton blocked Anthony's back door.

"Then what am I supposed to do?" Anthony tightened his grip on his bag. "I have to go after her."

"You think you do." Morton didn't understand the bond that grew between mates. It was such a full, unbelievable sensation that Anthony wasn't sure he could even describe. But it was so all encompassing that when it cracked it hurt. That crack felt like a deep crevice.

"Give her some time before you chase after her. If you're hurting, then so is she. She'll come back. And then you can let her take you to meet her family." Asher lowered his arms as if he knew what he said would get through to Anthony. It did, but it didn't stop Anthony from curling his lip up in a growl.

"Fine." He dropped his bag on the floor and stomped back to the kitchen to make more coffee. It didn't matter he'd already drunk half a pot. "I should be with her through this too." He spoke over his shoulder while he poured the water into the machine.

"Yes, you should, but it's too late for that now." Asher left his post at the door.

"Is it?" He could just show up, be the one beside her while she faced her family. But Asher was right about one thing. It would force her to deal with him first while she was in the middle of dealing with her parents. That wasn't fair and just another selfish act. As much as it hurt, he'd give her the space. "What do I do now?"

"What would you have done when you got there?" Morton leaned over the island.

"I don't know." Anthony shrugged. "Just been there for her."

"Then be here for her when she gets back." Morton spoke as if it was so simple.

"Here? She walked away from me. She flew away from me. Holly won't come back here."

"You're underestimating the mate bond." The quirk of Asher's know-it-all brow pissed him off.

"Where else would she go?" Morton's tone held a genuine inquiry.

Anthony met Asher's eyes across the room. "The safehouse," they said together.

"Safehouse?" Morton's features twisted and he looked between the two of them.

Asher gave Morton a quick explanation. "I built a safehouse further north in the woods for the purpose of shifters to use when they needed somewhere to stay."

"She might go to Zachary's, but even after that I think she'll still search for sanctuary. That's where I'll go. I'll wait for her there." Anthony abandoned the coffee and stalked back to his bag he'd dropped. He tossed it by the back door and turned back. "But I need to go shopping first. I could be there for a few days. Morton, I need you to find people to cover my shifts for the next few days."

"Sure, but you can't go shopping yourself. You're still in no state to drive."

"I'll drive him around." Asher said to Morton as if Anthony wasn't even in the room.

Anthony didn't want to take any chance that he'd miss her return. He had to be there waiting for her, waiting for his mate to claim her in the only way he could.

18

Her mom's arms tightened around her when Holly tried to pull away. She'd been here three days and the ache inside grew consistently worse. The urge to shift and fly was great, but she'd been warned about caving into that urge. Being away from her mate with no clear future for them was taking its toll. It was time to go back. Her parents had begged her all morning to stay longer.

Her father stepped around her and her mom when someone knocked at the door. He opened it and allowed Zachary through. Her mom lifted one arm off Holly's back and stretched it out to Zachary.

"Oh Zachary, thank you for bringing her home. But you have to make her stay."

Zachary joined their hug, placing a kiss against Holly's head while patting her mother's back. "I'm sorry, I can't do that." He used his arm around Holly to help extricate her from her mother's grip.

"I promise I'll come back. Soon."

"Holly, you're not feeling well." Her father squeezed her

shoulder and her mother brushed her hair back by smoothing both hands over her face.

"We can see it in your eyes."

"I'm fine." She couldn't explain to them what made her feel this way. She hadn't told them what she was or about Anthony. Coming home had been enough for them to handle.

After several more hugs and prying away of hands, Zachary helped Ezaray carry her bags out to his truck. She'd found some of her old clothes, her computer, and some of the other things she'd used for work.

Holly couldn't stay away from Anthony. She wasn't meant to. If she was hurting this bad, then he must be too. She only hoped he understood why she did what she did and that it had nothing to do with her trust in him.

"Do you want to stay with us?" They were halfway to Alder Ridge when Zachary first spoke.

"No." If things didn't work with Anthony, she'd stay at the safehouse until she could afford a place of her own. Maybe staying within close proximity to her mate would keep them both from feeling the pain of being apart.

"What happened, Squirt?"

"With what?"

"I know why you got yourself caught, but why didn't you tell us first?"

"It's over Zachary." She didn't want to talk about it anymore. Nothing would have changed her decision.

"Okay. Then what happened with Anthony?"

Holly closed her eyes and leaned her head against the window.

"I'll kill him," he muttered.

"You won't lay a hand on him." She kept her eyes closed,

knowing Zachary's threat was an empty one and only came from protection for her.

She pretended to sleep for the remainder of the drive. She didn't fool Zachary, but he didn't try to speak to her again until they reached town.

"Where am I taking you?"

"Anthony's."

"Okay. I'll wait outside."

"No, you won't." She'd left him. She needed to return to him, to show him that even when she flew away she'd always come back.

Zachary sighed. He pulled up outside of Anthony's. His truck was there, but still covered in snow. There were tire tracks in the snow, but they didn't look fresh. Zachary helped her carry her bags to the front door.

"Thank you for taking me home."

"Always, Squirt."

Holly waited for Zachary to drive away. He sat there stubbornly for a minute before shaking his head and backing out. She knocked. His house was quiet. She knocked again, louder. Still no footsteps echoed. Trying the knob, it opened. He hadn't locked his door. She stepped inside and stomped off her boots then took them off. There was no life inside the house. He wasn't home.

The silence of the house chilled her skin. The kitchen to her left had half a pot of cold coffee that was starting to mildew, based on the scent. The couch was turned around to face the back door and on it sat a box full of empty beer bottles. One sniff and she could tell they were at least a few days old. She would guess the night she left. Checking his bedroom, his scent wasn't fresh.

There'd been no sign of him leaving from the front of his house. She looked in the back yard and saw footprints leading off his deck. Tracks from a quad led out of his shed and to the woods. Holly found a bag to put her boots and clothes in. She cleared a spot on the deck for her to stand while she shifted. Grabbing the bag with her feet she flew, staying low to follow his tracks.

There was really only one place for him to go up here. The tracks led straight to the safehouse. Smoke billowed softly from the chimney. The front steps were cleared of snow. She landed there and shifted, quickly putting her clothes and boots on against the cold. She considered knocking, but instead just walked in.

Anthony jumped to his feet from sitting on the floor by the fire.

"Holly." He breathed her name. She took two steps into the house.

"You've been up here since I left, haven't you?"

"Pretty much. I wanted to be here when you came back." His eyes darkened. "I'm sorry."

Holly waited. She had her own apologies to make, but he'd been sitting here with his thoughts for days while she'd been reuniting with her family. He needed to go first.

"I said I couldn't wait to see you grow back into yourself and to your full strength, but at the first chance to embrace that I got mad."

"You were scared." His reaction came from fear for her safety.

He nodded. "But I was still wrong. I was the one that didn't trust your decision or your abilities. I will never doubt you again."

Holly smiled. "You will, but you won't mean it that way. You were scared of losing me."

His muscles tensed and she noticed his feet flex into the floor.

"I'm sorry too. Not for doing what I did. I can't apologize for that, not when I knew it was the right thing to do and when I'd do it again if needed. But I am sorry I couldn't tell you before. I'm sorry I didn't find some way to leave you a message. I hope you can accept that. I'm returning to work and part of how I do my job is flying off on my own."

"I won't lie. I'm not sure how I'll react every time you fly off, but I can accept it. I can do more than that. Holly, I'm proud of you."

"Proud of me?" She clenched her teeth to keep the tears that instantly formed from falling down her face. She had people in her life that were proud of her, but that had been before. Her life before being forced to be someone she wasn't, before her entire being changed and she'd had to find her way back. Those that had said they were proud of her for surviving only pissed her off. She'd been a coward. She hadn't deserved that pride. But pride from her mate was different.

"Of course I am." He closed the distance, finally giving her the contact she needed. Sweet relief heated her body as she touched her mate. "I love you, sweet owl."

"I love you too, Anthony." When she thought he would kiss her, he didn't. His hand ran down her arm to hold her wrist. "You'd packed your bag." He gestured to her bag she'd left at the front door. When she'd left with Zachary, she hadn't bothered getting it, borrowing clothes from Ezaray instead until she could get her own things.

"I did."

"Why?" His hoarse question was followed by narrowed eyes.

"I had planned to move in with you." A single shoulder lifted to her ear.

"I didn't ask you to."

"So?" She stretched her lips and shook her head. His lips cracked into a grin.

"I suppose it's the appropriate place for my wife to live."

"Your what?" Her words were only soft breaths between them.

Anthony dropped to one knee and pulled a ring from his pocket. A rose gold band nestled a small square diamond. "Marry me, Holly."

"Yes, Anthony." She cupped the sides of his corded neck. "I'll marry you."

He stood in a rush, wrapping an arm around her waist to crush her against him. He took her mouth in a heated kiss while he slid the ring on her finger. Flames engulfed them. Her blood pounded and a mating chant rang in her head. Her core throbbed and clenched, eager to take him into her body.

Clothes slithered to the ground around them as they frantically groped at each other. Only seconds had passed and her breasts were flush against his chest and his cock was rigid against her stomach.

Mate. The word rang with incredible force.

"Anthony, I can't wait."

"Neither can I." His hands cupped her ass and he lifted, carrying her back toward the fireplace. Lowering them to the floor, he entered her on the way down. She cried out at the sensation of feeling whole again. She dug her nails into his shoulders, urging him on, but he didn't need it.

Her teeth sharpened. This was happening all too fast. Her need built in a quick rush. Anthony leaned his head against hers.

"Holly." He said her name like a prayer.

She felt her magic swirl within her and her skin tingled. The fire flared, catching their attention. Twirling the flame was her wind, the colours of the sunset and amber mixing with the red and orange from the flame. Then it spun outward and surrounded them.

Holly pushed against him, flipping him onto his back then pulled on his arms to sit him up. She wrapped her legs around him, hooking her ankles at his back. The wind wrapped them together like a blanket. Her orgasm sat on the edge, waiting. And judging by Anthony's tense muscles, so was his. But they were held off.

The warmth seeped into her mind creating a chant she hadn't heard before.

"Fate bound. The winds blessed." Her whispered breath carried the words.

"Fate bound. The winds blessed. I'll always be here." Anthony repeated and added his own oath. Holly drank it in by kissing him, meeting him on equal ground. They came together in a rush of ecstasy as the wind faded away into the fire.

ANTHONY's entire being righted itself with Holly in his arms. They'd eaten by the fire on a bed of blankets he'd gathered to make them more comfortable. He'd taken her twice more in between periods of sleep, feeling a connection he didn't know existed.

"So, you were going to move in before I even asked?" He traced his fingers up and down her exposed arm over top of the blanket.

"Yes. You'd asked me in your sleep."

"I did what?"

"You talk in your sleep all the time. One night you asked if I would move in with you."

Anthony leaned up on his elbow to look down at her face. "I'm glad you came back."

"I never wanted to leave."

"Then we'll get you properly moved in the morning."

"I already left my bags at your house."

He laughed, loving how sure she was with herself. He may have a hard time letting her fly off on her own and sometimes possibly dangerous situations, but he'd never hold her back. Not when she shone with beauty and was whole.

Anthony kissed her, letting his lips play with hers. Then he laid his head back and down and pulled her against him to sleep the rest of the night.

The sun rose, shining through the windows to wake them. The fire was dim. Anthony kissed Holly's bare shoulder. She moaned and rolled on her back. It would be so easy to spread her legs and fill her, but he was eager to get her settled into his home. Their home now.

"Good morning, sweet owl."

She opened her eyes and tilted her head.

He stood and pulled her up with him. "Let's get going."

She helped him clean up from his stay up here then grabbed her tiny bag at the door. He'd brought his quad up here so he didn't have to do the hike again. The hike was long enough without having to trudge through deep snow.

Chloe sat in a tree. She'd visited him every day that he'd been up here waiting. She was how he knew Holly would come back. Chloe flew down to greet Holly. She landed on Holly's shoulder and rubbed her head against Holly's hair. Anthony took her bag and waited for her next to his quad. Holly followed when Chloe flew back to the trees.

Anthony got on and waited for Holly to settle behind him. He pulled her arms around his waist. "Hold on tight."

Her laughs of excitement pulled out his own laughter.

He parked the quad in his shed and waited for Holly to get off the back. Inside the house, he started to clean up from his drunken depression while Holly showered. When she came out, her eyes were bright and she stood a little straighter. She glowed with her confidence.

"So how do you start about going back to work?"

"Normally, I'd look for job postings for articles. But this time, I'm doing it the other way around. I'm writing about the trappers and selling the story."

"You know the news has already reported about them."

"Yeah, but I don't write like a news reporter." It sounded more like a threat than a statement of fact that would give her the edge.

Anthony finished cleaning and showered while she unpacked the few bags she had. When he came back out, she was sitting on his couch with a computer on her lap.

"Would you rather claim a bedroom as an office?"

"Why? Am I in your way?" Her lips twitched, but her eyes never left her screen and her fingers didn't stop running over the keys.

"Of course not."

"I'm used to writing on the go. I don't really want an office. I like to move around."

When he sat on the couch next to her, she set her computer on the coffee table and crawled over to straddle his lap.

"I'm happy, Anthony." Her eyes flashed a bright amber that danced in circles.

"I can see that."

"Are you?"

"More than you'll ever know."

He pulled her down for a kiss and ran his hands up

under her shirt. His skin heated and his heart pounded. He held the woman that made him complete, that fit into his life just as she was meant to. Now, he needed to marry her to claim her the same way she'd claimed him. He'd made an oath and he intended to uphold it.

EPILOGUE

Maggie wished the couch would swallow her. With cushions any softer, her wish could come true. Holly and Ezaray sat beside her with their bodies turned. Zachary stood as a bold presence. He scared her sometimes, but he was their rescuer, their protector. She knew in her heart he was safe. If only someone could protect her from the news Holly had just given her.

"I'm sorry, Maggie. Maybe if I had written the story and got it out there, been the first, I could have avoided identifying all of us." But Maggie wouldn't need to be named to be identified.

"It's not your fault." None of them had contact with the other victims of her step-brother. If one of them wanted to come forth with what they'd been through at the hands of Tyrone, no one could stop them. "Did you write about it?"

"I did, but it was my way of coping. I didn't intend to have it published. I considered it, but the risks of shining light on all the victims and those that saved us stopped me." Holly's fingers intertwined and she twisted her hands.

"But the police already knew of the organization, right?

Zachary and the others left them all the handlers and most of the guards. They went after everyone left. They won't need to come looking for the victims anymore. Right?" Maggie refused to go home after Zachary rescued them. She followed them to Alder Ridge, a place she'd never heard of, for a reason.

"They're searching for us, anyway. They don't need to find us, but they want to talk to us. They've already called my parents." Ezaray sat on the edge of the couch to lean around Holly.

"Mine too," Holly added. "Our parents agreed to talk to us, but haven't told them where we are. But I'm sure that's only a matter of time before they find us."

As long as they didn't come looking for Maggie here. But it had been Maggie getting a job in the first place that led Tyrone here. The police would find them.

Anthony, Holly's fiance, stepped in from the kitchen. He'd stayed in there to give them privacy. She'd overheard him say he worried it would intimidate her to have him in the room. "Maggie, you won't have to talk to them."

She wasn't so sure about that. What reason would they have to believe she hadn't been part of her step-brother's plans? They may not look her at as just a victim as the others. No one other than Holly and Ezaray knew she was Tyrone's sister, but the police would make the connection, eventually.

Maggie wanted to hide, blend in and become invisible. But she'd made friends in Ezaray and Holly, and that pulled her out. So what if the police wanted to talk to her, wanted to assume she was more than a victim? She'd get through it. She lived in Alder Ridge now. The people didn't know her here. Any talk would blow away with the next season. She'd never return to her childhood home to face that humiliation.

Tyrone loved to feed the rumors that there was something wrong with his step-sister. He had a twisted way about how he treated her. The entire town was probably at this moment in shock over Tyrone's true character. But they still wouldn't understand the abuse he'd put her through since the day their parents married.

Exposing her past had been her greatest fear since the escape. Even the people here, those she considered friends now, knew nothing more than her relation to Tyrone. She saw the pity lightening the colour of their eyes when they looked at her. Maggie didn't want them to know anything more. She wanted to start her life here. Not just a new life, or picking up where she left off. No—this was the beginning for her.

Her friends wouldn't find out anything she didn't tell them herself. That would be the same for any police that found her and wanted to talk. Her step-brother had been abusive, and she was just as much a victim as every other girl there.

And that's as far as any of this would go because Tyrone was dead and she was never returning home.

ALSO BY SARAH URQUHART

Join my newsletter to receive special content, the most up to date information on releases, and special promotions.

http://bit.ly/sarahurquhart

Also, visit my website at...

http://www.authorsarahurquhart.com

... to see my full book list.

Continue reading for an excerpt of **Emerald Promise, Wounded Winds Book Five.**

EMERALD PROMISE

CHAPTER ONE

Maggie turned her head down, tired of swiveling it back and forth to keep up with the conversations. The heat in the air was dissipating as the evening took hold.

"You burnt the burgers, doc." Zachary peered over Asher's shoulder at the barbecue.

"No. They're fine." He shoved his shoulder into Zachary's chest and flipped the next burger. If they weren't burnt, they would be soon. Maggie breathed in the faint, charred scent. But it wasn't her place to correct Asher.

"Take mine off now." Zachary thrust an empty paper plate toward Asher.

"And mine." Nathan followed.

Mine, too, Maggie thought. But she stayed where she was, attempting to shape herself against the picnic table. Her grey shirt camouflaged well against the aged colour of the wood. Ezaray and Holly dragged her along, claiming she'd kept herself hidden too often. For months, they'd visited, took her for lunch and coffee. Once in a while, they'd bring Gwen and Shaye along, but Maggie always cut those outings short—sometimes finding the four women overwhelming when all together. Now she sat in Asher's yard with not only the four other women, but their husbands and fiancés as well.

She knew there had been a time she enjoyed having friends, but those memories faded into dreams a long time ago.

"Really? You two want to complain about *my* cooking?" Asher took criticism with an ease that Maggie envied. His calm, jovial spirit attracted everyone around him. They all looked to him as if he was their leader.

"I don't have to cook to know what tastes good." Zachary grabbed another spatula and reached over to get his own burger from the barbecue.

Zachary wasn't wrong. She hadn't learned how to do much in the kitchen, but she'd discovered some strong dislikes in food since arriving in Alder Ridge.

At first, she'd only made slow progress. Space and peace had filled the last several months, giving Maggie the time to grow on her own. Everyone had been encouraging and friendly, helping her get used to what a normal life should be like. A job, friends, responsibilities. She was no longer nervous in crowds, worrying about what strangers would see when they looked at her. And a knock on her door didn't send her into a visible panic attack. Maggie felt her old self stirring within, starving inside her. Nobody pushed her to go past her limits, or what they thought were her limits. But Maggie wasn't sure what to do next.

Tires crunching over gravel that kicked up to ping against metal heralded a pickup truck speeding toward Asher's. The truck slid, creating skid marks as the driver slammed on the brakes, stopping an inch from the other vehicles.

"Asher!" the driver yelled as he jumped out, leaving the

door swinging open. Most of the group ran toward him, all stopping at different times, spreading themselves out. Maggie kept herself still at the table, although her curiosity had her leaning her head around the others. She couldn't get more than a glimpse of the man or the vehicle past all the bodies.

"What is it?" Asher stood closest to the new truck.

"A bear. He's been shot. I patched him up, so he'd survive the drive, but he needs a vet at the moment, not a doctor." A doctor. She knew that voice. A voice that sometimes echoed in her nightmares as a calming tone. He'd never hurt her, but she hadn't realized then that he'd been someone she could trust. Stretching her neck further she saw the doctor, a man that had worked for her step-brother, but had also helped them all escape the hell her step-brother had created.

But he'd brought a bear? The doctor brought a bear with a gunshot wound to a vet? Maggie gripped the seat of the table and hunched her shoulders. She'd only be in the way if she moved.

Asher opened the tailgate of the truck while the others lifted a tarp that covered the back. "Back the truck up to the deck."

The doctor got back behind the wheel. The others moved out of the way to give him room to drive across the lawn.

Asher waited on the steps. "Help me get him out. We'll need to get him stable."

Four of the men there worked together to pull the bear from the back, straining and struggling to get him up the stairs. The bear's head faced her as they pulled him from the truck. His eyes remained closed, hiding in his brown fur. Why weren't they concerned he'd wake up any second and attack? Seeing a bear, even an unconscious and injured one, made her want to back away.

They set him on the deck. Gwen had run inside and returned with a black bag, giving them space to settle the bear before handing the bag to Asher.

Asher's voice carried as he made the diagnosis, but she was too far away to hear it all.

"... bullet hit the bone. It's still in there." Bears were common in Maggie's hometown. She was certain that in a case like this they'd put the bear down. Holly's fiancé, Anthony, was a Fish and Wildlife Officer. Yet he stood there with his hands on Holly's shoulders, not saying what needed to be done.

Maggie didn't understand, and she was too far away. She pinched her lips between her fingers, fighting with herself. One hand gripped the table tighter to keep herself there, and the other pushed against the top to make her move. Pulling in a breath through her nose, she huffed it out when her butt didn't lift off the bench. Trying again, she stood. Years of practice kept her steps slow and quiet. She'd learned how to place her feet down when she walked to create the least amount of noise or disruption.

The closer she got, the more she heard.

"I'll need as many of you present as possible for the surgery. He's already started to heal around the bullet. I need to do this now. But I can only guess how much anesthesia I'll need. It's not as if I've ever had to perform surgery on one of our kind." Asher didn't look at any of them as he continued to work on the bear. Maggie moved around the truck. She stood behind the other women, but she adjusted to give herself a clear view of what was happening on the deck.

"How long have you been driving with him?" Zachary stood beside the doctor.

"Four hours, but I wasn't going slow."

"Do you know what happened?" Nathan had crouched on the opposite side of the bear from Asher.

"Not the specifics. I saw it from the sky. How the hunter got the drop on him, I'm not sure. He was running, not well, and the hunter gave chase, determined. The bear ran toward the road and the hunter stopped following him."

The sky? She hadn't thought the doctor had a hobby. Piloting wouldn't have been her first guess.

"That was a risky move. If someone else had found him, he would have been put down." Anthony confirmed what Maggie had thought. So why weren't they suggesting that now? And why did he drive him four hours to find a vet? There had to have been several veterinarians between wherever he came from and here.

"The outcome was looking the same no matter which way he went. He'd been slowing down. I stopped him before he broke through the trees. I did the best I could there, then *kindly borrowed* a vehicle. I drove for about an hour before I stopped and treated him better, then came straight here. I even found clothes hidden under the front seat." The doctor pulled on the shirt that hung loosely around his torso.

His story was a puzzle with missing pieces, but she was the only one that seemed concerned with filling them in. The others all understood everything he said. Flying with no clothes and able to see a bear through the canopy of the trees. The bear was their sole focus. What was so special about this bear that would have all these people gathering to save his life? Stepping to the right, she wanted to get a better look at him.

"Maggie." Ezaray spoke suddenly over the top of

everyone else and came to her side. All nine sets of eyes landed on her. A nervous instinct saying that the attention on her would get her hurt pulled at her spine, forcing her to take several steps back. "We can take you home. I doubt you want to see all of this." Ezaray scrunched her nose, but her voice pitched with the sound of a polite lie.

"I need Zachary here." Asher never stopped preparing for the surgery.

"Zee and I can take you home." Holly left Anthony's side and joined Ezaray beside Maggie.

Maggie only nodded, but she tried to get one last look at the bear while she walked between Holly and Ezaray. Questions gripped the tip of her tongue, ready to fly, but they wanted her gone so they could talk freely again.

The urge to run rocked through Caiden's limbs, but no more than a twitch stretched his paws. Pain sliced through his flesh under his skin. Strange scents filled his nose. He wasn't home. But shifters surrounded him. Two wolves, a bear, and a hawk. The hawk. The scent was familiar. He'd been running, fighting through the pain shooting through his upper body. The hawk stopped him from running into the road. Once he'd stopped, the adrenaline slowed its transmission through his blood. His flight instinct screamed through his mind, but he'd passed out after that. Caiden remembered the panic as his eyes had closed.

Voices hummed around him. He tried to focus—feeling the wood surface beneath him, the dryness of his mouth. He counted the unfamiliar scents surrounding him. There were more than the fours shifters. Others that carried an odd, wild scent. He thought he smelled an owl nearby, not close like the others. Unconsciousness tugged at him again. Struggling to hold on, he breathed deep. A euphoric scent drifted through the others, faint and distant, but it shot straight to his head.

"I need you ready to hold him." Male voices were right above him.

"Let's go." Females were there, but drifting away. He breathed in again to pinpoint the scent, but dizziness collided with the pain and nothing he did stopped his muscles from relaxing against the wood as darkness tightened its grip.

Spikes of pain interrupted his memories, pulling him in and out. Each time he regained consciousness, he tried to open his eyes. He got as much as slits of vision that showed deck railings and the legs of two men. Caiden couldn't smell his brother. The familiar scents of the lodge, of home, the mountains, weren't there.

When next he woke, the sky was dark and filled with the stars. The pain had subsided, but an ache tightened his front leg. He tried to move, to brace himself with his front paws, but collapsed back to the wood with a grunt.

"The big guy's awake." Someone moved behind him. Caiden lifted his head. With narrowed eyes, he watched two men get up from wooden chairs, throwing blankets to the side. He inhaled the distinct scent of shifters. Broken memories filtered into his mind. The hawk. Waking, surrounded by shifters. It was a hawk and another bear that walked toward him now. The bear tapped on a door as he passed.

"How are you feeling?" The hawk crouched in front of Caiden, squeezing himself between his front paws and the deck railing. Caiden stared back. How the hell did the hawk expect him to answer? "Your eyes are clear. I'd say you're out of the woods. But Asher will be down in a minute."

As if on cue, footsteps sounded on stairs from inside the house. The door swung open and the strong scent of wolf wafted over the deck with a breeze. He assumed this was Asher.

"Well, that's a good sign." Asher motioned the hawk away and took his spot. He met Caiden's eyes. "Don't bite me."

Caiden didn't have a reason to, for now. He might not know where he was, but these shifters saved him. Asher touched his front leg and Caiden growled. The involuntary rumble spiked in the top of his chest and vibrated his gritting teeth. Pain stretched outward from his touch.

"Sorry. But you're healing. You won't be able to shift for a few days. It's best to let this heal as much as possible first. Then the magic can finish it with a shift." Asher took his hands away and stood to lean against the railing. "Do you remember what happened?"

Did he remember? He'd been out for a run after a particularly busy rush at the restaurant, letting his bear free. He hadn't called Wyatt to come, and Caiden hadn't met up with Theo, his animal pair, yet. Forest debris crunching, heavy, short breaths—they were his only warning. The wind had been blowing over his fur toward the heavy breather until it was too late for Caiden to realize what was happening. Then pain sliced his front leg. Yeah, he remembered.

He met Asher's eyes and nodded. Then he looked at the hawk who'd stopped his run toward the road to lose the hunter. Caiden had two choices, face the hunter chasing him while injured, or take a chance that whoever he ran into in town was his brother or one of his cousins.

Caiden nodded at the hawk, his eyes closing. He owed the hawk his gratitude.

"You'll have to stay here. I have a cabin deep in the

woods that I built for this purpose, for shifters to use as a safehouse whenever needed. But you aren't in the shape to travel up there. You'll heal a lot faster if you stay off your front leg. I just hope I don't have any visitors for the next few days." A smile twitched on his face. "My name's Asher Morestead. I'm a veterinarian here in Alder Ridge. This is Garrett Daly. He brought you here. And that's Nathan Marks."

Caiden looked at the surrounding shifters. He hoped one of them shifted soon so he could talk to them. He needed to let his brother know he was okay. Wyatt would be worried. Dakota would be too, but Wyatt would hide it from their sister. She'd be pissed, but it was what Wyatt did. Protected their baby sister.

"Get some sleep." When they all walked away, Caiden groaned. He needed one of them to make the call. Three sets of eyes glowed in the dark. He groaned again, moving his jaw up and down. Nathan started undressing and stepped off the deck. Through the railings, Caiden saw an auburn wind encircle the other shifter. He stepped back onto the deck as a bear.

I'm sorry. This couldn't wait until morning, Caiden explained, the sound of his echoed voice rough.

That's okay. What is it? Nathan tilted his head downward.

I need you to call my brother. To tell him what happened and to be careful for a while until we can track down the hunter that shot me. Caiden kept his head lifted, but his strength was slipping away.

Of course.

His name is Wyatt Greer. I'm from Firebrook. He gave Nathan his brother's phone number.

Does he know you're a shifter? One fury brow lifted.

He's a shifter, too.

I'll call him right away. Anything else you want me to tell him other than you're okay?

No. I'll be home in a few days. I'm Caiden. He'd talk to his brother when he got home. Right now, he needed to focus on pushing away the pain and healing.

Nathan nodded. Caiden repeated his brother's phone number and ensured Nathan that he wouldn't be asleep.

Nathan stepped off the deck to shift. He repeated the phone number aloud to the others, and Asher stepped inside to retrieve a phone. He passed it to Nathan after he finished buttoning his pants.

Caiden listened to the call, hearing his brother's voice through the line.

"Your brother is safe and in Alder Ridge. A friend of mine found him shot and brought him here to get him help."

"Shot? By who?" Caiden pictured his brother storming through a room, growing with his anger to take down any threat.

"He didn't say, or he doesn't know."

Caiden shook his head.

"He doesn't know," Nathan confirmed for Wyatt. "He's safe here and welcome to stay to heal. Our resident shifter docs say he needs a few days to heal before he can shift."

"Shifter docs?"

"Just a doctor and a vet who happen to be shifters themselves." Nathan looked between Asher and Garrett.

"Are you sure he's okay?" Caiden heard Wyatt's skepticism in his slow, emphasized speech.

"I'm sure." Nathan mimicked Wyatt's tone.

"Thanks for calling." It wasn't often his brother sounded lost. He'd ask Nathan or one of the others to call him again in the morning.

Nathan hung up.

Caiden thumped his head against the wood, and his eyes closed with the impact. It would be a long few days. But he considered himself lucky that shifters and not humans surrounded him. He may not be alive if not for the hawk.

Where was it? Maggie searched behind the couch cushions, in the kitchen, her bedroom, and even the bathroom. She didn't carry a big wallet or purse. Just a hard case card holder in her pocket. But right now, it wasn't in any pockets of her clothes from last night. She was sure she took it to Asher's barbecue.

Maggie didn't keep much. A single bank account and a bit of cash. But necessary to get to work, buy herself lunch and groceries. Checking the time on the wall clock, Maggie was early. Always was. This was her chance at a new start. She'd do nothing to screw it up. And that meant taking her job, despite only being a maid at one of the bed and breakfasts, seriously. She had one other job in her life. A general store clerk. The few years when her step-brother lived away from home had provided her some freedoms.

Going all the way to Asher's on the other side of town might make her late. But she needed her wallet. There was no choice. She called for a cab and then called her boss.

"That's fine, dear. Don't you worry about rushing at all." Ruth was the sweetest woman Maggie had ever met. The last thing she wanted to do was take advantage of Ruth's kindness.

Maggie watched for the cab from the porch. A red hatchback pulled into the driveway. Jogging toward it, she hopped in the backseat and gave the driver directions to Asher's. She didn't know the address off the top of her head, only how to get there. Halfway through the drive, she realized she hadn't told them she was stopping by, not that they hadn't told her multiple times she was always welcome and to come by if she ever needed anything. In fact, they all seemed to go out of their way to make sure she knew that. Maggie sent a text to Gwen saying she lost her wallet and was stopping by to see if it had fallen out of her pocket last night. The driver pulled up to Asher's only minutes later.

He parked behind three vehicles, Asher's, Gwen's, and the truck the doctor had driven in last night with the injured bear in the back. Not waiting for a reply from Gwen, Maggie jumped out of the cab and jogged across the yard toward the setup of picnic tables. She didn't want to be any later than she already was.

"Maggie."

Maggie stumbled, startled by a male voice calling her name. She looked up at the deck, and the doctor stood at the top of the stairs.

"Is there anything I can help you with, Maggie?"

"Dr. Daly. I just came looking for my wallet. I thought I must have lost it here last night."

"You need to call me Garrett," he reminded her with a gentle smile. Last winter, she'd woken up in the hospital with him standing over her. Tyrone had come to Alder Ridge to take her, Ezaray, and Holly back. A fight in the woods led to Maggie getting shot. She was told Garrett showed up after she'd passed out and took her to the hospital. She hadn't seen him since.

"I'm just going to look around out here. I'm late for work." She wasn't late yet, but she would be by the time they drove back across town. Maggie searched the bench she'd sat on and the surrounding grass. She hadn't moved around much. It likely hadn't fallen out anywhere else. About to give up, the green stripe along the edge of the case caught her eye. Relief pulsed. She picked it up and held it up to Garrett before putting it in her pocket. An awkward grasp pinched her smile. She didn't have more to say to him and he came with so many negative memories. She trusted her friends here, and even Garrett fell into the same category, but that logic didn't always work for her.

Maggie started back for the cab, but a deep, rumbling growl sent a tremor up her body. She turned back to the deck. Garrett's mouth moved, and he stared to the side. The same spot they'd put the bear the night before. What the hell were these people thinking? They still had an injured bear recovering on the deck. And the doctor was stupid enough to stand there with his back to it.

She didn't have time to educate the doctor on bear safety. Taking slow steps back, her eyes on the brown visible through the railings and not on Garrett talking to the dangerous lump, she moved toward the cab. But she couldn't keep her tongue still.

"You shouldn't still have him here. None of you strike me as the type that wouldn't have bear smarts."

"I'll be fine." Garrett's lips moved to the beginnings of a grin, but the rumble from the bear grew louder and took his attention off Maggie. The sound instilled ice in her feet, but she needed to get out of there. She continued her steps toward the cab—small, slow, consistent.

Paws thumped against the wood, and his rumble buried into his stomach.

"What do you think you're doing? Stay still." Garrett turned to face the bear. His body relaxed, as if talking to a patient. The same way he'd talked to Maggie and the others when treating them after a fight. The image, the words, the tone—her stomach hardened as if it crystallized—the tiny rocks building on top of each other, growing. Her vision blurred. The bear's rumble turned to an angry growl, the sound ripping away the flashes of memory that played in her mind.

Maggie inwardly shook and focused on the doctor moving toward the bear. Words stuck in her throat. The bear's head popped up over the railing. His nose twitched frantically.

The commotion drew the attention of the others inside the house. Asher stepped out his front door, but the bear blocked his way. Gwen's head poked around him. The doctor seemed to gain some sense and moved out of the way. Asher didn't jump in, either. The bear wanted to go home and lick his own wounds rather than have humans do it for him. Maggie could understand that.

But she stood in the bear's path.

Maggie continued toward the cab, the same slow and steady steps, while looking back over her shoulder to gauge the distance to the cab. A single groan left the bear, who was now staring at her. She wasn't just in his way—she was his target. His stark eyes saw past her skin. She couldn't tell what colour they were from this distance, but they weren't brown as they should be. They calmed her for a moment until she remembered the animal they belonged to.

Her steps didn't stop, and the bear grew more agitated.

"Maggie, please stop. He shouldn't be moving the way he is. He's going to hurt himself." Asher's request was as ridiculous as the doctor treating the bear like a patient.

"It's okay, Maggie." Gwen stepped out from behind Asher.

She shook her head and took another step back. The bear growled and tried to take the steps down off the deck, but he stumbled. Asher and Garrett jumped toward him to catch him. They couldn't be that stupid, but they chose to offer themselves as snacks. Maggie took the opportunity. She turned and ran back to the cab parked behind all the vehicles. The driver's bored eyes stared at his scrolling thumb. She slammed the back door after jumping in, startling him.

"Go, now. Please." Her breath caught as her volume increased.

The driver shrugged and put the car in reverse.

The bear had been looking directly at her. She turned around and looked out the back window. They still had their arms around the grizzly and were trying to pull him back onto the deck with little luck.

He hadn't been trying to get away from them. He'd been trying to get to her.

ABOUT THE AUTHOR

Looking at a crossroads, Sarah chose to write. With a deep love of anything romance, it was natural that romance stories flowed into her journal. From the East Coast and living in Alberta, Canada, she enjoyslife with her family and the beauty of the province around her. She gets hilariously excited when new stories and characters pop in her head and can't wait to write them out whether in thesub-genres of romantic suspense orparanormal romance. She hopes her readers enjoy her stories as much as she enjoys writing them.

You can find Sarah on Facebook and Instagram @authorsarahu, in her reader group *Sarah's Wild Ones,* or on BookBub.

www.ingramcontent.com/pod-product-compliance
Lightning Source LLC
Chambersburg PA
CBHW030812210726
48290CB00002B/551